IN GOD WE TRUST . . .

In his spacious office atop the Headquarters Building of the Celestial Construction Company, Inc., the

Stellar #7
SCIENCE-FICTION STORIES

EDITED BY
Judy-Lynn del Rey

A Del Rey Book

BALLANTINE BOOKS • NEW YORK

A Del Rey Book
Published by Ballantine Books

Library of Congress Catalog Card Number: 81-66549

ISBN 0-345-29473-4

Printed in Canada

First Edition: August 1981

Cover art by David B. Mattingly

TO LESTER,
Husband,
Sweetheart,
Colleague,
and Friend . . .
All of the above—and then some!

Contents

Making Light

James P. Hogan

In his spacious office atop the Headquarters Building of
the Celestial Construction Company Inc., the General Operations Director hummed to himself as he sat at his desk
and scanned over Contract 10,000,000,000 B.C. The contract document was brief and straightforward and called
for the creation of a standard Mark IV universe—plenty of
light; the usual suns, planets, and moons; a few firmaments
here and there with birds and animals on the land; fish-
filled waters around the land. There was an attached
schedule for accessories, spares for renewable resources,
and some supporting services. Deadline for the contract
was seven days—a piece of cake, the G.O.D. told himself.
Design Engineering Department's final proposal for the bid
lay to one side of the desk in the form of a bulky folder
that constituted the Works Order Review Document. Until
final approvals were granted, the W.O.R.D. would be all
that existed of the universe . . . but it was a beginning.

What promised to make this project a little different
from the previous Mark IV's, and somewhat more interesting, was the optional extra that Design Engineering had
tagged on in the *Appendix* section of the proposal: *people*,
Unlike the species that made up the usual mix of Mark IV
animal forms, which simply consumed resources and multi-
plied until they achieved a balance with the environment,
the people would have the capacity to harness fire, make
tools, and generally think about how they could be better
off. This would produce an awareness of needs and the
motivation to do something about satisfying them. Eventually the people would discover that, as their numbers and
their demands increased, they would no longer be able to
satisfy their needs with the resources that came readily to
hand. At that point, the computer simulations indicated,
they could simply give up, they could fight over what they

1

had until it ran out and then be obliged to give up anyway, or they could develop the intellectual potential inherent in their design and apply it to discovering the progression of newer resources hidden around them like the successively more challenging, but at the same time more rewarding, clues of a treasure hunt. The way out of the maze lay in the third alternative.

Wood, growing all over the surface of the planets, would be the most obvious fuel following the taming of fire, but it would not prove adequate for long. It would, however, enable the more easily mined metal ores—conveniently scattered on top of the crusts or not very far below—to be smelted and exploited to make the tools necessary for digging deeper to the coal. Coal would enable an industrial base to be set up for producing machines suitable for drilling and processing oil, which in turn would yield the more highly concentrated fuels essential for aircraft and rudimentary space vehicles. The scientific expertise that would emerge during this phase would be the key to unlocking nuclear energy from crustal uranium, and the fission technologies thus brought into being would pave the way into fusion—initially using the deuterium from the special-formula oceans premixed for the purpose—and hence out to the stars and on to the advanced methods that would render resources effectively infinite for the lifetime of the universe. On planets set up for them in that way and with brains that ought to be capable of figuring the rest out for themselves, the people would have a fair chance of winning the game.

What the purpose of the game was, Design Engineering hadn't said. The G.O.D. suspected that it was more for their own amusement than anything else, but he hadn't objected since he was quite curious himself to find out how the people would handle the situation. A modicum of applied precognition could no doubt have revealed that, but somehow it would have spoiled things.

He was still browsing over the last page of the contract when the phone rang with a peal of rising and falling chimes. It was Gabriel, the Vice President of Manufacturing. He sounded worried. "It's proposal number ten billion B.C.," he said. "I think we might have problems."

The G.O.D. frowned. "I was just going through it. Looks fine to me. What's the problem?"

"Somebody from Equal Employment Opportunities Creation has been onto the Legal Department. They're objecting to DE's proposal for the people on the grounds that it would discriminate unfairly against the animals. I think we ought to get the department heads together to talk about it. How are you fixed?"

"Pretty clear for the next few millennia. When did you want to do it?"

"How about right now, while the large conference and congregation room's free?"

"Sure. Get the others over and I'll see you there in, say, ten minutes."

"Leave it to me."

The G.O.D. replaced the phone, slipped the contract document inside the W.O.R.D. folder, tucked the folder under his arm as he stood up from the desk, and began walking toward the door. Outside in the corridor he paused to pat the pockets of his suit and found he was out of holy smokes, so he made a slight detour to get a pack from the machine by the ascension and descension elevators.

"The EEOC says that we can't endow one species with that kind of intelligence," the Head of the Legal Department explained across the gilt-edged conference table a quarter of an hour later. "Doing so would confer such a devastating advantage that the animals would be guaranteed permanent second-class status with no opportunity to compete, which would constitute an infringement of rights."

"And we've been looking into some of the other implications," another of the lawyers added. "The people would eventually assume a uniquely dominant role. That could set us up for an antitrust suit."

All heads turned toward the Chief Design Engineer. "Well, we can't take the intelligence away from the people," he objected. "The physiques that we've specified don't give them any other means of survival. They'd have no chance. Then we'd still be in trouble with EEOC but with everything the other way around." He threw his hands out impatiently. "And besides, it would defeat the purpose of the whole exercise. It was the addition of intelligence that was going to make this project more interesting.

"Why not make *all* the species equally intelligent?" somebody suggested.

The CDE shook his head. "We planned the ecology so that the animals would do most of the work for the people in the early phases and provide a lot of their food. If we made them equally intelligent, the situation would qualify as slavery and exploitation. We'd never get it past the Justice Department."

"And on top of that they'd all become eligible for education, sickness benefits, and retirement pensions," the CDE's assistant pointed out. "HEW would never accept the commitment. They couldn't handle the load."

That was true, the G.O.D. admitted as he thought about it. Already the Department of Harps, Eternity-pensions, and Wings had insisted that all guarantees of benefits be deleted from the proposal. And that had been just on account of the projected numbers of people, never mind all the animals. "So why can't we change things so the people don't have to depend on the animals at all?" he asked, at last looking up. "Let's make them strong enough to do all the work themselves, and have them just eat plants."

"Not that easy," the CDE answered, shaking his head dubiously. "They'd have to be at least the size of elephants on an input of vegetable protein. Then food-gathering would become such a problem that they'd never have any time left over for mental development, which puts us back to square one." He thought for a second or two, then added, "Though it might work if we redesigned the food chain somehow."

The G.O.D. looked over at the Head of Research. "What do you say to that?" he asked.

The scientist didn't appear too happy as he pinched his nose and reflected upon the question. "We'd have to figure it out again all the way down to the bacteria," he replied after a while. "You're talking about a complete redesign, not just a few modifications. Setting up a whole new ecology and running it through the simulator is a long job. I don't think we could finish before the closing date on the bid, and that doesn't allow for having to rewrite the proposal from scratch. If we could use the new Infallible Biological Modeler we might have had a chance, but we can't. It's not up and running yet."

"I thought the IBM was supposed to have been installed last week," the G.O.D. said, sounding surprised.

"It was, but the systems angelists haven't handed it over yet," the Research Chief replied. "They're not through exorcizing the bugs."

The G.O.D. frowned down at the table in front of him. "Hell," he muttered irritably.

"Er . . . we don't say that here," Gabriel reminded him politely.

"Oh, of course." The G.O.D. made an apologetic gesture and then cast his eyes around the table. "Does anyone else have any suggestions?" he invited. No one had. He sighed in resignation, then looked at the Chief Design Engineer. "I'm sorry, Chief, but it sounds as if we're stuck. I guess there's no choice but to drop the extras and revert to a standard Mark IV."

"No people?" The CDE sounded disappointed.

"No people," the G.O.D. confirmed. "It was a nice thought, but it's out of the question on the timescale of this contract. Keep working on it with Research, and maybe you'll have it all figured out in time for the next bid, huh?" The CDE nodded glumly. The meeting ended shortly thereafter, and the Vice President of Sales went back to his office to begin drafting a revised *Appendix* section to be delivered to the customer by winged messenger. So the project wasn't going to be so interesting after all, the G.O.D. reflected with a pang of regret as he collected his papers. But at least that meant there was less risk of overrunning on time and incurring penance clauses.

The Chief Design Engineer was on the phone shortly after lunch on the following day. "Have you heard?" he asked. He sounded distressed.

"Heard what?" the G.O.D. answered.

"Feathers, Aviation, and Aquatics have been onto our legal people. They're trying to tell us that our birds and fish aren't safe."

"That's ridiculous! They're the same ones as we've always used. What's wrong with our birds and fish?"

"According to FAA regulations, all flight-control and navigation systems have to be duplicated," the CDE said. "Our birds only have a single nervous system. Also, we're allowing them to fly over water without inflatable life jackets."

The G.O.D. was completely taken aback. "What's gotten into them?" he demanded. "They've never complained about anything like that before."

"They've never really bothered to check the regulations before, but the controversy over the people has attracted their attention to this project," the CDE told him. "Our legal people think they're all at it—all the angelcies are brushing the dust off manuals they've never looked at before and going through them with magnifying glasses. We could be in for some real hassles."

The G.O.D. groaned. "But what do they want us to do? We can't go loading the birds up with all kinds of duplicated junk. Their power-weight ratios are critically balanced. They'd never get off the ground."

"I know that. But all the same it's regulations, and the FAA won't budge. They also say we have to fit bad-weather landing aids."

The G.O.D.'s patience snapped abruptly. "They don't fly in bad weather," he yelled. "They just sit in the trees. If they don't fly, why do they need aids for landing? It'd be like putting life jackets on the camels."

"I know, I know, I know. But that's what the book says, and that's all the FAA's interested in."

"Can we do it?" the G.O.D. asked when he had calmed down a little.

"Only with the penguins, the ostriches, and the others that walk. I called the FAA guy a couple of minutes ago and told him that the only way we could equip all the birds for bad-weather landing was by making them all walk. He said that sounded fine."

"I've never heard of anything so stupid! What's the point of having birds at all if they're only allowed to walk? We can't have planets with walking birds all over the place. The competition would die laughing."

"I know all that. I'm just telling you what the guy said."

A few seconds of silence went by. Then the G.O.D. asked, "What's wrong with the fish?"

"The shallow-water species don't have coastal radar."

Pause.

"Is this some kind of joke?"

"I wish it were. They're serious all right."

The G.O.D. shook his head in disbelief and slumped back in his chair. "Maybe we might just have to go along without birds and shallow-water fish this time," he said at last. "Would the rest still work?"

"I'm not so sure it would," the CDE replied. "The birds were supposed to spread seeds around to produce enough vegetation to support the herbivores. If we reduce the quotas of herbivores, we'd have to cut back on the carnivores too. And without the birds to keep down the insects, we'd have the Forestry Cherubim on our backs for endangering the trees. With the trees in trouble and no shallow-water fish to clean up the garbage from the rivers, the whole ecosystem would break down. None of the animal species would be able to support themselves."

The G.O.D. sighed and wrestled with the problem in his head. The CDE himself had precipitated the current crisis by introducing the idea of people in the first place, but there would be nothing to be gained by starting rounds of recriminations and accusations at this point, he thought. What was important was to get the proposal into an acceptable form before the closing date for the bid. "The only thing I can think of is that if the animals become unable to support themselves, we'll have to put them all on welfare. If I call HEW and see if I can fix it, would that solve the problem?"

"Well . . . yeah, I guess it would . . . if you can fix it." The CDE didn't sound too hopeful.

The G.O.D. phoned the HEW Director a few minutes later and explained the situation. Would HEW accept a commitment to supplying welfare support for the animals?

"No way!" was the emphatic reply.

"What in he— heaven's name do you expect us to do?" the G.O.D. demanded, shouting in exasperation. "How can we meet anybody's regulations when they always conflict with somebody else's?"

"That's not our problem," the HEW Director stated bluntly. "Sorry."

Another meeting was called early the next morning to discuss the quandary. After all avenues had been explored, there seemed only one solution that would avoid all the conflicts: an azoic universe. *All* forms of living organisms would have to be deleted from the proposal. The meeting ended on a note of somber resignation.

* * *

The Environmental Protection Angel was on the line later that afternoon. Her voice was shrill and piercing, grating on the G.O.D.'s nerves. "Without any plants at all, the levels of carbon dioxide, nitrogen oxides, and sulfur compounds from volcanic activity would exceed the permitted limits. The proposal as it stands is quite unacceptable. We would not be able to issue operating licenses for the volcanoes."

"But the limits were set to safeguard only living organisms!" the G.O.D. thundered. "We've scrapped them—all of them. There *aren't any* living organisms to be safeguarded."

"There is no clause in the regulations which specifically exempts lifeless planets," the EPA told him primly. It was too much.

"What kind of lunatics are you?" the G.O.D. raged into the phone. "You don't need a specific exemption. What do you need protective regulations for when there isn't anything to be protected? How stupid can you get? Any idiot could see that it doesn't apply here—any of it. You're out of your mind."

"I'm simply doing my job, and I don't expect personal insults," came the reply. "The standards are quite clear, and they must be met. Good day." The line went dead.

The G.O.D. conveyed the news to Design Engineering, who discussed it with Research. Without the volcanoes there wouldn't be enough planetary outgassing to form the atmospheres and oceans. Okay, the atmospheres and oceans would have to go. But the volcanoes were also intended to play a role in relieving the structural stresses and thermal buildups in the planetary crusts. How could that be taken care of without any volcanoes? Only by having more earthquakes to make up the difference, the CDE declared. The G.O.D. told him to revise the proposal by deleting the volcanoes and making the crustal formations more earthquake-prone. Everybody agreed that the problem appeared at last to have been solved.

The Department of Highlands, Undulations, and Deserts called the G.O.D. a day later with an objection. "I'm dreadfully sorry, old chap, but we seem to have run into a bit of a problem," the man from HUD told him. "You see, the mountain ranges you've proposed don't quite come up to the standards set out in our building codes for the increased level of seismic activity. We'd have no choice but to condemn them as unsafe, I'm afraid."

"What if we do away with the mountains, then?" the G.O.D. growled sullenly.

"That would be perfectly satisfactory as far as we're concerned, but I rather suspect that you might still have a problem in getting it passed by the Occupational Safety and Health Angelcy. All those fissures opening up and landslides going on all over the place . . . it would be a bit hazardous for the animals, wouldn't it?"

"But we've already gotten rid of the animals," the G.O.D. pointed out. "There won't be any."

"I see your point," the man from HUD agreed amiably, "but it is still in the jolly old rules. You know how finicky those OSHA types can be. Just a friendly word in your ear. Frightfully sorry and all that."

The G.O.D. was past arguing.

Design Engineering's response was to make the planets completely inactive. There would be no mountains, no fluid interiors, no mobile plates—in fact, no tectonic processes of any kind. The planets would be simply featureless balls of solid rock that could never by any stretch of the imagination be considered potentially hazardous to any living thing, whether one existed or not.

The Great Accounting Overseer didn't like it. "What do you need them for?" a GAO minion challenged a day later. "They don't serve any useful purpose at all. They're just a needless additional expense on the cost budget. Why not get rid of them completely?"

"They've got a point," the CDE admitted when the G.O.D. went over to Engineering to talk about it. "I guess the only reason we put them in is because that's the way we've always done it. Yeah . . . I reckon we should strike them out. No planets."

But the Dispenser of Energy wasn't happy about the idea of a universe consisting of nothing but stars. "It might be budgeted to last for billions of years, but it's still finite nevertheless," an assistant of the DOE declared in a call to the G.O.D. "We are trying to encourage a policy of conservation, you know. This idea of having billions of stars just pouring out all that energy into empty space with none of it being used for anything at all . . . well, it would be terribly wasteful and inefficient. I don't think we could possibly approve something like that."

"But it's just as we've always done it," the G.O.D. protested. "The planets never used more than a drop in the ocean. The difference isn't worth talking about."

"Quantitatively yes, but I'm talking about a difference in principle," the DOE assistant replied. "The waste was high in the earlier projects, but at least there was a reason in principle. This time there isn't any, and that does make a difference. We couldn't give this universe an approval stamp. Sorry."

A day later Design Engineering had come up with a way to conserve the energy: Instead of being concentrated into masses sufficiently dense to sustain fusion reactions and form stars, the stellar material would be dispersed evenly throughout space as clouds of dust and gas in which the small amount of free energy that remained would be conserved through an equilibrium exchange between radiation and matter. The DOE was satisfied with that. Unfortunately the EPA was not; the clouds of dust and gas would exceed the pollution limits.

With two days to go before the closing date for the bid, the G.O.D. called all the department heads and senior technical staff members together to discuss the situation. The ensuing meeting went on all through the night. After running calculations through the computers several times, they at last came up with a solution they were sure had to be acceptable to everybody. Sales forwarded a revised final proposal to the customer, and the company waited nervously for the responses. Miraculously the phone on the G.O.D.'s desk didn't ring once all through the next day. The proposal was approved, and the final contract was awarded.

Out at the construction site, Gabriel watched despondently as the project at last got under way. All that was left of the original plan was a pinpoint of exotic particles of matter, radiation, space, and time, all compressed together at a temperature of billions of degrees. The bizarre particles fell apart into protons, neutrons, electrons, muons, neutrinos, and photons, which after a while began clustering together through the radiation fluid as he watched.

After the grandeur of the previous projects he had witnessed, the sight was depressing. "I guess we just write this one off, forget all about it, and file it away," he murmured to the G.O.D., who was standing next to him. "It's not much to look at, is it? I can't see this even getting a mention in the report to the stockholders." He turned his head to find that the G.O.D.'s eyes were twinkling mischievously. "What's funny?" he asked, puzzled.

The G.O.D. tipped his yellow hard-hat to the back of his head and grinned in a conspiratorial kind of way as he scratched his forehead. "Don't worry about it," he said quietly. "We've worked out a new method. It'll all come out just the way we planned . . . everything."

Gabriel blinked at him in astonishment. "What are you talking about? How do you mean, *everything*? You don't mean the stars, the planets, the oceans, the mountains . . ." His voice trailed away as he saw the G.O.D. nodding.

"And the birds, and the fish, and the animals, all the way through to the people," the G.O.D. told him confidently. "It'll turn out just the way we planned it in the original proposal."

Gabriel shook his head, nonplused. "But . . . how?" He gestured at the expanding fireball, in which traces of helium and a few other light nuclei were beginning to appear. "How could it all come out of *that*?"

The G.O.D. chuckled. "The research people developed some things called 'Laws of Physics' that they buried inside it. The angelcies will never find them. But they're in there, and they'll make it all happen just the way we planned. We ran the numbers through the IBM last night, and they work. You wait and see."

Gabriel looked over his shoulder at the site supervisor's hut and then gazed back at the embryo universe with a new interest and respect. "I was going to go inside for a coffee," he said. "But this sounds interesting. I think I'll hang around a little longer. I don't want to miss this."

The G.O.D. smiled. "Oh, that's okay—you go get your coffee," he said. "There's plenty of time yet." ☆

Horn o' Plenty

Terry Carr and Leanne Frahm

Jamie had a weakness for magic tricks.

Not the "real" magic tricks magicians use on stage, but the junk tricks that fool no one but the people who buy them—usually after seeing a one-inch ad in the back of a magazine catering to those who are credulous about flying saucers or the sex lives of movie stars. Every time Jamie ordered one, he ended up with a bent piece of garishly colored cardboard or three wires twisted together.

"Never again," he'd tell himself. Then he'd see another ad. Somehow the tiny print blotchily reproduced on cheap paper made the products seem arcane and exciting, as if only people who persevered to read almost illegible things could be rewarded with miracles.

Even so, as soon as he had mailed his check for the horn o' plenty he felt like a fool. Nobody in his right mind would have paid any attention to such a phony advertisement—but Jamie had, if only, he told himself, to find out what the gimmick was.

The gimmick was that the horn o' plenty was real.

When he came home from work at the Dimmesdale mortuary, Jamie found a two-foot-square package wrapped in brown paper in front of his apartment door. He took it inside and cut the khaki string with his Italian Army Knife—the small white flag no longer popped out when he pressed its release, but the pizza cutter worked if you tried hard enough. Removing the wrapping, he opened a plain white box and burrowed into plastic peanut shells; he felt a solid object, removed it gently and set the thing on the floor, brushing plastic dust from its top.

Top? He wasn't quite sure, suddenly, that it was the top. It didn't look much like a horn o' plenty should look, at least any he had ever heard of. The shape was all wrong.

12

Instead of being spoutlike, it was more . . . well, what *was* it like? He studied it, blinking. It didn't seem to have any definite outlines; the moment his eyes focused on one part, it shimmered and disappeared. It was as if he could see the object most clearly from the corner of his eye.

Squinting hard, Jamie decided that it was mostly flask-shaped, but . . .

He poked here and there; there didn't seem to be any holes, but he had the impression there were openings . . . somewhere. No latches or hinges, either. The whole thing was very confusing.

When he began picking up the wrappings, he noticed a small piece of white cardboard still in the box. A note was typed on it: *This merchandice will begin operation thirty minutes after unpackign. Please store in a cool dry place.*

Jamie frowned. "Now what does that mean? *Will begin operation thirty minutes after* . . . How do you set a thing like this?" He tried to study the horn o' plenty again; it shimmered and wavered tantalizingly.

At length he stood up, with a vague sense of matters being out of his hands. Well, if it wasn't supposed to start for half an hour, he might as well have dinner while he waited. He put the horn in the corner by an open window, then headed for the kitchen to prepare dinner.

"A damn shame," he muttered as he opened a can of jumping beans con carne. "Having to eat this stuff when I've got a horn o' plenty of my very own. I ought to be dining on ambrosia and sipping mead—or is it the other way around?" He dumped the contents of the can into a saucepan and set it over a flame on the stove. The beans began to wriggle lethargically, and he reminded himself—remembering last night's fiasco—to eat around the tiny pieces of plastic embedded in them. Naomi, his girlfriend, hadn't appreciated having to pick bits of half-melted plastic out of her teeth.

Dinner ready, he spooned the now quiescent beans into a plate and poured himself a glass of Mauna Loa mineral water. He had found to his surprise that he rather liked its pungent flavor. He sat at the table and lost himself in a novel called *Slave-Tyrants of Lemuria* as he ate. At the end of an hour he suddenly put the book down. *"Damn!"* He dashed into the living room to see how his horn o' plenty was getting along.

It still sat silent and shimmering in the corner; but several new things had been added. In a haphazard jumble around it was the weirdest conglomeration of junk Jamie had ever seen.

There was a sort of papery thing, crumpled into a ball, and several mottled orange oblates that looked a little like some kind of fruit, although just offhand Jamie didn't feel like tasting them. And he noticed a few metallic things, maybe parts of some machine. Jamie wondered if the horn o' plenty was rattling out some vital moving parts.

Kneeling beside the pile, he began to sort through it cautiously, using the flyswatter from his Italian Army Knife. There were also, he discovered, two round spongy things, and a pool of greenish semiliquid that stank. Good thing it was near an open window.

"Curiouser and curiouser," he muttered. He considered the situation for several minutes, but no worthwhile explanations came to mind. Then he noticed that a bluish paste had been precipitated onto the floor and over some of the other items of clutter already surrounding the horn. He sniffed at it tentatively. It had no odor, but his eyes watered.

What could he do with a horn o' plenty that did nothing but make a mess in his living room? Complain to Ralph Nader?

What about the landlord? Jamie abruptly realized that it was not precisely *his* living room that was submerging under a sea of decidedly peculiar flotsam and jetsam. There was no clause in his lease about haywire horns o' plenty, though there was one forbidding pets that made messes. Jamie had a momentary vision of a courtroom and an irate Mr. Rankin standing ankle-deep in Exhibit A, charging him with owning an incontinent horn o' plenty.

Jamie decided to give up for the time being; he pulled out an old and frayed sheet and threw it over the whole mess. Then he went out for a calming walk.

He was heading up Fourteenth Street, debating whether or not to ship the horn o' plenty back to Varieties Unlimited, but wondering how to turn it off so that the package wouldn't burst in transit as more and more things materialized out of it, when he noticed he had automatically walked to Naomi's apartment. Naomi, it suddenly occurred to him, was just the person to take such a problem to—

after all, hadn't he fallen in love with her for her original mind?

He dashed up a flight of stairs and rang the doorbell. It chimed the theme from *Close Encounters*, and presently Naomi opened the door.

"Jamie! Come in." She hugged him briefly, then led him down the hall of her railroad flat to her workroom. At five-feet-ten, she was an inch taller than he. As they entered the room, her straight black hair glistened with moving highlights under a revolving ballroom light. She removed four leather-bound volumes from a virgin vinyl couch and sat cross-legged at one end.

Jamie settled down beside her, sighing. "I've got a problem, Naomi. A scientific one."

"I'm not a scientist," she said. "I'm a humble student."

"Well, you're not all that humble."

She grinned. "Perhaps not, *petit chou*. I try to study reality—all of it, whether or not it has anything to do with science." She swept a gesture around the room, which was dominated by a computer terminal and printouts typed on near-vellum—"corpse paper," she called it—with three walls of books haphazardly filed, many of them stuck in backward. A cheap book club copy of *Demonology Reconsidered* lay on her desk, held open by a roller skate.

"Right now I'm interested in necromancy, sorcery and alchemy. It's very seductive—maybe I'll turn some base metal into gold tomorrow."

"It's been done," Jamie said, impatient to get on to his problem. "By scientists, no less."

"Of course scientists have done it—but that's just the point, dear heart. They spent more on the process than the gold they made was worth! That's the way with scientists—they go by the book. They wouldn't change base metal into *salami* if they couldn't do it in a way that was strictly kosher."

Jamie said, "I have something that will interest you—it's very unconventional."

"Not a seven-toed cat, I hope. My friends are always bringing them to me."

"Nothing like that. It's a . . . well, a horn o' plenty. I got it from a mail-order house, of all places."

"Of course," she said. "Wonderful."

"You've heard of it?"

"No, but I'm not surprised. I once asked myself what I'd do if I found out how to make one. Why, *market* it, of course. I'm afraid such an offer would wreak havoc in this country, though—even destroy the whole capitalist system." Her expression indicated she wouldn't really be sorry about that.

"You're not very patriotic, are you?" Jamie asked, frowning a bit. The traveling colors of the ballroom light were casting him into a sort of vertigo, like that weekend when he and Naomi had mixed peyote with ginseng, belladonna and cilantro.

"You're the one with the subversive horn o' plenty," Naomi said. "What's the gimmick? I assume it *does* work."

Jamie told her about the horn o' plenty. It took a long time. He showed her the ad he had answered, described the horn as best he could, and bogged down in trying to describe the conglomeration of . . . stuff . . . that had poured forth from it.

He finally ran out of descriptions. "I guess you'll just have to come over to my place to see it for yourself."

She nodded briskly, rose and went around the room gathering objects and throwing them into a daypack. Jamie recognized a few of them—a handmade pulley, a piece of chalk, several small flasks filled with murky liquids, and something called *The Tibetan Cookbook of the Dead*.

Naomi pulled on a yellow ski jacket with *Purgatory's Angels* stitched on the back. As she reached for her pack, she paused. "Should I bring my toothbrush and my teddy bear?"

"Please," Jamie said. He led her back to his apartment.

As Jamie unlocked the door, a sense of foreboding gripped him, accompanied by an overripe cheese smell. He hesitated in the doorway, but Naomi impatiently urged him forward.

A trickle of green viscous liquid was oozing slowly across the floor, its exploratory path marked by puddles as it spread. Naomi moved up behind him. "All *right*. Looks interesting already." She slipped past him and went to the window corner.

Jamie closed the door quickly, then picked up a towel and stuffed it under the door, though he hated to sacrifice it; it was a designer-signed John Belushi. He joined Naomi beside the horn o' plenty, which by now was almost totally covered by a growing pile of junk. A fine reddish powder layered everything; it was from this that the new sour smell originated.

Naomi reached toward the nearest items. "Do you think you should do that?" Jamie asked apprehensively.

"Do what?"

"Touch anything. With your bare hands, I mean. There's a lot of funny-smelling powder, and that pasty stuff . . ."

"No doubt you're right," Naomi said, frowning. "We're dealing here with the unknown, and unknowns should be treated with circumspection. I . . . hmmm . . ." She prodded one of the spongy balls with a forefinger.

Jamie mentally reviewed what he knew about first-aid.

Naomi remained silent for a long time, gently lifting objects and peering at them closely. She rubbed the reddish powder between her fingertips, then stuck a thumb into the ooze and licked at it. She picked up the horn itself. Her eyes widened when she touched it, then she grimaced as she studied it from all angles. It didn't seem to have any angles.

There was a soft pop, and something purple plopped to the floor.

"There!" she said. "Did you see that?"

"Yes, but I didn't see where it came from. Did you?"

"No," said Naomi. "Wonderful." She chuckled and carefully placed the horn back on the floor. It wavered and shimmered, but nothing happened for some time. Eventually Naomi sat back, crossed her legs and closed her eyes.

Jamie looked on anxiously. "Well, what do you make of it?"

"Nothing," Naomi declared dreamily. "Absolutely nothing."

A touch of hysteria crept into Jamie's voice. "But do you know what it is? More important, do you know how to stop it?"

"Ah!" Naomi opened her eyes and raised a red-tinged finger. "I know a lot of things it *isn't*, which is always a good start. As for stopping it . . ." She had the grace to look slightly sheepish. "This is truly a mystery, you know," she said finally.

"I knew *that* before I came to you."

"Samples," Naomi said decisively. "We'll collect samples and go back to my workroom."

Jamie suddenly realized he couldn't have slept in his own apartment anyway, knowing what was taking place in the living room . . . and not knowing. What if the ooze worked its way into the bedroom and ate a hole in his waterbed? For one thing, the tropical fish inside would die.

"Okay—I'll get *my* toothbrush."

Jamie woke beneath the pyramidal canopy of Naomi's bed, but he couldn't remember when, if ever, she had joined him. He had sat up for hours the night before watching her at work, before finally retiring in the small hours of the morning.

"Work" wasn't exactly the word for Naomi's performance. She had leaped from petri dish to pentagram, fed data and queries into her computer and scrawled obscure notes in Latin on a blackboard. When he had gone to bed, she was sitting on the couch simultaneously speed-reading books by Einstein and Lovecraft.

Jamie rubbed his eyes and sat up. *"Aha!"* Naomi said, appearing in the doorway. "You're awake." She sat on the edge of the bed and kissed his nose.

"I'm sorry I couldn't stay up with you," Jamie mumbled around the fur on his teeth.

"Nonsense, my all. I didn't even notice you were gone till a few minutes ago. Let's have some breakfast—I've already called in sick for you at work."

Jamie did feel sick, especially at the thought of what old Dimmesdale would think of a young woman calling to excuse his assistant's absence. Morticians weren't very sympathetic about some things.

"But the stuff—the horn o' plenty. How did your research go?"

"Magnificently, of course," Naomi said. "Eggs all right?"

"Sure," Jamie muttered, feeling around for his clothes and then discovering he'd slept in them. He tottered off to the bathroom. "Then you know what that stuff is?"

"Oh, certainly. Concentrated protein, surrounded by an albuminous jelly and enclosed in a calciferous shell . . ."

"Not the eggs!" Jamie closed his eyes and spoke very

clearly and slowly. "Naomi, did you or did you not identify any of the samples we collected from that pile on my living room floor?"

"Yes, yes. I've established that they are, in fact, unidentifiable. Sunnyside up?"

Naomi spoke through a mouthful of fishcake toast. "Just small differences, you understand. An extra molecule here, a twist to the protein chain there—nothing all that outré, but totally different in the broad view. Totally different." She grinned. "Hate to think what a conventional scientist might have done if he'd had to explain that stuff—blown his brains out rather than admit it existed, probably. Or worse, applied for a ten-year government grant to study it."

Jamie's patience had worn thin during Naomi's contented humming as she had prepared one of her creative breakfasts. (He never had been able to stand it when she tried to sing melodies by George Crumb.) "All right, but what *is* it?"

Still chewing, she raised her eyebrows at him, then wiggled them Groucho-like. "Naomitium, Jamieite—you name it, literally. They're all brand-new."

"But where does all the stuff come from?" Jamie persisted. "How do they get in that thing? Why are they spilling out all over my apartment?"

"Aha, *mi amor*—spoken like a true student. We'll work on those questions today." Naomi pushed herself back from the table and idly scratched the side of her nose with a chopstick. "I suggest—'

"The mail-order house!" Jamie cried. "Varieties Unlimited—we can start there and trace the manufacturers!" His excitement abruptly died. "On second thought, I suppose we ought to inform the authorities first."

"Authorities?" Naomi's face became immobile.

"Yes," Jamie said. "The government, or someone . . ."

Naomi stood up so angrily that the director's chair with Torquemada's name lettered on the back crashed to the floor. "You seriously suggest going to the government and its pussycat scientists? What do you think they'd make of your horn o' plenty? Impossible, they'd say—a hoax! The horn would disappear forever beneath a mountain of stultified stupidity."

She placed her palms flat on the table and leaned over

Jamie. "I, Naomi Lokisson, will follow this investigation to the very end—for *you*. When I'm finished, no one will be able to deny the facts, and your name will go down in the annals of knowledge right beside mine as co-discoverer of all these new materials."

Jamie nodded weakly. "Sounds wonderful. But where do we start?"

Naomi held up the advertisement for the horn o' plenty. "Everton. That's where Varieties Unlimited's office is."

"I know. It's only an hour's drive from here. But Varieties Unlimited only has a box number; that could be hard to trace."

Naomi grinned. "Nothing simpler. We just wait at the post office and follow whoever collects the mail from that box."

Jamie reddened. "Right," he said briskly, trying to sound authoritative. "We'll take my car."

As they donned their coats, Jamie said, "I thought your name was Luckman."

"My grandmother changed it to that when her husband ran off to be a fire-eater in a circus. Don't ask."

"Pity about the weather," Jamie remarked conversationally.

Naomi huddled in her ski jacket and growled something in very Low German. Jamie sighed, turned the heater up and resumed peering out the side window of the car. The radio was playing a punk-synthesizer version of *The Nutcracker Suite*; he shuddered.

During their forty-mile drive to Everton a cold snap had scurried down from the north, bringing a late sleet storm. The street outside the post office was icy; the few pedestrians abroad hurried past the car, concentrating too much on their footing to pay attention to its occupants.

"No one's going to come today," Naomi grumbled.

"You never know." Jamie rummaged in her daypack and pulled out the Szechuan pizza they had bought that morning from a street vendor in Greenwich Village. Dividing it with his knife, he gave Naomi half, and they settled back to pass the time eating. The food warmed them—in fact, it warmed Jamie entirely too much when he unthinkingly chewed a whole chili pepper, and he coughed violently.

Naomi hissed for him to be silent. "Look!" she said softly, pointing. "No, don't look like that! He'll see you. Look without looking like you're looking."

Inside the post office a small man fumbled at the box whose number they had checked earlier. Jamie excitedly gulped the rest of his pizza and reached for the door handle.

"No!" Naomi said. "Not here. Let's follow him when he comes out."

Jamie nodded. Adrenalin mounted rapidly, especially as the half-chewed pizza began to churn in his stomach. They waited while the little man withdrew a sheaf of envelopes, closed the box and left the post office. When the man reached the corner and turned, Jamie started the car and took off after him. Peering ahead, he rounded the corner as rapidly as the wet street would allow and accelerated.

"Where is he?"

"We just passed him—he's walking very slowly."

"Damn. We can't stop next to him; he'll notice."

"Park at the end of the block, *pobrecito*. We'll start again after he passes us."

With a feeling that this was not at all the way these things were supposed to be done, Jamie continued down the street and parked. As he turned off the engine, Naomi lurched to the floor of the car. Surprised, Jamie quickly joined her. "Do you really think all this is necessary?" he whispered. "I don't think he'll pay any attention to us."

She stared back at him in equal surprise. "I dropped my pizza," she explained.

Jamie groaned, and sat up just as their quarry walked past. The man entered a doorway in the next block. Jamie smiled with relief.

"Come on," he said. They left the car and hurried to the storefront where the man had disappeared. It was a delicatessen.

Jamie hesitated, reading a hand-lettered sign announcing a special sale of Afghanistani goat's cheese. Then a sloppily typed notice in a corner of the window caught his eye: *Varieties Unlimited. "2nd Floor."*

They found the unlighted stairway and ascended.

Jamie wasn't at all sure what to expect when he knocked, so he braced himself for anything. Anything turned out to be an eye that peered at them from the crack made when the chained door opened two inches. The eye was bloodshot, surrounded by wrinkles. The voice was hoarse. "Yeah?"

"We're looking for the management of Varieties Unlimited."

"You got it."

"Then could we come in and talk to you?"

The eyebrows rose slightly. "You wanna buy something?"

"No, actually it's about something I already bought," Jamie said.

The door began to close. "Nah, no refunds."

"I don't want a refund," Jamie said quickly. "I—I'm interested in a franchise."

"Franchise?" The door opened again to two inches.

"Yes. I'd like to buy distribution rights to one of your products." Jamie sounded as confident as he could.

The eye narrowed, studying him dubiously. Jamie realized he didn't look very prepossessing in his faded Boston Marathon jacket and deerstalker cap with flaps that only half-covered his ears, but he forced himself to meet the man's gaze.

"Okay," the voice said grudgingly.

The door opened completely. They entered a dusty room walled with shelves crammed full of cardboard cartons, most of them with auction lot numbers scribbled on their sides. A skylight in the middle of the ceiling admitted pale light through spiderwebs. Jamie noticed a stack of parcels wrapped in brown paper and tied with khaki string. Maybe a dozen of them, he thought. Varieties Unlimited couldn't be making very much money.

The man was lean and slightly hunched; his hair was sandy and thinning, combed forward with unsuccessful vanity. "I'm Mervyn Pilk," he said heartily, and Jamie was reminded of quite a few heirs-of-the-deceased he'd met. "I hold the distributorships for all the products of Varieties Unlimited." His face was wrinkled into a permanent frown that looked all the worse for the expression of amiable interest now overlaying it.

"James Sloughborough," Jamie said. Pilk's handshake was almost firm. "This is Naomi Luckman, my research associate."

Pilk glanced at her and nodded. "Which product are you guys interested in?"

"Lokisson," Naomi muttered. "And we're not both guys."

"Anybody's got money, he's a guy," said Pilk. "Which product?"

Jamie decided to plunge right in. "It's about the horn o' plenty, Mr. Pilk."

The wrinkles in the small man's face darkened. "That's not for sale," he said flatly.

"We may be able to work out a percentage transaction." Jamie had automatically fallen into his mortician's voice. "But first we'll have to know more about the product."

"Like what?"

"We'll need specifications. How it's made, and the cost per unit. Who the manufacturers are."

Pilk's sudden grin was almost a leer. "That's a trade secret. But there's nothing about it that's against the law, if that's what you're worried about."

Naomi wasn't about to be put off. "Actually it violates several laws, my friend. Mostly those of chemistry and biology. Not to mention—"

"So don't," Pilk said, suddenly nervous. He glanced at the pile of horns o' plenty that were packaged for mailing. Jamie decided to press the advantage.

"You see, Mr. Pilk, we've analyzed some of the items that came out of the horn. We know they don't exist on Earth. We require that you tell us where they *do* come from."

Pilk's eyes shifted from point to point around the room. "The whole thing's legit," he muttered.

"I'm sure it is, one way or another," Jamie said. "Still, we'd like to find out what the government would think of it—and of the rest of your little business here."

That was a shot in the dark, but it worked. Pilk jumped.

"No! . . . No." He looked sourly at the wrapped packages, as if they were cartons for Cuba. "Okay, so the horns aren't exactly supplied by the Bell Company. But no way I'm gonna tell anyone where they come from. I can't. I won't."

Jamie was surprised by the little man's desperate stubbornness. He was thankful when Naomi interrupted.

"Look, *amico*, surely we can discuss this in a friendly way—without threats," she said, glaring ostentatiously at Jamie. She pointed to some overstuffed chairs that were heaped with empty cartons. "Let's sit down and talk . . . guy to guy."

It was the good-cop-bad-cop routine, Jamie realized admiringly. He wouldn't have expected Naomi to play Ms. Nice Guy, but she was nothing if not adaptable.

And it was working. Pilk quickly tossed the cartons onto the floor as Jamie and Naomi removed their wet jackets. The little man seemed relieved as he settled into the swivel chair behind his desk and his visitors took the overstuffed chairs, which had managed to become understuffed over the years.

"Have some of this," Naomi said, drawing a bottle of ouzo from her pack. Pilk's eyes widened as he took it and read the label. Imports from Eastern Europe were rare these days. He tried a taste, followed by a fervent gulp.

"Nice," he said hoarsely as he handed it back. Jamie reached for the bottle, but Naomi grabbed it and placed it invitingly on the desk. Pilk took another long pull.

"Now then, Mr. Pilk," Naomi said with her most encouraging smile. "You were saying, about the horn o' plenty . . ."

Jamie watched in amazement as Pilk's face seemed to dissolve. The wrinkles around his mouth smoothed and would have disappeared entirely if they hadn't collected so much grime; his eyes dilated and became dim pools of contentment. Jamie decided the man must have had more than a few nips against the cold before he had ventured out this morning.

"Funny about those things," Pilk said with a giggle. "There were these two guys, see, come up to me one day. Must of heard about my reputation for business. 'Course,"—he took another pull—"I wasn't always in *this* business. Used to sell previously owned cars. What a life. The old Toyotas sold for more than a Mercedes. And some stiff was always complaining about his worn-out carb. Now *this* business"—he gestured airily around the room—"this business, nobody complains, 'cause he don't want to admit he's a sucker." Pilk waggled his head knowingly and managed to connect with the bottle again.

Naomi had cast an amused glance toward Jamie at Pilk's last remark; Jamie frowned to say get-on-with-it.

"The horns," Naomi suggested gently. She leaned forward, giving Pilk a glance down her low-buttoned disco shirt. He hiccuped.

"Yeah. Like I say, these guys come up to me one day, ask me if I'll distribute the things. So I say what's in it for me? You know." Pilk winked. "And God *damn*, they say almost a dollar a sale. Adds up to maybe two thousand the first month—new product and all, it grabs a lot of curiosity."

He swallowed again from the bottle and held it out to Naomi. She passed it to Jamie, who took a sip that went down his throat like spiced lava. He handed the ouzo back to Pilk, certain that it had been fortified.

"So okay. I say what's in it for them? They say . . . they say . . ." Pilk guffawed and belched. "Sorry. They say thirty cents worth o' tin for every sale. *Tin!* I say you crazy? They just smile." With a canny look he set the bottle on his desk. "They say don't worry, they make something over on their side too."

"Their side?" Naomi asked, leaning forward again.

Pilk looked away with exaggerated disinterest. "That's what they said. I didn't ask what side that was. They didn't have no accents, though."

"Tin," Naomi mused. "That must be something so rare to them that—"

"How do you get the tin to them?" Jamie asked. "Do they come and pick it up?"

"Nah." Pilk pointed to an octagonal device in the shadows of one of his shelves. "They left that thing, and boxes come out of it after I stick tin cans in. You should see how fat my cat is—looks like he oughta be a Sumo wrestler."

"What happens to the tin cans?" Naomi asked.

Pilk was drinking again; Jamie watched his Adam's apple go up and down like a pogo stick. The small man stoppered the bottle and laid it in a side drawer of his desk. "The cans go pop, pop, and disappear. The boxes show up going pop too, only a different pop. Never mind. Beats the hell out of the post office, I'll tell you."

Naomi, who had been regarding the octagonal frame thoughtfully, leaped up and headed for it, her hand out-

stretched to reach into it. Pilk lurched after her, crying
"No!" He grabbed her arm and fell, pulling her to the littered floor with him.

"Don' . . . do that," he gasped as they untangled.
"They tol' me it was only designed to take tin, an' never
put anything else in. Never! Should see what it does jus' to
labels on the cans. An' if . . . and if I don't wash all the
food out o' the cans, this *stuff* dribbles out." He looked
sick. "So don't stick your hand in. Godsake."

Somewhat disappointed, Naomi nodded, her eyes sweep-
ing around the room. They landed on a jumble of empty
cans nearby; Jamie saw them at the same time, and realization dawned on both of them at once.

Before the groaning Pilk managed to focus his eyes and
protest, Naomi had gathered up several cans and was tossing them into the dark interior of the frame. The cans vanished with a sound more like a burp than a pop. Shredded
paper from their labels sprayed out like strangely colored
confetti.

Pilk found his voice at last. "Hey, cut that out! Wattaya
tryin' to do, overpay 'em?"

Surprisingly, Naomi obeyed. She dropped several cans
back onto the pile, her eyes never leaving the frame. In a
moment a deeper sound came—a bump rather than a
burp—and a neatly wrapped parcel slid forward out of the
frame. It was identical to the one Jamie had received in the
mail.

Naomi opened it; inside was an oddly shifting and shimmering horn o' plenty. She glanced in satisfaction at Jamie.

"All right; he's telling the truth," Jamie said. "But we
still don't know very much."

"A lot more than we did an hour ago, *conquistador*."

Pilk struggled to his feet, walked carefully back to his
desk and settled gratefully in his chair. He sighed. "I been
honest with you, like you said. Right? You see anything
crooked goin' on?" He belched. "Simple business deal,
trade for trade."

"It doesn't look crooked," Jamie admitted. "But I
wouldn't call it simple."

"Yeah, I guess not. God damn weird, if you ask me."
His eyes narrowed cunningly—or was he just trying to fo-
cus? "Look, this's a . . . good business. But I might sell.
Got other opportunities too, see—happens I know this

broad, this guy, can tell every hurricane that's comin' in jus' by throwin' down matchsticks. Always figured there must be an angle to selling insurance . . ."

Jamie looked at Naomi; she shrugged. Pilk was becoming too drunk to supply any further coherent information.

"We'll be in touch," Jamie promised, and reached for his jacket.

Jamie sat morosely on Naomi's couch. He had been thinking hard for two days now, disconsolately watching the clutter mount around his horn o' plenty by day, spending his nights with Naomi.

Naomi refused to speculate about what they should do—she was absorbed in working on the samples Jamie brought her, calculating, precipitating, irradiating to her heart's delight. The bell, book and candle seemed to have lost place with her in favor of the more customary scientific methods.

It seemed to Jamie that he should turn the whole matter over to the authorities, those nebulous figures who would deal with it efficiently and thoroughly. But he was reluctant to do so. Besides his very practical fear of Naomi's wrath—he remembered the time he had called in the fire department to deal with a poltergeist salamander—Jamie had to admit that deep down he wanted to hold onto this secret. There just might be a lot of money in it, if he and Naomi could figure it all out.

But short of tying up Pilk and sending the . . . whatever . . . a note etched on a cat food can demanding a summit meeting, he couldn't see how to take charge of the situation. Furthermore, he doubted that those on the other side would bother to read cat food graffiti.

He was roused from his worries by Naomi's cheerful call.

"Dinner!"

Jamie groaned. Naomi's creative meals had already passed from the impressionistic to the surreal; he was afraid to think of what might come next. Last night she had served a health-food dinner starting with cream of yogurt soup and culminating in seaweed mousse. He wasn't sure just what the entree had been, though he had had the opportunity to contemplate the problem all night as his stomach churned and gave forth its effluvia.

Jamie approached the table cautiously.

"What is that?"

"Dinner," Naomi said happily.

"Why is that dinner?"

"What a charming way you have with words, *mon fou*. It's dinner because there is nothing else it could be, of course; that is its True Name. Sit down. Enjoy."

Jamie sat, staring at the plate in front of him. On it lay an octagonally molded substance that was pale green and quivered slightly. It was tastefully garnished with miner's lettuce. He looked blankly at Naomi, who smiled proudly.

"You see, all has not been wasted. What else did you expect of me?"

"I've been hoping to lower my expectations," Jamie said weakly. "Less is more." He watched apprehensively as she raised a forkful of the substance to her mouth and began to chew. "What *is* it?"

"Food, of course," Naomi replied indistinctly. "Nutriment, energy—*you* know." She swallowed.

Jamie asked faintly, "Where did it come from?"

Naomi waved the fork expressively before gathering another mouthful. "You remember that green liquid that came out of the horn?" Jamie nodded, suddenly nauseated. "Well, would you believe that just three drops of it, added to a piece of bread, convert the starches into one of the purest and most easily digested forms of protein ever known?"

"No."

Naomi blinked. "It's true. Oversimplified, perhaps—there is a bit of chemistry involved—but that's basically the process. And this is the result."

"It's safe?" Jamie asked, staring at his plate.

"Absolutely. I had a snack last night, when you woke me up with the tossing and turning. It's very filling too, and it really does provide a lot of energy—if you'd stayed around today, you'd have seen me as practically a blur of motion."

Jamie had seen her that way before, on nothing more than TV dinners from CBS-MacDonald's. He took a tiny, dubious bite of the food. It tasted . . . brackish, maybe, but pleasant. He swallowed. Whatever it was stayed down.

He took a deep breath and some of the miner's lettuce, and began eating.

* * *

For the seventeenth time since dinner, Jamie felt his pulse and his forehead. He catalogued the various sensations within his body, waiting for the first twinge, the sudden stab of pain, the blurring in his mind. Nothing abnormal happened. He felt fine—full of zest, in fact.

He looked in wonder at Naomi, who was busily programming Adelle Davis recipes into her computer terminal. "Do you realize what this means?" he asked.

"Mmmm?"

"A revolution, nothing else."

"Of course." Naomi scanned a printout full of chemical formulae and their translations to minimum daily requirements of vitamins. She underlined three of them.

"I mean a *social* revolution, Naomi: the capability of feeding the whole world's population by adding just a few thousand gallons of that green stuff to the amount of grain we're already producing. And considering how much of it came out of *one* horn, imagine owning as many of them as we want!"

"You're thinking again about marketing them, right? Money. . . ." She waggled a finger at him. "Naughty, naughty. What about supply and demand, and your patriotic duty? Do you want to put our beef farmers out of work? Do you want the Third World nations to become independent of our handouts?"

Jamie shifted uncomfortably on the couch. "But if we handle things properly . . . Look, this can be bigger than nations; it could even make the world one single nation."

"If handled properly," Naomi said softly. "What are the odds?"

"I don't know—but we can't just ignore this." Jamie paced around the small room. "Dear God, can this be all it seems to be? How much of what Pilk said can we believe? He was drunk—and I wouldn't trust him when he was sober, would you?"

"*In vino veritas*, love."

" 'It was the wine that was talking,' " Jamie countered. "Anyway, the whole thing is so unlikely—people from another world sending us gobs of miracle substances in trade for tin. That octagonal thing could have just been another magic trick, after all—I wouldn't put anything past Pilk."

"There is one factor you're overlooking. The horn o' plenty and its byproducts are real."

Jamie nodded reluctantly. "Then maybe the whole thing's real. . . . Yes, it must be. And that means we've *got* to buy that franchise from Pilk. Can you imagine what he might do if he ever stayed sober long enough to figure out what he's got? He could make the late Khomeini look like Mahatma Gandhi."

"Why did I have to fall in love with an altruist?" Naomi sighed, switching off the computer terminal. Then she smiled wryly. "I suppose I must be a closet messiah too. . . . All right, Jamie, how much cash can you raise?"

"I've got a few thousand in the bank. What about your inheritance?"

"Mostly gone, *kochkeleh*. My grandfather's business went downhill after the Depression; people wouldn't spend as much on feeding horsemeat to their pets as they did for themselves, even then. I could put in a thousand, maybe a little more."

"So we'll need a loan. No, I can't see any bank accepting the collateral. . . . Maybe we could sign a contract with Pilk to buy him out completely within six months."

"I think he'd prefer cash," she said.

"We'll try anyway." Jamie stood up and burped. There was no aftertaste, which he took as a good omen. "Anyone who'd make a deal like he did with a couple of anonymous aliens ought to be a pushover for humans."

It took four days, counting the weekend, for Jamie to get a satisfactory contract drawn up by a lawyer for Dimmesdale Eternal Sanctuary. The lawyer raised his eyebrows ever so delicately when he read the description of the business, then efficiently produced forms in quintuplicate that were only four times as long as Jamie's draft. Everything was covered in them, from patent rights to indemnity clauses including Acts of God—a paragraph that, under the circumstances, required an hour of discussion couched in the vaguest of precise terms.

It was late afternoon on Tuesday when Jamie and Naomi arrived at Mervyn Pilk's office in Everton, so they weren't surprised when the eye behind the two-inch crack took several seconds to focus on them.

"You remember us," Jamie said.

"Crap. Yeah."

"We have to talk with you."

"Busy," Pilk said, and the door began to close. Jamie mentioned a sum of money, whereupon Pilk nearly tore the door open. He gestured more expansively than necessary to the chairs in front of his desk. Jamie sat, forbearing to loosen the gray mortician's tie that seemed to smell of formaldehyde; this was a business as serious as any he had conducted at his job. Besides, Pilk's bloated face reminded him of a drowning victim he had once handled.

Naomi removed her ski jacket, the only one she owned, and deposited it on the messy floor beside her chair. She leaned forward and cleaved unto Pilk's words.

"You got cash?"

"Not exactly," Jamie said, "but—"

"No cash, no deal," Pilk said firmly.

Jamie glanced around the room and saw many neatly wrapped parcels that bore no addresses. Evidently Varieties Unlimited wasn't doing very well this week. "We've formulated our offer," he said. "It begins with five thousand dollars up front, but that's only the beginning. Tell me, Mr. Pilk, how long will it take you to clear five thousand from the horns o' plenty?"

"Month or two," Pilk replied, obviously lying.

"No, Mr. Pilk. At least a year. The horns o' plenty are a very small part of Varieties Unlimited's operation. Remember that we've investigated some of your other, ah, services."

"That bastard ex-partner o' mine! But you can't prove anything!" Pilk rummaged in a desk drawer and brought forth a bottle of vodka; he gulped it.

"We don't have to prove anything if we can strike a simple business deal." Jamie drew one copy of the contract from his jacket and laid it before the little man. "See for yourself. Further payments to comprise the entire purchase price are specified in paragraph six."

Pilk began to read, running his left hand across the page as he drank from the bottle in his right. Doing so required some pauses, since he was evidently incapable of reading without moving his lips. At length he looked up, his eyes not so much narrowed as drooping.

"You got an angle, huh? Something I don't know about but you're gonna make a lot o' money out of."

Naomi spoke up: *"Cher voleur,* of course we know something you don't. But it is something no ordinary scientist would think to discover. Only I have the mental ability and agility to find that something. Only by stepping out of the muddy rut of scientific erosion can the true—"

Pilk snickered. "Is she for real?" he asked Jamie.

"For very real. You won't be able to make a cent more from the horn o' plenty than you're making now, unless you sign that contract. And I assure you, we won't make the offer again. We have other business to pursue."

"All of which is legal," Naomi added.

Pilk stared from one to the other of them, then with a doubtful grunt turned his eyes back to the contract. He muttered his way through all of it. Jamie forced himself to keep any expression from his face; glancing at Naomi, he saw that she had closed her eyes and was evidently saying her mantra. He occupied himself with wondering what that might be. Something from Descartes? Castañeda? More likely Aristophanes.

Pilk roused him by setting the bottle down with a thud. "You guys oughta be in my line o' work. Okay, okay, you got a deal. Lessee the down payment."

Jamie produced a cashier's check and the other four copies of the contract. Pilk glanced at the check and put it in his shirt pocket; he signed all five copies of the contract.

"There's one more thing," Naomi said.

Pilk glared at her as if he wished they were married so that he could divorce her.

"We'll have to meet your contacts on the other side," she said.

The small man giggled. "My pleasure to introduce you. You guys deserve each other—you're all weird. Except they're even weirder. Creepy, in fact."

"What's creepy about them?" Jamie asked.

Pilk waved a hand vaguely. "Their eyes—they're shifty, like they almost aren't there. Never trust no guy when you can't see his eyes, know what I'm sayin'? I like to do business on trust, but these guys . . ." He shook his head.

Jamie could imagine why Pilk liked to operate on trust. "How do you get in touch with them?" he asked.

"Ahh, it's easy, once you know how. Jus' stick some glass in that thing over there"—he nodded at the octagonal transporter—"and get the hell out o' the way. Makes a noise like King Kong farting an' the glass shoots back out in pieces like a shotgun. Five minutes later these guys show up at the door, an' they ain't happy. They're pretty mealy-mouthed, though; they calm down quick enough."

Naomi stood up and shook Pilk's hand. "I'm sure we're both satisfied with what you say, and we'll proceed with our business immediately. A pleasure to have met you, Mr. Pilk."

The small man grinned broadly. He raised the vodka bottle in salute, took three gulps and extended it to Naomi with a slightly clumsy bow.

Naomi took the bottle and whirled, striding across the room to the octagonal maw. "*Hey!*" Pilk cried. Naomi stood carefully to the side of the device and hurled the bottle in.

There came the sound of tangent worlds grinding exceedingly coarsely; a white spray vomited forth like the wake of a snowplow, covering the dirty floor and several boxes.

"Christ; now you've done it!" Pilk snatched his porkpie hat from the corner of his desk, briefly looked around for his jacket and abandoned the search. He hurried to the door. "You guys get yer stuff done, an' I'll see you."

Pilk tore open the door. Two men stood outside.

They were no taller than he, and each wore a porkpie hat and a frayed plaid overcoat; their trousers were wrinkled and shiny in the wrong places, and they seemed to have no eyes, only shadows beneath ragged eyebrows.

"You are very careless," said one of them.

"Very," said the other.

Pilk stepped back, making patting motions at the air in front of him. "No, listen, it wasn't me. These guys . . ."

Eyeless faces turned slightly toward Jamie and Naomi, then turned back to Pilk. "Yes?" Were there two voices, or only one that echoed?

Pilk took control of himself; he stood straight and drew a breath. "These guys just bought me out. You gotta deal with them now; I'm not in it no more."

"Ah. And who are these guys?"

Pilk waved a hand that almost got away from him. "Mr. James Slobro and Ms. Naomi Luckman. They now own the rights on this side to all your stuff."

Jamie stepped forward and held out his hand. "Good to meet you." He felt his hand being shaken formally; the grip was as strong as if two hands held his.

"Naomi *Lokisson*," he heard, and saw Naomi actually curtsy.

Mervyn Pilk took the opportunity to slip past the two visitors and scurry down the stairs.

Jamie watched him go, then forced himself to say lightly, "Please come in. Let's chat."

The two dark faces turned to one another for a moment. "Chat. Yes." Jamie was relieved to see that at least one of their mouths moved.

The men entered and, without removing either hats or overcoats, sat in the understuffed chairs. Naomi dragged a box from the corner to sit on, and Jamie, after a moment's hesitation, sat behind Pilk's desk.

"Well," he said. "As Mr. Pilk told you, my associate and I have bought his interest in the, ah, the horns o' plenty. Is that what *you* call them?"

"You must never put anything in the chute except tin," warned the man on the right.

"Mr. Pilk said that was how he called you," Jamie said.

"We do not like to be called." Low voice. Echoes. Shadows stirring sluggishly around the two men even though they weren't moving. Jamie noticed that they had very small feet. Their shoes were unpolished, scuffed; and there was something odd about the way they had tied their laces.

"I'm sure you must be very busy," Jamie said.

"We do not like to be here."

Jamie glanced at Naomi, hoping for a cue. She was leaning forward, elbows on knees, looking pensively at the visitors.

"May I ask," Jamie continued, "just where you come from? We have reason to believe you aren't from this world."

The faces looked at each other, then back to Jamie. "Our world is very similar. Different smells."

"Due to different elements," Naomi said helpfully. "In different combinations. But not *too* different, I suppose?"

Heads turned to her. "Very similar. But they smell better."

"Surely that's just because you're used to the smells of your world," she said. "To us, the green paste that comes through the horns o' plenty has an unpleasant odor."

"Green paste . . ." said one.

"Chloroprote." Both nodded. Both smiled. Their teeth

were small, and not long. Grinders in the front of their mouths? Jamie felt obscurely relieved.

"We don't like chloroprote either."

Their voices had gradually become lighter, and there was less echo now.

"Is your world in what we'd call an alternative time stream?" Naomi asked. "A place almost like here, only a few things happened differently? Mostly at the submolecular level, I'd imagine."

Smiles again, wider this time. They had no canines.

"Very good. Of course, during history these differences have produced larger variations."

"We produced tin thousands of years ago, but it lacked tensile strength."

"It becomes very soft in warm weather."

"We have a long tradition of tin sculpture. It is very delicate in design, but details are lost quickly."

The visitors had become almost animated; their tiny feet shuffled, and one of them had begun to make soft gestures with his hands. Jamie wasn't sure, but he thought their fingers each had an extra joint.

"So you want the stronger alloy we can produce here," he said. "And you trade us chloroprote and . . . that red dust, for instance."

The shadowed faces turned to each other. "Ruddy pollen," said one.

"Yes." The second face turned back to Jamie. "We vacuum it up each spring and bury it. Our lazier ones who don't have land dump it into their garbage."

Tiny feet moving more quickly now. Was it excitement or agitation?

"I think I see," said Naomi, sitting up and adjusting her shirt. "The substances you're sending us are things you don't want, things you usually bury. But someone found a better way to get rid of them—someone invented an interprobability transporter, or whatever you call it."

"Chute."

"Okay; a chute between our worlds. Two kinds, actually—the simpler one just ships stuff from there to here, and that's the horn o' plenty. The other kind can transport things from here *back*."

One of the faces turned to Jamie. "This person is a female."

"Then you wondered if you could get anything useful from us," Naomi went on. "So you came here yourselves, and you found our tin . . . and you met Mervyn Pilk."

Dark faces turned to each other, and Jamie could hear excited gabbling. When the heads turned again, the men's eyebrows were raised, and Jamie saw that they really did have eyes. Their irises were red.

"We did not meet Mervyn Pilk for some time. But no one else believed us—many were rude, and all of them went away when we spoke. We were called names."

"I'll bet," Jamie said.

"We altered our clothing for each person, but it didn't help until we met Mervyn Pilk. He listened to us and was friendly. He said nice things to us, though his accent was hard to understand."

"He was drunk; he slurs."

One face turned to the other; the second continued. "We made an arrangement with Mervyn Pilk—he has been supplying us with much tin, and he accepts what we send him in return." The man who was speaking drew himself up proudly. "We are now men of substance in our world."

The other dark man turned away from him to Jamie and Naomi. Very, very calmly he said, "We do not wish to change our arrangement. Do you plan to continue the exchange as it has been?"

Jamie noticed that Naomi was looking at him with a slight smile and lifted eyebrows. She seemed very pleased with herself, with everything.

"I believe . . ." he said. "Yes, of course we'll continue."

The two dark men settled back in their chairs. But Naomi had something to add.

"We may want to make *some* changes, but"—she held up her hand—"don't worry, they'll be mutually beneficial. You see, gentlemen, so far we've only scratched the surface of the possibilities. I'm sure there are other substances in your world that will be new and useful to us; we'd like to see and test them. In return, we'll find things here that will produce wonders for you. That is—"

She regarded them closely. They fidgeted, moving their tiny feet, fussing with long-fingered hands.

"That is, *mes associés*, if you have the means to analyze and use what we give you. Forgive me, but since your business success has come only recently, I doubt that you've yet set up an organization that can make the most of the possibilities before us. You'll need someone on your side who has the knowledge to advise you."

"Oh," said one dark man, and "Yes," said the other. They were nodding eagerly.

Naomi smiled. "We're going to do a lot of *very* profitable business together. Much better than your previous line of work, I'm sure."

Jamie watched their heads bob, and frowned. "Naomi, I don't quite—"

"Until recently, love, our friends here were garbagemen."

Shadows shifted reproachfully. "Removal executives," said an echoing voice or two.

"You know," Jamie said to Naomi's back, "it's not as easy as you'd think, being a millionaire."

They were relaxing in Naomi's workshop, which she had refused to give up when Jamie had moved into a twenty-room townhouse. Naomi had added a good deal of research equipment, including a new computer terminal that responded to input from her voice alone.

She merely grunted in reply to Jamie's remark.

But Jamie was serious. There was an enormous amount of work to keep up with: buying storage warehouses and conversion plants for the green liquid, making business arrangements with bakeries and distributorships around the world, the endless details of patent rights and setting up a financial empire. Not to mention political pressure from everyone including the Food and Drug Administration.

With an eye to the future, they had incorporated under the name Varieties Unlimited. Not that Naomi took much part in these plans. Her only interests lay in continuing her study of more and more substances that came out of the horn o' plenty, and in her voluminous wire-recorder correspondence with researchers on The Other Side. Jamie knew she had some involved plan for sending as much of the scientific community as possible into permanent trauma, but he had been far too busy to pay much attention.

Sometimes he wondered if it was all worth it. What if the world's supply of tin were exhausted before they could find an alternative? And what about all those new substances for which they hadn't yet found a use? He also worried about the huge amounts of waste that were being thrown away, and the fact that Naomi had insisted on cornering the market in garbage dumps hadn't helped his state of mind.

Jamie tried to shrug off the mood. Money was, after all, supposed to bring happiness. And the business was certainly worthwhile: starvation and malnutrition around the world were disappearing. Already he had received awards and testimonials from Werner Erhard and a number of vegetarian organizations. He should feel like a benefactor instead of a harried businessman.

"Responsibility," he mused aloud, getting up to wander restlessly around the room.

"Don't step there," said Naomi. "Pentagram."

Jamie looked at the floor. "It has eight sides," he pointed out.

"Very good, love. It's really an octogram—experimental Hieronymus chute."

Jamie stepped around the configuration and continued pacing. "We've taken on an enormous responsibility—I'm not sure the two of us can handle all the ramifications. Maybe we should call in some experts. The World Health Organization—"

Naomi guffawed, looking up from the microfiche reader she had been studying.

"Look," he said, "I know you think you're more competent than people who've been working all their lives—"

Naomi held up a hand, then beckoned him over to her littered workbench. "Look at this."

He bent over a large mortar—cauldron?—then drew back hurriedly. "What's that?" he gasped, fighting for fresh air.

"Basically, just sewage. Raw human sewage."

"Yuck."

"Basically, I said. It also contains a certain amount of bat's blood, ground sprigs of deadly nightshade, and a couple of foreskins." Jamie looked blank. "I got the basic recipe from that." She indicated an antique volume written in brown calligraphy, with illuminated chapter headings that looked, at a glance, somewhat obscene.

"Now watch. When I add a pinch of this . . ."

Jamie recognized the reddish powder. A horrid surmise rose in his mind.

"*No!* I am *not* going to eat *that!*"

Naomi stared at him. "Of course not. Why on earth would you want to? There's very little nourishment in hydrocarbons, you know."

Relief washed over him. Then: "What did you say?"

She smiled winningly. "Hydrocarbons."

"But that's . . ."

He stared into the bowl, at the thick black sludge that lay viscously in the bottom, now smelling very different indeed.

". . . oil," said Naomi.

Jamie sat down suddenly, his face in his hands. "Oil from sewage," he muttered. He felt himself shaking, and realized that he was laughing.

He looked up, trying to compose his features into something approaching solemnity.

"You know, being a billionaire isn't going to be easy either."   ☆

Excursion Fare

James Tiptree, Jr.

Several curious events were in the news that year, but young Dag and Philippa had been too busy to notice. And right now they were overwhelmed beyond thought of all else.

They were dying, or about to die, all alone in the reaches of the northern Atlantic Ocean.

"Letting up," Philippa gasped through crusted lips.

Feebly, she began to bail again. She was wedged into the rope-holds of the swamped, inflated raft that had been the passenger-pod of their balloon. In the gray-churned sea around her writhed bright tatters, all that was left of *Sky-Walker*.

They had been driven down into the ocean fifty scream-ing hours ago.

"No," Dag croaked from the other end of the pod, his voice startlingly loud in the sudden quiet. The wind-shriek had dropped, and the hail of spume upon them was subsid-ing. "It's only the eye. We're in the eye. Look up."

She looked and saw, above the great storm-walls curving away on either side, a strange gray-yellow patch of clear sky. It seemed to be evening, far away up there. But she could see, too, that the clear patch ended; dimly in the distance, the terrible storm-walls joined again. Beneath them would be raving, driving mountains of sea, air that was smashed and flying brine. The North side, too—worse even than what they'd miraculously lived through. Now the miracles were over.

"We can't—possibly—"

"No. Oh, god, fuck it," Dag groaned for the hundredth time. "This wasn't supposed to be here. 'Degenerated into a low'—aaagh!" He gave a bitter bark, and in the increasing

40

calm, pried loose their last canteen and crawled over to her with it.

"Might as well finish this."

As they drank, pale sunlight touched them. "Goodbye, sun," Philippa whispered very low. They grasped each other in numb arms and kissed deeply.

"I got you into this. I got you into this," Dag said into her neck.

"It's all right, darling." Her lips were too cracked for her to speak clearly.

A big brownish flap of something dead slithered over the swamped side, washed away again. She shivered harder. "Do you think . . . I'd want you to be alone in this?"

There was clearly no hope, but he pulled away and crouched up to wrench loose and jettison the remains of the heater-struts that were weighing down one side of the raft. Their transceiver had doubtless long since ceased bleating out its SOS. He started to send it over too.

"No," Philippa protested weakly.

He tried to grin at her—a salt-crusted, sodden, red-eyed specter—and let it be, even straining over to straighten the antenna and give the emergency generator a few more cranks. Then he collapsed down in the water before her, grasping her cold legs with water-wrinkled hands. She dropped her futile bailer and clumsily caressed his head and shoulders, pulling him up into her lap. The sun-gleam had gone; they were both shivering uncontrollably now.

Over his head she could see the oncoming wind-wall, the end of the eye: Great yellow-black spume-walls, racing from right to left.

"Let's . . . let's hold together now."

"No," he said unclearly. "Better chance if we balance it."

She nodded. They both knew there was no chance; he made no move to leave her. A burst of rain hissed onto them, mingled with a last light-ray. The roaring, howling mountains of death loomed louder, nearer. Already their raft was starting to move with it. As they waited for the end, Dag mumbled incomprehensibly: She caught the repeated word "prove" and held him tighter. He was affirming for the last time the deep dream, the drive that had powered their attempt: That lone human beings were still

free to achieve high adventure, free to master fate, and
defy the edicts of an over organized world . . .

Their pathetic little raft was already tossing in the first
great chop before the roaring, racing mountains took them.
Dag had forced himself away from Philippa when the raft
was almost doubled end-over-end, but she had made her
frozen fingers tie a rope from his waist to hers, and he had
stretched his numb legs to clamp his feet around her an-
kles.

Darkness was all but on them now. The roaring grew.
The tossing and spinning became more violent. Soon the
first torrent of water broached over them. As they surfaced
again, each struggled simultaneously to breathe and to see
if the other lived.

Suddenly he heard her cry out so loudly that it pierced
the storm. A terrible fear for her took him—and then he
heard it too: Through the howl and slamming came the
pound of a powerful engine.

An instant later a blinding light poured on them through
the spume, lost them, and came back from windward.

The two young people had only a momentary glimpse of
something huge and white rising and falling alongside a
few yards away, when a cable shot over their heads and
their pod lurched, tilted, folded in on them and physically
flew, struck something that might have been a plunging
gunwale, and tumbled them out half smothered and
drowned, onto a solid floor.

Quick hands cut them loose, a white-capped bronzed
face with the name *Charon* in gold on the visor looked
briefly down at them, then vanished. Great sobs were rack-
ing them both. They tried to say "thank you" through the
spasms at half-seen grayish faces in the gray light as they
felt themselves piled onto a bunk. Presently they realized
the bunk was sodden, and more green water suddenly
poured into what they saw was a cockpit.

The strange craft had seemed utter safety, steady as a
rock, after the helpless raft, but they now could feel that
she was pitching wildly. They were in fact far from safe
yet, they were only in a lifeboat, with a hurricane still upon
them. But they could feel no more fear, only trust in the
tall white-clad man at the helm, and in his quick, silent
crew.

"Okay, let's get out of here," the tall man said now. "Give 'em masks."

Scubalike masks were pressed over their faces. Philippa's head was gently pulled away from Dag's neck. She offered no resistance, but only reached for Dag's arm just as his hand found and gripped hers.

"Breathe. Breathe," ordered an accented voice.

The mask-air was fresh and sweet. The last thing they remembered was a swiftly increasing motor-roar, and a heave as if the lifeboat were planing up on foils as she drove into the gray-lit gale.

They came to in the beds of a pleasant room; only a calm, almost imperceptible engine-throb, and the slight swaying of the sunlight on the window-curtains, told them they were still at sea.

Dag twisted and groggily scanned a discreet panel displaying dials, lights, an outlet marked Oxygen, and then located Philippa in the next bed. Her dark eyes were on him, glowing and merry with love.

"I've been waiting for you to wake up. Watch it, you're hooked to a zillion IVs. The thing is—uh, oh!—" She retched noisily into a yellow basin she was holding.

"Are you okay? Hey, Phil!"

"The problem *is*," she continued with great dignity as the spasm waned, "you have to throw up a lot of salt water. Your basin's on the stand there. Maybe nausea won't hit you."

But it did; he grabbed his blue basin just in time, discovering in the process that his ribs on one side were bandaged and so was one knee.

When he could look up again, a red-haired nurse was in the room.

"You kids both with us again? I'm Anna Boyd." She wasn't pretty, but she had a great smile. She produced two shot-glasses full of green, syrupy-looking liquid.

"Drink this now, it'll help."

"Where are we? What day is this?" Dag asked.

"Tuesday. The rest later—here's Dr. Halloway. Drink up."

They drank, looking over the rims of their glasses at a middle-aged, slightly rotund man with sandy hair and very bright eyes. The name on his lab coat breast pocket said

Charon. A little like a big chipmunk, Dag thought. But his eyelids were very heavy, and before Halloway could finish checking the knee-bandage he was drifting off. He had just time to hear Philippa call sleepily to him, "We're on a hospice ship."

Halloway smiled and nodded. "That's right."

But his patients were already lost in sweet, dreamless sleep, their bodies busy repairing the endless days and sleepless nights of *Sky-Walker*'s end.

At one point during the night Dag woke to dim lights and saw, or dreamed, a tall man in gold-braided whites standing by Philippa's bed. This bothered him a little, until he saw that the man was looking, not at Philippa, but at something or someone beside him, by the foot of his own bed. A child? No—the presence moved away and became a blurred or veiled shape in a wheelchair. A vague sense of disquiet stirred in him, but then he remembered "hospice ship," and the wheelchair seemed somehow appropriate. The presence said something very deep and blurry. But Dag couldn't concentrate. Almost sure that this was all a dream, he let himself slip off the corner of consciousness, still grateful for their comfort and safety. Phil's okay, was his last half-thought.

Next day was blurry too, and emotional. One moment they thrilled again to their finding by the great hospice ship's lifeboat, and the next they collapsed into sadness and wept into their broth and custard at *Sky-Walker*'s fate.

"It was m-more than just an adventure," Philippa repeated. "We wanted to p-prove, to prove what one person can, to show you still can, that we c-could—"

"We were . . . crazy," Dag said in a bitter, flat voice. She'd never heard him so down. It roused her a little.

"That was a freak," she said. "Anybody can be hit by a freak thing. It doesn't *mean* . . ."

They were silent awhile, weighed down by reaction to the long nightmare.

Then Dag started to say something, but she got there first, in a tentative, little voice like a kid's. "We could . . . do it again."

He sat bolt upright, then painfully rose from his bed and moved over to hers.

"Do you mean that, Phil? Think. Would you really?"

She nodded hard, her lips set.

"We can. I mean, *we will* . . . You can't have *two* freaks."

"You really would?" He reached for her, grunting with the pain of his rib. She nodded hard, hard.

"Even if we have *three* freaks. Dag, we're going to."

"Oh, my god, my darling . . . it'll be hard."

"So it's hard."

He choked up again.

"We'll call it the *D-defiance*."

"Yick."

"Okay, okay. The *Horatio H. Fish-Flattener*."

They giggled through tears, holding each other, thinking of the long hard year ahead—years, maybe. Raising the money. The talk-talk-talk. But they would succeed. Somehow they would. They'd start right away, while some of the stuff they needed to work with was still around.

Then Dr. Halloway descended on them with two nurses and a battery of tests, chasing Dag back to his own bed in mock scandal. He seemed extra-cheerful, a happy chipmunk. Halfway through the second tissue sample it occurred to them why. Typically, Philippa said it. "We must be some of the first healthy patients you've had in a long while, Doctor."

Halloway looked up, suddenly sobered. "That's right. My lifework is spent with the dying."

"People you can't help."

He grunted. "Well, I can help some. I don't mean save them, I mean we're learning a lot about how to make dying—also an important part of life—go better. For instance, we've come light-years beyond the old Brompton cocktail, though we still call it that. Here on the high seas—great old phrase, isn't it?—we're not subject to the stupid drug laws of any nation. We can experiment with whatever seems promising for the patient. Only prejudice on our parts makes this gloomy work, you know. One of the last taboos. Because doctors hate what they can't fix. But I must say you certainly are a pair of splendid young specimens, especially after what you went through." He patted a bandage on Philippa's shoulder. "It does me good to see healing like that. One forgets."

Dag squinted at him, wondering if maybe Halloway

would like to find and extract some kind of magic health-juice out of them for his patients—real mad-doctor stuff. But he didn't look crazy, just hard-working and pleased.

"When do we get up? It better be tomorrow or we'll start to go sour on you."

"Tomorrow you take a walk on the ward. With Miss Boyd."

"I want to see the ocean," Phil said.

"I'd think you'd have had enough of that. But okay. I guess I really have got into the habit of over-caution. I'll tell Anna Boyd to take you out on deck. If the weather's fine."

"Over-caution," Dag said sneakily, and Halloway laughed.

Next morning Anna Boyd brought them each a new blue hospital jump suit with *Charon* emblazoned in bright yellow on the breast pocket and presently led them through what seemed a mile's maze of corridors. Pleasant carpets, paintings ("By patients," she told them), doors ajar from which came normal-sounding voices and a laugh or two in the distance—nothing seemed like a hospital, except for the occasional IV stand or oxygen-breather outside a door and the number of nurses, male and female, passing by.

Only twice did they pass doors from which came sounds they didn't like. One was open; they edged gingerly past the rasping sobs and were startled to hear the weeping change to "Hello!" They looked in; a sobbing old woman in a dressing gown held the hand of an even older woman on the bed. She was sobbing too, but her free hand was waving to them. Nurse Boyd herded them to the doorway.

"H-hello," Philippa essayed.

The old woman peered at them. "You're not dying?" she asked hoarsely.

"No."

"Not yet," Dag added.

"Good!" She blew her nose and said, "So young! But you will someday. When you do, I hope it's as nice as this."

Her companion had pulled herself together enough to nod and add, "That's right," through a teary smile.

They stared helplessly, noticing a male nurse standing in the shadow by the port.

"I mean it," the older woman rasped. "Oh, we're just

crying because of—somebody we both knew. He didn't
have all this, you see. He . . ." She choked up, forced a
grotesque smile. "Sometimes it's hard, remembering. But
it's better to let it out."

"I see," Philippa said gravely.

"Bye now, dears. Thanks for stopping." Her companion
lifted one age-warped hand in the ghost of a farewell wave.
Her other hand clutched some knitting.

They went quickly on, into a sunlit lounge with someone's easel in the corner.

"I think I know what she meant," Philippa said in a low
voice.

"Me too." Dag's tone echoed hers, and he took her hand
and pressed it briefly. They needed no more words. They
had in fact met each other in the visitors' lounge of the
hospital where her father and his grandmother were dying
of cancer.

The experience had been almost more than they could
bear. The once-loved people, now helpless bodies who were
waked from inadequate "sedation" only to scream in ag-
ony . . . the gray back wards, where the nurses came ever
slower and less frequently, and the doctors scarcely at all
. . . the insane laws denying certain drugs on the grounds
of preserving the dying from addiction . . . and deeper
yet, the unspoken fear for self—that this was how one
would end.

And now they were on a hospice ship—on one of the
controversial death cruises itself, where no one but the
dying were allowed. Immoral swindle or genuine benefac-
tion? Well, they would see.

"They tried to keep them secret at first, didn't they?"
Dag asked. "What was it—oh, yes, the *La France*, sixty
thousand tons."

"The S.S. *Gabriel* now," said Anna Boyd.

"I guess it was very hard to get on then. They had quotas for rich people, and middle income, and charity. And
no relatives."

"They still do. There *are* a few relatives, though, for the
very young and very, very old patients."

They were passing a poster offering short shore trips at
the upcoming ports of call. There was a photo of a green
and white bus that looked familiar. Had they observed
some of the "death trips" without knowing it?

"Hey, we're going to North Africa," Phil said.

"Yes, we've found people enjoy the tours—wherever the narcotics laws are, er, negotiable. The Sphinx is very popular, even with stretcher people." Anna Boyd smiled warmly.

"What happens if someone dies?"

"We do the best we can to handle the situation tactfully. S.A. Hospice Ltd. is good at that. Now—there's your sea!"

Strong glass doors opened onto a section of open deck that looked like a pleasant patio hung with live plants. Heavy storm shutters by the rail were folded back. It was a beautiful day.

They made for the rail and craned over, fascinated by the surge of water below along the great ship's sides. By peering they could just see the gleaming bow-wave curling out, and sternward, the tremendous churn of her wake. Refreshed by the breeze and sunlight, reveling in the huge ship's mastery of the element that had so nearly killed them, they didn't notice that someone else had come out, until a horrid fit of coughing made them turn.

The man was obviously a patient, a small, bone-thin man whose jump suit hung slack over his collapsed chest, with sunken, haggard eyes above his handkerchief. The coughing ceased; he grinned almost frighteningly and tottered to a bench.

"Hi! You're the kids who made the balloon trip, right?"

"Yes."

"Wow. Crazy. I like it." He turned away to complete another ghastly coughing fit. When it was over he gasped, "Told me—you were here. Sure am glad I met you." His eyes were going from Dag to Phil and back, hungrily yet somehow happily. "Rosenthal's the name, by the way. Not that it matters. Doc says I'll probably die tomorrow or Saturday, but I sure don't feel it. I used to be a C.P.A. Tell me, how was it? Was it worth it to you?"

"Oh, yes."

They went on to tell him a bit about ballooning, the wonderful part before the storm, the silent flights over waving people they could call to, the birds that came with them. Unconsciously they swung into the back-and-forth duet they had used so often in interviews, while their eyes tried to grasp the reality of the macabre figure before them.

He seemed delighted by every aspect, from the charm

and wonder of this old-new way of flight to the smallest detail of their precarious financing.

"So you're going to try again, eh?"

"Yes, we are."

"Good for you. Geez, am I glad I lasted long enough to meet you."

A second, very small nurse had come out, carrying a nautical wooden tray of crystal wine-goblets. Anna Boyd, who had been listening from the rail, stepped forward.

"I feel pretty good, Shirl," Rosenthal croaked at the tray-bearer.

"And that's the way we want to keep you." She handed him a goblet. "Down with it, Mr. R."

"I was just kidding." He drank it quickly. "Great stuff, but they sure could improve the flavor."

"We're working on it. I brought you something to help." She set the tray down by Anna and produced a packet of lifesavers and something else which she slipped quickly into his breast pocket. It looked suspiciously like a cigarette.

"Ah, Shirl, you're an ange. When I get up there, first thing I do is make sure you're in the book."

"And how do you know you're going up there, Mr. R.?" Shirley asked mischievously.

"No doubt whatsoever. Can you think of any place they must need a C.P.A. more?"

In the general laughter, Dag and Phil had been looking curiously at the beautifully set tray.

"Ah-ah-ah!" Shirley whirled and snatched it up again. "This you stay strictly away from, kids. The big no-no. Not even a lick at an empty glass. It's a Brompton cocktail with a few improvements that have side effects. One taste and you're up the wall for life."

She grinned at Rosenthal, took his glass, and trotted back inside.

Anna Boyd stepped back to the rail. "Hi, look. Porpoises!"

Rosenthal got up to see too. Self-consciously giving him space, they leaned out to watch the sleek olive bodies playing in the bow-wave, apparently scornful of the mighty ship bearing on them.

"Ah, glorious!" Rosenthal tried to breathe deeply and was doubled over by coughing. Back on his bench, he grinned ruefully. "Funny. Maybe you kids can figure it out."

"What?"

"All this." Feebly, he waved one bony hand around at the charming patio, the great ship in general.

"I can figure out ordinary costs. Top quality, every little thing. And the *Charon* used to be the *United States*, she's a fuel hog. Plus—I was on three or four hospital boards before I got sick—I couldn't begin to cost out this kind of care. And I know I paid full price—in fact I kicked in double, my heirs are richer than god and don't give a damn. Even assuming twenty percent of the others did the same, it doesn't begin to add up."

Phil and Dag looked about speculatively, but their work with *Sky-Walker* offered no basis for any such extrapolations.

"Plus—" Rosenthal held up bony fingers to count. "This Society Anonymous Ltd. has the S.S. *Mercury*, that was the *QE II*; the S.S. *Gabriel*, you know her; the *Queen Mary* that was once a museum is now under work as the S.S. *Saint Martha*; *plus* the old *Michelangelo* and the *Da Vinci* are in drydock for rebuilding. I think they have options on every damn thing afloat over thirty-five thousand tons. I know because I bumped into a couple of get-rich-quick medical outfits that want to jump in. This S.A. Hospice is not about to let that happen, no way. God knows, they may even raise the old *Queen Elizabeth*, she's down off Singapore."

He paused for a brief coughing bout.

"I tell you, it doesn't begin to add up."

The two young people could only frown thoughtfully.

"They must have an angel," Philippa offered.

"Hey, that's good." Rosenthal grinned. "Don't make me laugh, you trying to kill me?" He laughed anyway, and only coughed a little. "Well, just a thought to leave you with."

"Time you two *wunderkinden* went home," said Anna Boyd.

"Great meeting you, fan-tastic. And keep on flying, hear?"

"We will, Mr. R., and—"

Anna Boyd hustled them out before the farewells could become awkward.

As they walked back along the serene corridors, Philippa observed quietly, "*Brave New World*?"

"Huh? Oh, yeah. Remember the death ward—and roses and kids and candy, all sweety googoo. And some awful drug—I mean, weren't they all spaced out?"

"Yes. To think the mother didn't even know her son. Or didn't care."

"This place isn't like that though. Those old ladies, they weren't spacey, they were remembering. And Rosenthal was sharp."

"And their feeling bad about whomever, that was rational. But it's so hard to believe . . . Miss Boyd—"

"Anna, to you."

"Anna, is Mr. Rosenthal *really* going to die tomorrow?"

"He wasn't supposed to last to yesterday, my dear. We don't know *what* he's breathing with."

"Lung cancer, isn't it?"

"Yes, and badly metastasized. The only thing we've noticed is that people who aren't in pain, and have interests, sometimes seem to last just a little longer. Pain helps to kill, you know."

"Lung cancer," Dag said. "Look, I don't mean to talk out of turn, but, well, you had to have seen it too . . ."

Anna frowned, then suddenly understood. "Of course. Shirl's cigarette. She slips him one every few days. Naturally Dr. Halloway okayed it first."

"But—"

"But why not? If he can have some pleasure. Mostly he just carries the thing around and finally lights it and sniffs the smoke."

"And coughs like mad?"

"Oh, yes."

"I'm starting to understand it," Dag said slowly. "Granted, these people really are all absolutely one hundred percent dying—they are, aren't they, Anna? No maybes, no cures possible?"

"No maybes," she told him. "There's a screening board. The decision has to be unanimous. I think there was one long remission case on the first cruise—it was a four-year-old girl, kids are the hardest to judge. But she went, on the second trip, while they were still arguing. Those whom I feel sorry for are the ones the board turns down, wrongly."

"Oh, my god, little kids," Phil murmured.

"Okay," Dag went on. "So they're absolutely one hundred percent goners. So then the rule is that whatever makes a person feel good is okay. If it really makes him happy—I mean, as herself or himself. Whether he or she goes happy on Monday instead of being miserable or hurting to drag it out to Tuesday doesn't count. Right?"

"That's right, my dear."

"Of course, it could be a problem," Phil said thoughtfully, "if, for instance, a person is an alcoholic."

"That's right too—in theory. Luckily we don't get alcoholics, so far. But even if we did—it's strange, but in practice, things are often simpler. You can always think up a good theoretical dilemma; but what we actually have to deal with just about solves itself, with common sense . . . And now we have arrived at the practical issue known as your bedroom, and I'll bet somebody has trouble not going to sleep in his or her dessert."

She would have lost her bet—the dessert was delicious—but not by much. The wisdom of their young bodies took over, and afternoon merged into all-night in a sweet, dreamless, drugless blur.

Early next morning they discovered that all their own clothes, plus what few possessions had been salvaged from *Sky-Walker*'s pod, were neatly cleaned and stored in their closet. Even Philippa's bright scarf was there.

"Hey, let's get dressed! Then they'll have to let us out."

They were out of hospital garb and into their own in two minutes. Just as Philippa was cinching the belt that made her army fatigues a showcase for her tiny-waisted, healthy body, Dr. Halloway walked in.

"Well, well, well." He looked them over, twinkly chipmunk. "And where do you two think you're going?"

Dag stuttered for an instant, then inspiration struck. "Well, sir, we were going to ask you something. We met Mr. Rosenthal yesterday. Somehow he knew who we were, and he wanted to hear all about the balloon flight. He seemed to enjoy it too. So I thought I'd ask you if some other patients feel that way. If you like, we could stroll around the decks and chat with anyone who cares to. And of course it'd be better to do so in our own clothes. Or is that a no-good thought?"

"Far from it! In fact it's a delightful meeting of the minds." Halloway's merry grin contained only the faintest, most benevolent suspicion that Dag had just made up the whole escape plan. "It's amazing how word gets around this ship—I'll never understand it. You two are the sensation of the cruise. Everybody wants to see you, and half of them want to ask questions. Just strolling around wouldn't do at all. I've already talked to Captain Ulrik, and he'll be delighted to hear you're ready to give a little talk."

"Oof," said Philippa. "Some people are too smart."

Halloway winked at her.

"But it'll have to be done on a slightly more organized basis, to give the nonambulatories their chance. There's a nice big enclosed patio back of the main swimming pool; and it's obvious from your speed in getting dressed that you're both up to standing on a bench for a few minutes. There'll be a P.A. there too. Do you think you could be ready to give them a little story of your flight, and answer a few questions, by, say, four this afternoon?"

"Oh, *Dag*," Phil said reproachfully. "I can't, I just cannot."

"Well, why not, Phil? We've done it a million times. All but the storm part. And you can do that, it's fresh in our minds."

"Fresh?! Oh, you—"

"Now, now, now," chuckled Halloway. "Remember, my dears, this is one audience which—" his face sobered for a moment—"cannot take many postponements. Wouldn't it be a shame if a person who is very interested and able to hear you today should be, shall we say, too sick tomorrow?"

"Oooh," said Phil, and then muttered rebelliously, "That's blackmail. But—okay."

"Good girl." His twinkle was back. "Then I take it we're all agreed. I'll put the word out for four o'clock. But I'd like to collect you about three—there are a few very special people you should meet first. And now how about choosing a nice nourishing lunch?"

At three sharp Halloway and Anna Boyd ushered them out through still another corridor, which ended at the old main staircase, now largely converted to a wheelchair ramp. They seemed to be near the bottom; the hospital was evidently deep in the center of the *Charon*—for maximum stability, Dag guessed.

"Want the elevators?" Anna asked. "How's that knee?"

"No, thanks—he needs the exercise," Phil answered for him, a trifle tartly. She had not quite forgiven Dag for getting her into speechifying which she loathed.

As they climbed up, they noticed that advantage had been taken of the high old ceilings to install a number of mezzanines. The first three landings featured a number of tastefully curtained-off chambers. Glimpses into some of those with drawn drapes revealed altars of various forms, the soft glow of candles. Chapels.

"We have provision here for nearly every faith," Halloway told them. "I would have said every one, but last voyage we had a Bahai, and a member of an obscure Albigensian sect, which required some speedy new construction. I've suggested to Ulrik that we better be prepared for an altar to the Unknown God, as the old Romans were."

"Or goddess," said Phil.

"You'd be surprised what we have in that line already. What's the problem, Dag, knee acting up?"

It was, slightly, but Dag wasn't in the mood to confess in front of Phil. Instead he pretended interest in the heavy seals on the entrance to the mezzanine they were passing.

"The oxygenation ward," Anna Boyd told him. "We can do that another day; it only has two patients both in rather bad shape now, and you have to wear special static-free clothing."

"Is—Mr. Rosenthal there?" Phil asked as they climbed on, "or . . ."

"No, he's still with us, believe it or not. We got him to carry a portable respirator, so he gets some oxy from time to time. He'll be there, you'll see!"

"Here are my first specials," Halloway said, leading them off the stairs and down a hall furnished with oddly low benches.

The "specials" turned out to be children.

About twenty of them were in the lounge; they ranged from toddlers to a girl and two boys who might be fifteen. Scattered through the group were four adult women and a man, all in civilian dress—doubtless some of these few parents permitted aboard.

Not many of the kids showed any obvious signs of illness; they were reading or drawing, or listening on earphones; two were constructing a wooden village, and one fat child was industriously disassembling a digital clock. Indeed, had it not been for the occasional roll-bed or wheelchair, and a certain quiet aura of maturity, they could have been any randomly assorted group waiting, say, in a dentist's office. Only the ravaged faces of the parents told another story.

Anna Boyd explained that Dag and Phil were the balloonists saved from the sea, and she introduced them around—so many Terrys, Kevins, Karens, and Jennys that Phil lost count. Dreadful to think that these ordinary names were soon to be inscribed on a stone headmarker or on the bronze plate of an urn.

"Phil and Dag are going to tell us all about their trip and the wreck in the big storm," Anna said. "It'll be in half an hour up by the pool. We can send some people to help you get there. Do any of you want to come?"

There was a chorus of assents, some very feeble. Philippa noticed that the plump little clock-dissector, whose name was Mike, only scowled.

A woman was sitting by a roll-bed containing one of the teen-age boys. His assent had been soft-voiced, but his eyes were luminously eager. Now his mother spoke up.

"Dr. Halloway, I think this is most unwise. The exertion'll tire Terry much too much. He can't possibly go."

The boy on the bed turned a beseeching face toward her. "Mother! Can't you understand? It doesn't *matter*." His voice, when he raised it, screeched and gurgled in his chest. "I'll be dead soon, *dead*. Maybe next week. Then I'll be getting all the rest there is. Meanwhile this is something I want to do. And it doesn't matter if I'm tired, it doesn't matter if I break both my legs. I can do anything I want to now, because soon I'll be dead! *Dead, dead!*"

"Ohhh—oh, *no*—my darling baby," the mother wailed hysterically. "Don't make jokes. Don't even think it. It's all a horrible mistake, you just need more rest and the right medicine. I'm going to take you off this dreadful boat. I won't let you die—I won't have it! You're going to live, my dearest! Live!"

"Die!" he croaked, grinning horribly, his voice a deliberate mockery of hers. He panted for a moment and then said, in his former quiet tone, "Dr. Halloway, you'll see I get there, won't you?"

Halloway nodded. He was writing swiftly in a notebook he carried.

"Not to worry, Terry. You may find your mother resting when you get back."

A smile of great sweetness lit Terry's face, and he lay back, exhausted.

Meanwhile there had been some interactions between Nurse Boyd and other parents, which Dag and Phil had missed. Anna said something to Halloway, and he made another short note in his book.

As they turned to go, the fat little clock-disassembler, who had so far shown no interest, presented himself somberly in their path. Philippa smiled at him; she couldn't tell whether his fat was normal or an outward sign of disease. He offered no response, but said to her in a surprisingly deep, loud, challenging voice: "I betcha don't know the pithagean the-rem."

Taken aback, Philippa replied, "Uh—do you mean the Pythagorean Theorem, Mike?"

"Betcha don't know it."

Phil glanced wildly at Dag, at Halloway and Anna. No help. "Well, if you do mean the Pythagorean Theorem, it's—wait a minute—yes: It's 'The square of the hypotenuse of any right-angled triangle is equal to the sum of the squares of the other two sides.' "

"All right," the child said, still scowling. "I'll come."

"Glad to have you," Dag said somewhat acidly. But the boy, who might have been around six or eight, had stumped back to his clock.

"That Mike," Anna half sighed, half grinned as they left the children's lounge. "You wouldn't believe it—I'll miss him . . . Oh, wait; you go on ahead. They weren't all there. I better check on Tammy and Jane. Tammy's father may be acting up again."

They went on to the last of the "special" people, who turned out to be eight very, very aged and frail people in roll-beds. All but one were women. And beside each bed sat another of the relatives, in civilian clothing, and all extremely old themselves. Quite probably daughters—or in a few cases a son. Again it was the same scene: The grief-ravaged faces of the relatives—the first such faces Dag and Phil had seen on *Charon*, they realized—contrasting with the serenity or even gentle cheerfulness of the patients'.

Dr. Halloway introduced them around, his voice loud. "These are our near-centenarians," he told Phil and Dag. "Or wait, you're a real centenarian, aren't you, Mrs. Tombee?"

"I am," stated the old lady firmly. She appeared to be part black. "I made it. Last July."

"And have any of you heard of this young pair of balloon flyers we saved from the sea? They're going to be telling their story upstairs in a few minutes. If any of you feel like coming we'll bring you up, or if any of your children here would like to go, I'll send someone in to take their places."

There was a general chorus of negatives from the "children."

"Oh, yes," another old lady spoke up feebly. "Lucy tells us all about it. Come over here, girl, so I can see you. And you too, boy."

Phil and Dag moved from bed to bed, turning around self-consciously, and once or twice even bending over to be felt by shaking, gnarled old fingers.

"I'm glad I saw them," the lone old man said huskily. "But going upstairs—I don't think so. Can't see much, probably couldn't hear, might fall asleep."

This provoked a trembling flurry of laughter from the other patients.

"Tell you what," Halloway more or less shouted. "We're going to make a tape—a tape recording—of the whole thing. Now you've seen them. Any of you who want to can play over the tape with your earphones any time."

"That'd be just fine," a third old lady wheezed. "We'll probably never do it, but we'll always think we could. Goodbye, young people. Be careful."

This sentiment was generally echoed by those who had followed it, except for another aged patient who hadn't spoken before. "I want to go upstairs and hear it," she declared in a surprisingly firm voice.

There followed another version of the scene with Terry

and his mother; this time it was her old daughter, at least eighty herself, tearfully, angrily, repeating, "It'll *tire* mother so!"

But the outcome was different. The aged patient gave in. "If I go up there, Effie'll have to come," she said crossly. "And she'll get exhausted and probably make a scene. And I'll have to leave halfway. You be sure and send that tape, won't you, Doctor H.?"

"I will," he promised her. "And maybe we can have a little chat about things."

"I'd be grateful," Effie's mother said and lay back, worn out, while her daughter fussed at her.

"One of our real dilemmas," Halloway told the young people as they returned to the stairs. "I'm not a man who often dreams of arranging fatal accidents, but— Ah, Anna, what news of Tammy and Jane?"

"Jane just wants to go on reading, but Tammy's got the problem with her father. You'll have to send Flink and his boys in there too."

Halloway made another notation as they climbed the last flight. "You carry on, Anna; I'll be along. Oh, you kids, that reminds me. I don't want you to get a shock. You know they fished up strips of your gas bag or whatever along with you. Well, you may see your raft, or maybe some hunk of *Sky-Walker* with the name, by the bench where you'll be talking. That bother you?"

Dag and Phil glanced at each other.

"Thanks for warning us," Phil said quietly.

Halloway took himself off, and Anna led them along immaculate sunlit decks to a large glassed-in solarium by the aft-pool. Inside was warm and light, and so jammed with arriving patients and their attendants and equipment—some had roll-beds, IVs, and oxygen tanks—that no individuals stood out.

They were grateful for Halloway's warning when they saw the huge red and yellow name-sheet of *Sky-Walker* hung above a large low bench at the center of one side.

"Hop on up," said Anna. They did so, and presently from nowhere a grayish arm stretched up through the throng bearing two hand-held mikes.

"You . . . cahn using these?"

"Oh, yes!"

The sight and accent of the little crewman brought back

to Philippa in vivid detail their rescue amid the terrors of the great storm. She found it no longer threatened her badly, so perhaps she could deliver a good talk after all. Much as she hated speaking, it was her belief that audiences deserved the best she could do.

Dag led off with his usual fine balloon-enthusiast speech, spiced with his unquenchable zest and vision—and throwing in as many interesting figures and ratios as he could recall for little Mike's sake—while she faced and organized her memories: The hours of limping just above the wave-crests, throwing everything overboard—the fantastic updraft that carried them almost to the stratosphere and threatened to freeze or strangle them in vacuum even as it saved them—only to be followed by the more terrible smash-down finally, all the way into wild water, the butane heater drowned, the bell of *Sky-Walker* collapsing over them so they had to cut free for air—and then the four— four!—dreadful days and worse nights of sheer survival in the foundering raft; the last pause in the storm's eye, and then what would have been the end had it not been for the miracle of the hospice ship's lifeboat.

Apparently she did it well—she ended to clapping, cheers, pounding of canes.

In the after-chat, Dag added, "That transmitter must have kept functioning to the very end. When I get back I'm going to kiss the guy who made it."

"Let *her* kiss him!" An old voice cackled—and Phil was able to spot and wave at Rosenthal, now crumpled in a wheelchair and feebly waving back through his coughs.

Dag's eye had been caught by two figures quietly leaving through a side-door at the back—a tall, erect figure in whites, accompanied by someone veiled, in a motorized chair. He nudged Phil. "Captain Ulrik came to hear us."

"Who was that in the wheelchair with the captain?" he asked Anna on their way back, after over an hour of questions had finally emptied the solarium.

"Oh, some big shot on the permanent staff—Dr. T., we call him. Head of Multidisciplinary Research. Nothing to do with actual medical practice, like Halloway. The Big Think. He's the one we could get the use of a nuclear reactor from, or a super-computer if we needed it. Outside research projects come in through him, I believe . . . He was in some bad accident, even his face is all messed up, poor man. He's always wearing those cover-ups the few times I've seen him. I imagine he finds the privacy of ship life more peaceful . . . Well, that was quite a show, kids. I think a good early supper and some beddy-bye are the prescription. Get those combat clothes off and have a tray in bed. How about it?"

They couldn't have agreed more.

When Halloway came in to congratulate them, Phil was drowsing over her pecan pie. Halloway seemed enthusiastic over the effect of the speech on his special people. "And the tape is *good*," he told them. "You really get beautiful technical work here. Old Mrs. Brattle, the one who wanted to go, has listened to your part three times, Phil—hey, Miss Philippa, open those eyes a minute—and Mrs. Tombee is running hers."

"How about the kids? That little fat boy?"

"Great. Mike announced he is going to design an improved balloon. You know—" Halloway was abruptly serious—"I think we have a real loss coming there. He's only five, you know. Late five. He'll die too young for any serious work he might have done."

"Five!"

"Yeah. We had to give him the College SAT math section to get a score." Halloway sighed. "Speaking of losses, I don't know how this'll hit you, but you have to get used to remembering where you are. Terry—the boy with the mother, remember?—he died about an hour after he got back on the ward."

"He *died*? Oh—but did *we*—did we—?"

"Did you kill him? Of course not. His disease killed him—helped along by his mother. Almost his last words were, 'I'm so glad I heard them.' See? We always get a few people who go after any excitement. Often the more pleasant the event, the higher the after-rate. Terry was just one of four so far tonight . . . it's as if an unpleasant thing—like, say, the time a dead patient's mother got away and went berserk, dashing all over the wards, making scenes—it was exciting enough but it didn't satisfy people as a last experience. They seemed determined to outlast it. And then something nice gives them just the right feeling or memory; they feel they can let go."

Dag and Phil stared at him; this was something to absorb.

"Four people have died—"

"But we—"

"Not to fret." Halloway stood up and his voice took on a good-doctor authority they hadn't heard before. This was a new aspect of him: The friendly-chipmunk disguise dropped for a moment, revealing the strength at the core. "We all have to grow up, you know. The child refers everything to itself as cause . . . And—" his tone softened—"I think it will make you feel better to know that the highest death-rates we have come after a really first-rate serious musical evening. You're nowhere near *that*! . . . Good night, now."

They didn't talk it over much; Halloway had said it all. Serious, but in no way depressed, they sank into another night of marvelous sleep.

Sometime after midnight Philippa roused to use their bathroom. Automatically putting on her robe, she felt unusually alert—perhaps they really were getting "slept out."

In this she was not alone.

When she returned, Dag was in her bed, two muscular arms reaching for her. She melted toward him, and then an impulse of mischief rose in her. She laughed and bolted over behind his bed, which was near the door. He leaped after her onto that bed, erect and wild-looking in his inadequate hospital gown. Oh, god, she loved him!

But mischief still held her, and since she still wore her robe, she ran out into the corridor, expecting him to delay for his robe to give her time to hide. Instead he came bounding straight out after her into the empty corridor, making a horrible face as he lunged to grasp her.

"Rapist!" she called out, loving him in every fiber. But youth and some archaic zest of the chase carried her fleetly down the silent halls. If he didn't care, she didn't either; she tucked up her robe like Atalanta and flew giggling up a small ramp-way, pursued by her laughing and swearing naked incarnation of the male. Clearly, when he caught her there would be no return to their room—so, womanlike, as she sped she kept an eye out for a clean stretch of carpet, and at least a corner that would afford minimal privacy.

Up and up—he was gaining fast, and her own desire was gaining faster—the carpet was deep and unused-seeming here, and the next landing was a corner! She saw a shallow niche in the wall just as she came to it, stopped dead, and pressed herself into it, eyes shining, one hand to her mouth to stop her laughter, should he pound on past.

He rushed up the last bend after her, so aflame with love that to her eyes the absurd gown was the tunic of a running god. Oh! He was here, upon her—passing! She could all but feel his breath as she backed hard into the niche.

Just as he went by he saw her, whirled, and reached with a soft triumphant laugh. She pressed back to fling herself bodily at him.

—And the niche behind her gave way.

She half fell, half staggered backward, into what she assumed was a broom-closet, or something of the sort, and was amazed to find herself in a very large, palely lit space before a great translucent wall with double doors in it. The oxygen ward, was her first thought. But the air here was half gagging her—it was quite abnormal.

Then she found that the niche door had closed behind her. The whole wall containing it was curtained, or upholstered in some way. There was a set of large official-looking double doors much farther along in the wall, but that way would take her farther from Dag. She wanted the little secret service door. But her half-fall and spin had disoriented her, and she couldn't make out any edge outlines. She began to feel about and push frantically.

Just as panic started, she realized that Dag must of course be frantically searching for her on the other side—it was only a question of moments and he would find his way in too. She should warn him not to let the niche door close.

Meanwhile her sexual glow had receded a bit under the impact of strangeness, and curiosity—one of her dominant traits—was taking over. So she turned with her back to the wall and looked about.

Not ten feet from her stood a rolling bed, completely canopied in translucent greenish netting or plastic. Behind the curtains she could see a small dark figure—why, it was a black child, sitting up cross-legged and staring at her with white-rimmed eyes!

Evidently it was waiting to be rolled into the big closed ward. Perhaps she had frightened it terribly when she crashed through the wall?

She smiled. "I'm sorry. I just fell in. It's all right."

The child's mouth moved, but no sound came out. Instead she saw what seemed to be its arm, making a beckoning gesture at her.

Momentarily forgetting about Dag, she approached the canopied bed. The curtains were quite opaque, when light was not behind them. Was this some particularly difficult breathing problem? She raised a hand and waved hello to the child.

It continued to beckon. When she did not respond further, it reached up and parted the curtains beside it a crack, and she bent and looked in, smiling.

As she did so, she heard the sound of the niche door opening behind her and called out, "Don't let it close."

But her warning ended almost in a squeak—her eyes had taken in the creature sitting under the canopy, and her world was turning upside down. At first she thought the child was hideously deformed—so deformed as to be beyond even the most dreadful of side show freaks. Everted organs, extra limbs—she could scarcely bear to look. But its bright eyes held her, and then she felt its touch—her hand, too, had been at the curtain-slit, and the child had grasped her wrist.

Had its grasp been rough or greedy, she would have jerked loose and run to Dag. But its touch was very gentle, delicate, and fragile-feeling.

Meanwhile her eyes and brain were busy, were bringing her one overwhelming, convincing message: This was no deformed human child, if indeed it was a child at all. Nor was it any earthly animal. Her breath choking in her throat, trembling from head to foot, she understood.

The creature before her, actually grasping her hand, was an intelligent being of no race that ever walked on Earth. An alien, an extraterrestrial. At her first full sight of it, the antique phrase "an imp of Hell" had flashed through her mind; and she almost screamed out. But that feather-light touch seemed to quench terror. Instead she simply looked.

The creature was not human "black," but deep blood-crimson, with bright vermilion spots, and accessory organs that pulsed. Its nose was an intricate red vertical slit; the mouth was sharply triangular, with an extraordinary number of tiny sharp bluish teeth; there was no chin or lower jaw. But the eyes! They were very large, and what she had taken for white rings extended threadlike into the pupils, which were great star-shaped black abysses, surrounded with flecked jewels of many colors. Beautiful . . .

In the short time she had to look, she was never sure how many limbs it had, save that there were far too many, of different lengths. Afterward she recalled one prehensile member that might have been a foot, holding a pen.

Meanwhile the creature was examining her wrist and hand with great but gentle thoroughness. It turned her hand, flexed and wiggled her wrist, fingers, and thumb, stopping at the slightest resistance: it put its eyes close to skin, nails, and palm-lines, smelled carefully between the fingers, even nibbled with exquisite delicacy at the forearm skin. Between its teeth something very hot—perhaps a tongue—touched her. It seemed prepared to continue up to her elbow and beyond.

At some point during the reeling and reshaping of her world, she realized Dag had come behind her. He bent to look in. As he did so, she heard his breathing change. As he went through the realizations she had endured, she could feel emotions jolting him. Almost at once he grasped her arm to pull her away.

"N-no," she whispered. "It's gentle. Listen—go look inside those big glass doors. I don't think it's any oxygen ward, I think I see . . . more . . ." A belated shred of common sense came to her. "Just take a peek. I bet we're not supposed to be here."

He walked over to the translucent wall, behind which moving shapes could be glimpsed as they momentarily came near the glass, and cautiously opened one door a crack. Instantly he began to cough. But still he stared in.

"Oh, my god—" she heard him explode.

"What?"

"Different—they're all different—"

A growing murmur of strange sounds began coming from beyond the open door.

"I want to see." She spoke directly to the creature who held her arm, pulling gently back. "Will you please let me go now?" It stared. "You have beautiful eyes," she said. "But please, may I go?" She tugged again, a little harder.

What the response would have been she never knew.

A squad of ten short, grayish crew members materialized through the "official" doors and surrounded them. "No-o,

no-o," one said to Dag, pulling him from the glass doors. It
was the only sound any of them made. Her arm was abruptly drawn from the red-imp's grasp—it made no protest—and its curtains were firmly closed. In instants they
found themselves being marched up a curving ramp. No
doors opened off it. Six led with Dag, four followed with
Philippa.

Dag had made one or two attempts to struggle—he said
afterward it was like fighting with an oversized granite
bowling ball—and Phil tried to pull away from the hands
on her arms. But their grip, though not tight or painful,
felt like stone bracelets too.

Up and up they went, Dag becoming increasingly dis-
comforted by his nudity.

"Listen, can't you fellows lend me some pants? Or even
a towel or a rug?"

No response whatever.

"I think they're aliens too," Phil called to him. "Our clothing customs probably don't mean a thing."

"Yeah, but I have a feeling we're about to meet some
humans," he called back. "Can you spare that robe?"

"I think you've just broken the chivalry record," Phil
told him. "If they give us a chance you can tie that gown
thing around your middle. And if I can I'll give you the
one I have *under* my robe and we can build you sort of a
dhoti."

"Oh, honey, I'm sorry. I forgot you don't have a real
nightie under that, and I feel pretty weird. We're going to
get some kind of chewing-out—it's a hell of a note to take
with no pants."

"Just tell yourself you're Socrates or Alexander the
Great—you'd be well-dressed."

"Hey, you realize we're way above deck level? I think
we're being taken to the bridge. Oh, god."

"But we didn't do anything or hurt anybody. And we'll
keep what we've seen a secret if they want."

"I have this feeling that they want just that, all right. We
may get dumped in solitary, and disembarked in Macao
. . . Hey, I can see the top of the ramp around the next
bend."

But at that moment they were turned aside and marched
into a long, narrow, quiet, dim room, one seemingly just
under the bridge. It was divided into two halves by a boxy

enclosure which might be a stairwell to the bridge. The end they were in was bare, save for a few unused-looking chairs and a table, but they could glimpse what looked like a highly functional office at the other end. It was empty of any other people. Two of their captors stationed themselves on each side of the central structure to block access to the office part. The rest left, as ever, in silence.

The tall, bronzed man whom they had first met in the lifeboat—whom they knew now as First Mate Ted Brandt—came in from the ramp.

"Well, youngsters, you've certainly bought yourselves a mess of trouble. Captain Ulrik and the professor will be along soon."

His voice was hearty, but indefinably lacking in some normal human resonance; it sounded in some way dead. They had both noticed this before, but put it down to the press of work and fatigue. Now they were not so sure, and it made them uneasy.

But Dag had a more urgent matter on his mind. "For god's sake, Officer Brandt, can somebody lend me some pants before the party?"

Brandt snorted, seemingly having just noted Dag's state. He said something very fast in a strange tongue to one of the guards, and the man trotted out the ramp door. Meanwhile Philippa was protesting to Brandt.

"I don't understand, sir. We didn't do anything at all—we only looked. I know we didn't hurt anybody. That—that person wanted to touch *me*. The only thing I can think of is that our breath or something spoiled the air—is that it?

"No," Brandt said. His face was flushing; his voice mocked hers savagely. "You didn't 'hurt anybody' . . . you 'only looked.' "

"And of course we won't say anything about their being there or anything they don't want us to. We really can keep secrets. I mean, important ones."

Brandt stared at her in explosive silence, his face changing complexly, as if something chronic had begun to hurt him deep inside.

"Oh, you'll keep their secrets, all right." He shook his head in mock wonder. "Babies! Oh, god, goddamn babies I fish for now! Listen—"

He was interrupted by the return of the guard, bearing, to Dag's disappointment, another hospital robe like Philippa's. But he put it on and at once felt better and more assertive.

"Officer Brandt, sir, I don't know exactly what you're saying or what we're into here. But there are a few laws, and plenty of people know we exist."

"Oh, yes. Human laws." He took a deep breath. "Now listen, kids, and listen good. In a couple of minutes the Captain and—another person are going to be talking to you. Catch every word they say and believe every word they say. It won't be repeated. Don't argue. Don't protest. You have some growing up to do, very, very fast. Start by understanding that our total human concepts of right and wrong, or what's important, don't apply here—any more than do a goldfish's. And that you're being talked to by a person who can eliminate this planet, or our entire solar system, and regard it at worst as a budgetary nuisance. There's only one thing that applies here, and that's whatever that person happens to want. As for your yatter about keeping secrets, he's not about to endanger one iota of one project by putting it in the power of any person—any person whatsoever—to mess up. Now, lesson one. You tell me: What kind of people are absolutely guaranteed-certain to keep a secret?"

There was a moment's pause.

"D-dead people," Dag said.

"I see at least one of you is getting the idea. You can also add in people with their brains cut out. Living vegetables."

"But that's like the Mafia!" Philippa protested.

"Little girl, compared with these jokers, the Mafia is a bunch of nursery delinquents. They could pick the Mafia up like a chicken and wring its neck tomorrow if they wanted. Unfortunately, they don't want. But that's not a bad place to start your thinking, baby."

"Wait one minute," Dag said. "You're alive, and I don't think your brain's been cut out. Are you telling us this bunch of aliens is taking over the world—and you're helping them?"

Brandt's face was now very sweaty, but it had lost its flush and was becoming clay-covered. He took out a bandanna.

"Take over the world? They couldn't care less . . ." He mopped his face. "This is . . . hard for me to talk about,

even when it's okay . . . No. Just the opposite. They don't
want to change anything. We just go right on, like always.
Except there're a few things we can't do, like start a nuclear war. Or invent an FTL drive, maybe . . ."

He mopped his pale face again, looked at his watch.

"Then what are they doing that's so secret they kill people?" Philippa asked.

Brandt drew a couple of painful breaths, and they could
see the sweat spring out on his lips again. "Studying . . .
just studying us. You ran into the students' floor, that's
all."

"Then what's the big secret?"

"Use—use your heads . . . I can't talk any more.
They'll be here in a minute or so . . . use the time to
grow up all you can."

He half sat on a corner of the table as if recovering from
an ordeal.

"One thing," Dag said. "Is the other person, the professor—is he that person in the wheelchair, all covered up?"

Brandt nodded tiredly.

Phil and Dag had drawn very close together during
Brandt's speech.

"Remember, Phil," he said to her in their "special"
voice. "We made it through the storm. This is just a different storm. Can you keep your cool and watch for every
wave or break, like we did then?"

She nodded silently, Yes; her eyes large and grave.

"Time's up, kids." Brandt went to the central enclosure
and opened it, revealing indeed a stairway. White-clad legs
could be seen descending.

The two young people instinctively straightened their
shoulders and stood side by side as Captain Ulrik entered
the room. Quietly Dag's hand found hers and gripped it.

"Professor Tasso's on his way, sir," Brandt said.

The captain nodded and took up a position facing the
ramp door.

"I've had a little talk with them, sir. They're of course
very sorry, but I explained that's beside the point."

Ulrik glanced over at the pair, lips tight. "Good. I hope
we need waste no time on emotional irrelevancies. Your
apologies are registered. It remains for Professor Tasso to
determine what he wishes done. I hope it has been explained to you that he's not kindly, nor is he cruel. In past

instances, he has been as decent as he could be in human terms, given his priorities. His priorities and interests are simply not ours. And they are totally paramount."

"Captain Ulrik, sir," Philippa said shyly, "may we ask, are you human? I mean, not an alien too?"

The captain smiled frostily. "Why, yes, I am, little miss. But that won't help you."

"Oh, I realize that, sir. I was just curious . . . And of course if you are, I wonder why, I mean, why you'd do all this for them."

He stared at her, and they glimpsed in his eyes a fanatic gleam, like a distant light across the waves of night.

"I have no family . . ." he said slowly. "And I doubt if you can understand this, missy. There are men who would sail a load of devils to Hell for the permanent command of a ship like this . . . and I'm one of them."

"I think I do see, sir." Her voice was soft. "It's like *Sky-Walker* was to us." Dag covertly squeezed her hand. The captain's posture had relaxed ever so slightly. Dag decided against a question he was going to ask.

A brief moment of silence—and then one of the guards jumped to the big ramp doors and opened them wide. The large canopied wheelchair rolled into the room.

"Professor Tasso," Officer Brandt announced formally.

Even at close quarters, little of the alien could be made out behind the greenish translucent canopy, save that he seemed to be very tall and of superficially human form. The veiling material was a little thinner or clearer over the face region, revealing occasional glimpses of light, inhumanly long eyes, but no suggestion of nose. In the silence, a tank fastened beneath the chair seat hissed very faintly; there was a not-unpleasant chemical odor in the room.

The frighteningly long eyes had completed a brief inspection of Dag and Philippa. "Well, Ulrik," a cool inorganic voice said from somewhere near the wheelchair arm, "your impulsive act . . . has caused . . . trouble. You should have consulted . . . with me . . . first."

The voice was accentless, with odd pauses. Dag decided it was some kind of super-voder. He wished he could hear the alien's own voice.

"In this particular case, Professor Tasso, it would have made no difference." The captain spoke at normal speed, in his natural tone. "Their SOS—the emergency signal—was widely received. We were in a thickly traveled sea-lane, and the *Charon* was known to be the closest ship. Had I failed to respond, it would have attracted great unfavorable attention, possibly an investigation. It is an inviolable law of the sea to respond to such an SOS, and, for your information, one which I personally will not violate as long as I remain in command of this vessel."

"Perhaps . . . I should know more of these laws of your . . . sea before I receive . . . any more surprises."

It might be only the voder, but there seemed to be a very faint donnish or academic humor to the alien's remark. The exchange did not seem to be really hostile. Dag and Philippa felt a faint revival of hope.

The next words dashed it.

"Now as to what is to . . . be done with . . . you. I can offer . . . you two choices. You may elect to die . . . as soon as you choose, but certainly before we reach the next port. When, Ulrik?"

"Next Friday. Eight days."

"And there . . . would be no difficulty, Mr. Brandt?"

"No, sir. Like the Doven case. A fatal accident."

"I would dislike too many fatal accidents on my ship," Ulrik put in. "Instead I suggest an apparent suicide. Motive, despondency over failure of their ambitious flight, and no finances or some other impediment to repeating the attempt. This would also be acceptable to human public opinion, of which they have attracted a great deal."

"Approved," said the voder voice. "Perhaps I should assure you two that your . . . actual—as opposed to reported—deaths would be—is humane your somewhat . . . curious term?"

Dag and Philippa were forcing themselves to remain unemotional, composed. In this they were aided by the growing conviction that they were in a nightmare from which they must soon awaken. In this state they were able to notice again the flavor of the academic in the alien's words. Philippa in particular was reminded of a professor she had long suffered with. Dag was reminded of another aspect of bureaucracy, and recalled that this creature was in charge of what must be a fairly major and expensive research project.

But could an alien—an *alien*—be compared with and

treated like a human type? Each, in frightened silence, summoned courage to try the only clue each had.

Meanwhile the passionless voice was outlining their second choice. To be released freely, but only after a brain operation which would extirpate all memory of the aliens aboard.

"Officer Brandt mentioned this alternative, sir," Philippa said. "It appeared to us that an operation which would surely remove all traces of our memories would be so extensive that we would be in pretty bad shape afterward. Not ourselves. Is that correct?"

"There does appear to be considerable . . . deficit," the alien voice replied. "Four such operations have been done by one of our people—Dr. Halloway is not involved with us—and while all the patients lived, only the third appears to have been very successful. In this case . . . the individual achieved independent life in some form of . . . motor maintenance work, I believe. He had been previously occupied in . . . some aspect of your . . . music. The problem is that your brains, like some of ours . . . display considerable redundancy, so that extensive . . . separate incisions are required . . . But doubtless I go beyond the limits of your understanding."

"On the contrary, sir," Philippa said bravely. "I have received some training in neurology while in school, and I understand exactly what you mean by brain redundancy. From the scientific viewpoint—the *human* scientific viewpoint, of course—it's a great pity that your student's actual experimental work could not be published. It would have created intense human attention and settled many theoretical arguments. Or started new ones," she added daringly.

From the canopied figure itself came a totally new sound—a sort of rhythmic squeak. Could it be laughter?

"Very good," said the voder. "Captain Ulrik, am I correct that this one of the pair is a young . . . egg-bearer, ah, female?"

"You're very expert, sir," Dag interjected, equally daring. "Many humans find it difficult to distinguish us without more clothing cues."

Again a brief, strange bell-note from within the canopy. But the metallic voder voice continued unchanged. "I had not been informed that your young, and females in particular . . . were intelligent enough to hold converse."

"Sir." Dag dared the ultimate—what was to lose? "If I may deduce that your human contact have been limited to humans like Captain Ulrik and Officer Brandt, that is, to mature males of highly specialized but very narrow interests, there may be much—uh—behavioral information about humans which has not been available to you."

"Possible," said the voder. "Um. Ahem. But now remains your choice."

"Sir, in order for us to choose more promptly, may I ask one more question? I can guess the demands on your time, and I hope I am not asking too much."

"Is it . . . relevant—and not too long?"

"Sir, we have already caused trouble, and we want to make amends by cooperating and being rational and helpful in every possible way. But we humans have a peculiarity—maybe a primitive weakness—and we find it almost impossible to function, to make decisions and do as we're told, unless we have at least a rough idea of the most important facts around us. You and your research group are the overwhelming mystery in our situation. Now, without some understanding of the simplest facts, we will deteriorate so quickly that it really would be a time-saver and a help to those who have to deal with us if you could spare a moment now. Because only you can do it."

"That seems rational—and you are not the only race with this need. What are your main unknowns?"

"Well, if we could have merely the barest outline of what you intend to do to our world, we could die or undergo surgery quite calmly. For example, we gather that you wish your presence here kept secret. Is this because you plan a massive change in our world, or, conversely, because you wish to observe us unchanged, and knowledge of your presence here would certainly alter our behavior? We see also that this is a very large, beautifully run, innovative project. Is it so large that all hospice ships carry your study teams?"

"And why our world?" Philippa put in. "*You* know countless other worlds, while we know only ours. So we're painfully confused: What could there possibly be about us worth your while to study? It must be just that we're so ordinary, a super-average. Or is there some unique thing here?"

"That too is rational, given your premises." The being

paused and made an obscure movement beneath the canopy, then spoke rapidly over his shoulder to a guard, who left the room at once.

Meanwhile Dag and Philippa exchanged glances. Phil knew Dag's blood was running as icy as hers; he knew that the same knife twisting in his vitals was agonizing her. But he was proud of her. "Grow up," Brandt had ordered. Well, they had grown. From free human beings they had "grown up" to helpless captives, "specimens" of a world that itself had changed from being unique and free and its own master to being merely one of many planets dominated by alien powers. From life they had "grown up" to accept their own on-rushing deaths, for each knew that the other would never endure becoming a brain-cut zombie.

And they had grown even further—to the shared, tacit realization that their mere deaths would accomplish nothing but leave this outrage unchanged. Whereas their intact life, on any terms, might hold some crazy hope. So—from playing the game of nightmare, which had worn thin and abandoned them, they who prided themselves on free expression had grown into the courage of the slave's guile, and were playing for their very lives with only the weapon of sycophancy, likely to win nothing but the pain of encouraging a world-eating monster to explain its plans for cooking and garnishing their Earth.

"It's true that your type of world and culture is ordinary, but you are a unique find. In every other such world we know of, your *Wrrg*—let us call it your Alpha cycle—or the much rarer cycle we may call Beta—has run the full course. Apart from a very few tertiary late-starters where life is only just emerging, we have found usually only the Alpha remains: Blasted cinders, with perhaps a few surviving forms of no interests, such as your crab-grass. An essentially dead world."

"You mean, from nuclear war, sir?"

"Yes. They were self-destroyed. That's your most probable, or Alpha, cycle. Then there is also the rarer Beta, or entropic, cycle, where war has been somehow avoided, but where unchecked population growth has consumed all resources and destroyed all possibility of change. There the once-intelligent dominant species exists in some irreversibly degenerate form in huge, though periodically ravaged, numbers, with no other species left alive except a few simple external and internal parasites of no evolutionary potential. Some of them hang on for a surprisingly long terminal phase, but we mostly find the Beta planets dead too. They're quite unmistakable.

"Your planet is thus a unique find. Not only is it preclimactic, but the Alpha and Beta processes are both underway simultaneously, one might say, in competition with each other. And because of your unusual history, your development is so unbalanced that you show limited areas where entropic degeneration is almost complete, especially in urban enclaves like, say, Calicut—while in other areas, like North Amrica and Roosh, the Alpha demolition is almost ready to let go. Additionally, a host of other areas in every conceivable intermediate stage, or combination of stages, right down to your so-called wildernesses. Unparalleled! The sociobiological equivalent of watching a star go through its climactic stages before our very eyes."

"Sir," Phil asked, "does this mean you plan to sit by and watch us destroy ourselves? Your interest is in seeing which of the Alpha or Beta deaths win out?"

"Oh, by no means. I am disappointed with your lack of vision—although I must say I've seen high-placed administrators make the same error . . . Oh, my, no—that would be a terrible loss to science!"

At some point during this exposition, he had done something to the voder which caused it for moments to speak in tones throbbing with electronic emotion. Under different circumstances the effect would have been grotesquely funny. Here no one smiled.

"The proper scientific approach is quite the opposite. The incomparable scientific value of your condition dictates that we must maintain it intact just as long as we possibly can, so that generations of students may profit. Nothing fundamental must change—the delicately balanced potentials, with every variant tendency coexisting, must be preserved at all costs. And with very small, imperceptible interventions here and there, this is easily do-able. For instance, maverick nuclear strike attempts simply encounter malfunctions. Fully entropic areas can easily be limited in spread. Lines of activity which totally deplete one resource or another can be diverted, or the supply covertly replaced. Massive conventional land warfare can be quashed overnight by disease. Over-homogenization can be checked in any number of ways. Interesting utopian efforts can easily be undercut if they become too successful. The accidental loss of pivotal culture complexes can be prevented. And all on a minuscule budget and with personnel requirements near zero. The only necessity is for constant, informed watchfulness—and most of this is achieved by the very activities which different student observers automatically provide! Nor is a hundred percent effectiveness required—changes within certain limits are certainly permissible, and desirable, as long as the overall balance is retained. One might say that never has as great a scientific object been presented along with virtually all means of observing and preserving it, at so small a cost . . . 'Watch you destroy yourselves'? What an appalling thought!"

Midway through his speech, Dag—who had had some limited experience in obtaining grants—recognized what he was hearing—fragments of the oft-rehearsed expository enthusiasm of a high-level project application for a long-range, big-budget grant. Somewhere in the unimaginable bowels of an interstellar research hierarchy, was there a dossier, a computer address for a Project Earth, by whatever name or number it was called? The mere thought gave him the coldest shudder yet.

"And moreover—" Professor Tasso was wrapping it up —"your peculiar development has left a number of other interesting species still alive, some actually with evolutionary potential. It might not be beyond the realm of fantasy one day to observe man's replacement by an entirely different intelligent species! This would probably require some administrative assistance, budgetary considerations, and so forth; but since such events have been known or deduced to have occurred, to observe one actually taking place would be a scientific and educational event of the first magnitude."

"What wonderful vision!" Dag heard Philippa say, and made himself chime in too. "I shall be really quite resigned to dying tonight, after having heard such an inspiring plan, and even glimpsing it in action."

There was a slight pause before Professor Tasso's voice asked, "Your choice, then, is to die? But—tonight? It seems a bit abrupt."

"Oh, no," said Dag. "We could never be content with life as brainless subhumans—especially after having heard you. And it's characteristic of our race that this type of decision is best carried out quickly." He turned to Captain Ulrik. "We can write the suicide note right away, sir, and even let a few nurses or somebody see us being despondent and so on, if you wish. I'm sure you have something lethal handy. Or we could take some sleeping pills—break into Dr. Halloway's cabinet, if you wanted—and just jump overboard. Nice moon too." He turned back to Professor Tasso. "But you know, sir, I'll be a bit sorry to leave you, and all this. It's so wonderful. And that alien who felt Phil seemed really interested in actually touching a human. And of course we were fascinated too. It made me wonder for a minute if we could somehow find a role as specimens, on the same terms as Mr. Brandt here, not seeing any other humans. But you've undoubtedly considered all that, and no use bothering you further."

"That's right," Phil said. "And, my, it was interesting to feel his interest. A nice last memory. Oh—if it isn't one question too many, after you've been so kind. As Dag asked, are all the hospice ships like this?"

"No. Only this one so far," the alien replied. The voder voice sounded a little abstracted. "Although if the research interest continues to grow—you're a . . . very popular subject, you'll be glad to know—we may have to have another. And I may say the purely human interest in the hospice movement has taken us by some surprise—it's creating its own budgetary problems!"

"Well," Philippa offered, "if you're getting many big hospice ships, why not have a small, fast, all-alien ship and disguise it as a supply and service vessel? You could have a sister ship that actually was a support ship; you'll surely be needing one soon." She checked herself apologetically. "But of course you've thought of all that. Still if we'd been around, we certainly could have warned you to expect the human part to go like a bomb!" She chuckled shyly. "Maybe you do need an average specimen or two to give you access to typical human responses, the way our marketing researchers maintain a panel of human samples."

The alien made another of his undecipherable personal squeaks, or moans, all the while staring at her. The voder remained silent. After a moment or two Officer Brandt stood up, followed by Captain Ulrik. The alien guard moved toward the doors.

"Well, goodbye, sir. And the best of luck," Dag said, heart in mouth. There was another tiny pause.

"A moment, Ulrik." The voder was normally cool again. "Halloway's report . . . am I correct in recalling that these two young humans are of excellent health, intelligence, and so on?"

"First rate," the captain answered. "You couldn't easily find a better pair."

"And they're from a mutually compatible subgroup? Presumably fertile?"

"In theory, yes, sir. But they're untried. As you doubtless know, human fertility varies. In this case all we can say is that there is no known impediment."

The alien's voder made an inconclusive sound.

"I believe I wish to discuss something, first with the captain and then with my staff. Meanwhile—" his uncanny long eyes slid to Dag and Philippa—"I wish you to allow me to revoke my permission to die as soon as tonight. Brandt will conduct you both to some comfortable place where you will have complete privacy, and see you get good meals and beds. It is possible, even probable, but *in no way definite*, you understand, that I may have a third alternative to offer you. That is to be evaluated and decided on its merits to us. Then I shall indulge in the custom of *my* race and visit you at sunrise to announce my decision. That will not defer your deaths unendurably, if my decision is negative or you still so elect, will it?"

"No, sir," Dag said. "I believe we can hold out. However, could I ask Mr. Brandt the favor of supplying some musical recordings, or reading matter? We aren't likely to sleep much."

"Mr. Brandt, you will supply everything they wish, excepting contact with any others. If this is all, you may go now."

"Goodbye, sir," they said in unison. "And however it turns out, good luck and thank you," Phil added.

Brandt said something quietly to Ulrik and received his assent. Then he led them out and down the ramp to a small unnoticed door, which gave onto a utility deck studded with ventilator shafts and gratings. They were startled to find it seemed to be midafternoon, a cheerless gray day.

Totally disoriented, tired beyond ordinary exhaustion, they followed Brandt numbly, barely aware that a squad of four small crewmen brought up the rear. These simply followed along, untouching, until Philippa stumbled over a cable and found herself being courteously and briefly upheld.

When it seemed that they must have walked at least a mile, they came to covered stairs leading up to a high, largely glass-enclosed crosswalk, a sort of shadow-bridge, across the stern. Their escorts opened the stair doors, and they climbed effortfully behind Brandt, to come out into a long narrow white-carpeted room, not unlike the subbridge they had left, except that there was no office nor other signs of occupancy. Through the glass walls the great gray track of *Charon's* wake was hypnotic.

Four more crewmen arrived, struggling in with a non-hospital bed. More largely white furniture kept appearing as if by magic before their benumbed gaze. The last load featured a stereo record player and sound system, and several attractive ferns and flowering plants in white pots. The sad gray day outside was now only a foil for summery coziness within.

"Fantastic," Dag said dully.

"Is this your doing, your selection, Mr. Brandt?" Phil asked. He nodded. "You have lovely taste." She stared at him hard; he didn't meet her eyes.

"Oh, Mr. Brandt, how did you ever get into this?"

"I was doing three ninety-year consecutives, in a max security federal brig." He looked directly at her then. "Ulrik knew me, and thought I'd work out. They fixed it so I died. There's a headstone back of Clintonville that's ten years old. I don't guess I'll ever get to see it, not that I care. We only do absolutely essential shore trips, see; most of the supply and refitting are done right at the pier. People come on, of course. Before every port they reinforce the hypnotic clamp; you may notice we're a little strange then. If you're around, that is."

"If we're around," Dag echoed somberly. "Listen, I wish we had something to leave you. Your getting us out of that storm will be one of the great things I'll think of at the end. Sorry we had to mess up on you."

"Take my scarf, Mr. Brandt," Phil said. "I'll try to get it to you. You can use it for a bandanna."

"Ah, for shit's sake." He started out the door, then paused. "There's a better-then-even chance, kids. If you want it. You really did a job on the professor. I admit, I didn't think you had it in you."

"You did it, Mr. Brandt. We took your advice. If there is a chance of—of life as laboratory hamsters, it's due to you."

"Ohh, great flying turds of duckshit!" Swearing hideously, he started down the stairs, turned back to stick his head in. "Since you like my advice, here's one last piece: If any of your thinking involves escaping, now or ever, forget it. Just save your skull power and forget it. *I know.*"

He was gone.

With one accord they turned to each other and simply held together, human heart to heart, in a long silent communication without words, without passion, while the room darkened around them. Ultimately Dag started, staggered, and discovered he had been sleeping on his feet, with Phil, asleep too, holding him up.

What seemed to have waked them was a soft, persistent knocking at the door. It turned out to be a crewman bearing a tray of steaming bowls of oyster stew and plates of big fresh strawberries.

They were young and stunned by despair; forced to believe, yet scarcely able to grasp, that the deepest premise of normal human life, the independence of their world, was a delusion. Now this reality had been turned inside out, revealing the great cancer of alien intervention. And for them there would be no more *Sky-Walker*; all dreams had died. Tomorrow's sunrise would bring only confirmation of their own imminent deaths, or—perhaps more dreadful— the offer of life as the study objects, playthings, of nonhuman monsters.

Life? Would it be even life, lacking all freedom, even all privacy? If they bore or were forced to bear young, their children would be for the prying fingers, lenses, noses of unknown aliens, subject perhaps to unthinkable experimentation. Their very acts of conception and birth would be open to the view, perhaps the interference, of their masters. Was this life?

They could almost find it possible to envy ordinary humans the pathetic freedom of their ignorance.

And yet—though it was far indeed from their dream of conquering the winds of a free Earth—they were not without one very small victory: All on their own and unarmed, they had met the enemy, diagnosed a weakness, and used it to manipulate the inscrutable, all-powerful master of their fate. They had made him acknowledge them as something slightly more than mere "specimens"; had at the least caused him to reconsider, to take unanticipated action recognizing their existence.

If sunrise brought only his refusal and their forced deaths, they would go knowing their killer was not wholly content. And if he brought an offer of life, they held it in their power to negate his plans, to die by their own free choice.

Such was their victory: A slave's triumph, tiny, gained by ignoble guile, but real—how very real, only those who have fought from total helplessness and nonbeing can know. They had no idea what they would choose or suffer, come morning, but meanwhile they were alive and young, and not without pride.

They ate the excellent oyster stew and strawberries, finding also crisp greens with vinegar, hot buttered muffins, cheeses, milk, and a small bottle of cold sparkling wine.

By tacit consent they didn't discuss their own plight then. Only with his mouth full of cheese did Dag say thoughtfully, "On the brink . . . that must mean they think it's a close thing with us."

"We all think that." Phil poured the wine.

"But how do they keep us that way?"

"Hmm. Hey—that earthquake in Iraq or wherever. Could they do that, to stop the wars?"

"Sure. What's a little pinch of earthquake-juice?" He sobered. "We didn't read enough news. Remember that big fire that got zapped in New York, and that crazy oil find off New Zealand? And those so-called nuclear misfires— maybe they were all them."

"And the fog-bank over the whales," Phil added. "He said something about saving some other species, remember? . . . And that funny place on, what, New Caledonia everyone decided was a sacred Moslem thing. Maybe that's where they land! Nobody's allowed near, and that big mosque-building could be anything."

"I bet you're right. My god . . . Well, I guess that does supper . . . Phil, come sit by the window. Let's just sit close."

"Oh, darling. My darling . . ."

There was of course no more sleep for them that night. For the first hours they sat with room lights dimmed, watching a magnificent full moon rise toward the zenith and simply vacillating. They were so deeply together that speech needed only fragments.

"Fertile," Dag or Philippa would say now and then, knowing that in the other's mind would unroll images of a laboratory hamster giving birth under the eyes—and fingers—of a dozen kids.

"Maybe not right away," one would comment.

"Hardest on you," Dag would add each time. Once he said, "No worse than human gynecologists, maybe. But what if it—if *they*—grow?"

"Pass along secret tradition?" Phil speculated.

"Possible."

"Or persuade them it has to be adopted out," Dag suggested. "My aunt could take one . . . Lots of possible stories. Like, we had brain messed up by wreck. No oxygen. *Charon* kindly consented to let us end days here. Too far gone to visit. But you get pregnant, see. Kid's okay."

"But persuade them? How?"

"Tell them we all die, or kid dies, without humans. Get sick, starve like Gandhi . . . If we're good little hamsters they might not want to lose us. If it's perfectly safe for them, baby can't talk. Use it only for really major stuff, though."

"They don't know very much," Philippa said.

"Yet."

Now and again one of them would say simply, "It's cleaner."

And the other, sharing the overpowering yearning for a quick, near end, would agree with increasing relief. "Right."

Occasionally one or the other would say, "No friends."

"Interesting to meet aliens?"

"Medical students don't socialize with hamsters."

"Still . . ."

"Yeah."

"I don't think that Captain Ulrik really knows very much either," Philippa commented. "He's just a sailor."

"Brandt's got more to him. But he's morbid."

"Yes."

Considerably later Philippa said, "I can't get over that 'on the brink.' That's how they want us—*forever* on the brink."

"All the brinks," he said, reaching for her again. Sometime after midnight they had rather solemnly decided to make better use of what was either their last night of life or of privacy.

Later still, he made quite a long speech: "What's beyond the brinks is a lot worse, I gather. Maybe Earth should be grateful. Gives us time. Some people might find a different way."

"Wouldn't they stop it?"

"Only if they recognized it. Administrators get old, students get sloppy. We're the only representatives of our race here, maybe we could help. Unlikely, of course."

"But . . . it's the only game in town." Philippa was rubbing his sore knee. "After all, *they're* alive. Their worlds must be okay. How? Could we find out?"

"That could be really important," Dag said slowly. "I mean *really*. To us humans."

"But then what? Send out secret messages? Notes in bottles?"

"I don't know. Something. Oh, no use, I guess."

"No . . . Regardless; it's still the only game in town," Phil repeated stubbornly. "Only it's dirty work. Like this afternoon, Dag . . . flattering them. Yassuh, Boss . . . Dirty, dirty."

He reared up and caught her bare shoulders, looking deep into her eyes.

"Which is the real challenge, darling? An hour ago I was pretty sure we'd just go. If we get the chance to stay, you'd have to bear all the shit part. Of course I'll be with you all they let me, but I might have trouble not killing some damn freak. But nobody can help you through some of it."

"They couldn't back home either . . . I feel like you do about the challenge and maybe our duty. But I think it's pretty hopeless too . . . But so was *Sky-Walker*."

"Listen, sweetheart—" only in their most serious moments did he use the old, old endearment—"this may all be beside the point. But if we get the chance, the toughest part falls on you. So I want you to decide which. I'm with you all the way either way."

"Oof. Okay."

* * *

When the first light grayed the ocean, they were sitting by the big windows, watching the phosphorescence fade slowly from sight in the wake.

"Cleaner." Philippa sounded final. "A clean goodbye."

"Right," he said slowly.

They held hands quietly. The light grew. The high top overcast turned pink. Suddenly it parted here and there to reveal bright blue beyond.

" 'That little tent of blue that prisoners call the sky,' " Dag quoted.

For the first time tears really threatened them. But suddenly Philippa drew herself up. " 'For each man kills the thing he loves'?" She took up his quote, sarcastically. "Stupid crap. An elderly faggot in Reading jail. Fuck it. Let's stick to our own words."

He laughed, deep and free, even if for the last time. "My great woman. God, I love you."

"And me you. Listen—about the 'clean goodbye.' The clean part is okay. But I'm not sure I settle for the goodbye. Dag, I just *don't know*. You decide."

"Maybe we won't have to, is as far as I get. Hey! I just thought of another way to try: . . . Which would you be most disappointed about if we had to do? Or maybe, if we couldn't do?"

Phil gave a surprised grunt, and they stared hard at each other, aware that the light was growing fast. The eastern horizon was clear; a great neon-orange blur showed where the sun would shortly rise.

"If we . . . gave up, I guess . . ."

Suddenly from the corners of their eyes they saw movement in the blinding glow on the deck. They wheeled and stared intently, hands gripped.

It materialized into a crewman trotting toward their staircase with a tray. Steam was rising from little jugs and covered dishes. He disappeared below them, and presently they heard him ascend and quietly open the door. The scent of hot coffee drifted to them. He went out.

Still they stared at the deck, only now and then glancing at each other, then back at the big white deck-well from which would come their fate: Death, or the offer of deathly life. Behind it the orange glow changed to a blaze of gilded white. An intolerably bright diamond chip was suddenly on the horizon, blinding them momentarily.

When they could see again, a big translucent-green canopied wheelchair was rolling toward them. Their fate, but no clue. Suddenly, from the doors behind it, Brandt's arm appeared. He held his hand up, finger meeting a thumb, and the arm vanished.

"Okay," Dag said. They both breathed out hard.

They were human, and young and brave. They knew they would find a way to try something, to try some way out for themselves or others. Now they had their chance.

War Movie

Larry Niven

Ten, twenty years ago my first thought would have been, *Great-looking broad! Tough-looking, too. If I make a pass, it had better be polite.* She was in her late twenties, tall, blond, healthy-looking, with a squarish jaw. She didn't look like the type to be fazed by anything; but she had stopped, stunned, just inside the door. Her first time here, I thought. Anyway, I'd have remembered her.

But after eighteen years tending bar in the Draco Tavern, my first thought is generally, *Human. Great! I won't have to dig out any of the esoteric stuff.* While she was still reacting to the sight of half a dozen oddly shaped sapients each indulging its own peculiar vice, I moved down the bar to the far right, where I keep the alcoholic beverages, expecting her to take one of the bar stools.

Nope. She looked about her, considering her choices—which didn't include empty tables; there was a fair crowd in tonight—then moved to join the lone qarasht. I was already starting to worry as I left the bar to take her order.

In the Draco it's considered normal to strike up conversations with other customers. But the qarasht wasn't acting like it wanted company. That bulk of thick fur, pale blue striped with black in narrow curves, had waddled in three hours ago. It was on its third quart-sized mug of Demerara Sours, and its sense cluster had been retracted for all that time, leaving it deaf and blind, lost in its own thoughts.

It must have felt the vibration when the woman sat down. Its sense cluster and stalk rose out of the fur like a python rising from a bed of moss. A snake with no mouth: just two big wide-set black bubbles for eyes and an ear like a pink blossom set between them, and a tuft of fine hairs along the stalk to serve for smell and taste, and a brilliant

85

ruby crest on top. Its translator box said, quite clearly, "Drink, not talk. My last day."

She didn't take the hint. "You're going home? Where?"

"Home to the organ banks. I am *shishishorupf*—" A word the box didn't translate. "Like bankrupt, except I die." The alien picked up its mug; the fur parted below its sense cluster stalk, to receive half a pint of Demerara Sour.

She looked around a little queasily and found me at her shoulder. With some relief she said, "Never mind, I'll come to the bar," and started to stand up.

The qarasht put a hand on her wrist. The eight skeletal fingers looked like two chicken feet wired together; but a qarasht's hand is stronger than it looks. "Sit," said the alien. "Barmonitor, get her one of these. Human, why do you not fight wars?"

"What?"

"You used to fight wars."

"Well," she said, "sure."

"We could have been fourth-level wealthy," the qarasht said, and slammed its mug to the table. "You would still be a single isolated species had we not come. In what fashion have you repaid our generosity?"

The woman was speechless; I wasn't. "Excuse me, but it wasn't the qarashteel who made first contact with Earth. It was the chirpsithra."

"We paid them."

"What? Why?"

"Our ship *Far-Stretching Sense Cluster* passed through Sol system while making a documentary. It confuses some species that we can make very long entertainments, and sell them to billions of customers who will spend years watching them, and reap profits that allow us to travel hundreds of light-years and spend decades working on such a project. But we are very long-lived, you know. Partly because we are able to keep the organ banks full," the qarasht said with some savagery, and it drank again. Its sense cluster was weaving a little.

"We found dramatic activity on your world," it went on. "All over your world, it seemed. Machines hurled against each other. Explosives. Machines built to fly, other machines to hurl them from the sky. Humans in the machines, dying. Machines blowing great holes in populated cities. It fuddles the mind, to think what such a spectacle would have cost to make ourselves! We went into orbit, and we recorded it all as best we could. Three years of it. When we were sure it was over, we returned home and sold it."

The woman swallowed. "I think I need that drink," she said to me. "Join us?"

I made two of the giant Demerara Sours and took them back. As I pulled up a chair the qarasht was saying, "If we had stopped then, we would still be moderately wealthy. Our recording instruments were not the best, of course. Worse, we could not get close enough to the surface for real detail. Our atmosphere probes shivered and shook and so did the pictures. Ours was a low-budget operation. But the ending was superb! Two cities destroyed by thermonuclear explosions! Our recordings sold well enough, but we would have been mad not to try for more.

"We invested all our profits in equipment. We borrowed all we could. Do you understand that the nearest spaceport to Sol system is sixteen-squared light-years distant? We had to finance a chirpsithra diplomatic expedition in order to get Local Group approval and transport for what we needed . . . and because we needed intermediaries. Chirps are very good at negotiating, and we are not. We did not tell them what we really wanted, of course."

The woman's words sounded like curses. "Why negotiate? You were doing fine as Peeping Toms. Even when people saw your ships, nobody believed them. I expect they're saucer-shaped?"

Foo fighters, I thought, while the alien said, "We needed more than the small atmospheric probes. We needed to mount hologram cameras. For that we had to travel all over the Earth, especially the cities. Such instruments are nearly invisible. We spray them across a flat surface, high up on your glass-slab-style towers, for instance. And we needed access to your libraries, to get some insight into *why* you do these things."

The lady drank. I remembered that there had been qarashteel everywhere the chirpsithra envoys went, twenty-four years ago when the big interstellar ships arrived; and I took a long pull from my Sour.

"It all looked so easy," the qarasht mourned. "We had left instruments on your Moon. The recordings couldn't be sold, of course, because your world's rotation permitted only fragmentary glimpses. But your machines were becoming better, *more* destructive! We thanked our luck that you had not destroyed yourselves before we could return. We studied the recordings, to guess where the next war would occur, but there was no discernible pattern. The largest land mass, we thought—"

True enough, the chirps and their qarashteel entourage had been very visible all over Asia and Europe. Those cameras on the Moon must have picked up activity in Poland and Korea and Vietnam and Afghanistan and Iran and Israel and Cuba and, and . . . bastards. "So you set up your cameras in a tearing hurry," I guessed, "and then you waited."

"We waited and waited. We have waited for thirty years . . . for twenty-four of your own years, and we have nothing to show for it but a riot here, a parade there, an attack on a child's vehicle . . . robbery of a bank, a thousand people smashing automobiles or an embassy building . . . rumors of war, of peace, some shouting in your councils . . . how can we sell any of this? On Earth my people need life-support to the tune of six thousand dollars a day. I and my associates are *shishishorupf* now, and I must return home to tell them."

The lady seemed ready to explode. "We make war movies, too," I said, to calm her down. "We've been doing it for over a hundred years. They sell fine."

Her answer was an intense whisper. "I never liked war movies. And that was us!"

"Sure, who else—"

The qarasht slammed its mug down. *"Why have you not fought a war?"*

She broke the brief pause. "We would have been ashamed."

"Ashamed?"

"In front of you. Aliens. We've seen twenty alien species on Earth since that first chirp expedition, and none of them seem to fight wars. The, uh, qarasht don't fight wars, do they?"

The alien's sense cluster snapped down into its fur, then slowly emerged again. "Certainly we do not!"

"Well, think how it would look!"

"But for you it is natural!"

"Not really," I said. "People have real trouble learning to kill. It's not built into us. Anyway, we don't have quite so much to fight over these days. The whole world's getting rich on the widgetry the chirps and the thtopar have been selling us. Long-lived, too, on glig medicines. We've all got more to lose." I flinched, because the alien's sense cluster was stretched across the table, staring at us in horror.

"A lot of our restless types are out mining the asteroids," the woman said.

"And, hey," I said, "remember when Egypt and Saudi Arabia were talking war in the UN? And all the aliens moved out of both countries, even the glig doctors with their geriatrics consulting office? The sheiks didn't like that one damn bit. And when the Soviets—"

"Our doing, all our own doing," the alien mourned. Its sense cluster pulled itself down and disappeared into the fur, leaving just the ruby crest showing. The alien lifted its mug and drank, blind.

The woman took my wrist and pulled me over to the bar. "What do we do *now?*" she whispered in my ear.

I shrugged. "Sounds like the emergency's over."

"But we can't just let it go, can we? You don't really think we've given up war, do you? But if we knew these damn aliens were waiting to make *movies* of us, maybe we would! Shouldn't we call the newspapers, or at least the secret service?"

"I don't think so."

"Somebody ought to know!"

"Think it through," I said. "One particular qarasht company may be defunct, but those cameras are still there, all over the world, and so are the mobile units. Some alien receiving company is going to own them. What if they offer . . . say, the Soviet Union one-tenth of one percent of those enormous profits on a war?"

She paled. I pushed my mug into her hands and she gulped hard at it. Shakily she asked, "Why didn't the qarasht think of that?"

"Maybe they don't think enough like men. Maybe if we just leave things alone, they never will. But we sure don't want any human entrepreneurs making suggestions. Let it drop, lady. Just let it drop."

Folger's Factor

L. Neil Smith

Bernie Gruenblum lifted a foot, hopping awkwardly out of the way as the tiny pedestrian skittered between his legs. Momentarily, he considered bringing his heel down on the resilient—but eminently breakable—shell, then thought better of it. No use precipitating a diplomatic incident.

The freenie squeaked an ecstatic salutation as its hundred-or-so legs whisked it rapidly out of sight down the city corridor. Bernie felt a shudder rising in his frame—how he *ever* could have thought the revolting little things were *cute*—then sighed. Shucks, wasn't their fault they looked like fluorescent pink army helmets flopped over the business-end of a pistachio-flavored wet-mop. The leathery orange periscope atop the carapace, which brought the creature's full height to fifteen inches, could be incredibly expressive in attitude and posture; the iridescent optic at its end admitted a far wider spectrum of frequencies than human eyes, could focus down to a bacterium or out to distant galaxies, and often twinkled with a quick, sophisticated humor.

And that, after all, was the problem. The little bastards were talented *and* cute. Perhaps too talented for the sake of *Homo sapiens'* future, almost as cute as the tiny iridium-plated plasma-gun his latest girlfriend—a beautiful and shapely blonde who worked in factory personnel somewhere down here—carried in her billfold.

And potentially about as deadly.

Or was he, after all this time, simply turning into a bigot? He glanced at his Academy-issue Nukutron—too early yet. The old priest would still be puttering around the church, and Bernie would never adjust to the elderly cleric's perpetually intolerant frown and self-righteous mutterings. Not that he didn't understand the poor old guy. This recent upswing in conversions must have some pretty ignominious aspects from the professional's viewpoint.

So instead, Bernie hunkered down on the gritty concrete steps of St. Wernher's and amused himself watching the people—chimpanzees, gorillas, orangutans, and a smattering of humans—passing by along the sublunarian thoroughfare. People *and* freenies, he amended to himself. Even in this blue-collar industrial burrow, they had begun constructing special little sidewalks for the aliens, tucked up safely against the storefronts and apartment buildings like miniature garden walls so the creatures wouldn't get stepped on, narrowing the sidewalks till there wasn't room enough for *real* folks to walk abreast.

Somewhere a whistle blew; tunnels leading to a dozen factories and nanoelectronics plants began pouring workers into the streets. The simians chattered and swung their lunchpails. Many would be coming here in a few hours for midnight Mass. Above the racket, Bernie could hear the shrill piping of an alien minority, consultants and observers. He took a long and pensive puff on his cigar.

Freenies even *talked* cute. Like the sound a kid's balloon makes when you blow it up, grasp the nozzle, and stretch it, releasing just a little air. Whatever they used for vocal chords were a bit more versatile than that: they could make sounds in the lower ranges as well, anything from nearly perfect human speech to something reminiscent of the morning after a big bowl of green chili. But they had quickly learned this wasn't polite, and limited themselves now to the innocuous noises which had given them their name.

Their cute, innocuous, goddamned little name!

Bernie looked at his watch again:

+22.8256	+22.8256
JUL 24	JUL 24
2100:35.6	2100:35.6

The twin faces, in rare accord, told him they were changing shifts inside the church as well. He decided he had loitered out here long enough and climbed the treads, stepped through the massive portals into the remodeled atrium. Hard to believe this place had once been an Earth-shuttle maintenance barn.

The old priest passed Bernie on his way out, gave him the same long, disapproving scowl with which he favored everyone these days, and was gone.

They hadn't really done too badly with this overgrown garage at that, Bernie thought for the dozenth time. Translating Earthbound cathedral architecture into something cheap and suitable for the underground warrens of Luna had deprived the church of its traditionally soul-humbling exterior, but they had almost made up for it on the inside, particularly with that intimidating vaulted ceiling a hundred yards overhead, supported in a dozen places by brilliantly pulsing columns of Navy-surplus, fusion-powered pressor beams.

Room enough in here to fly the Escadrille *and* the Baron's circus.

But the pressor-columns reminded him of starships, which reminded him of Spacers, which reminded him once more of the freenies teeming cutely in the streets. That soured his mood all over again. He put his cigar out in the font and walked into the nave.

The new priest wasn't in sight, no doubt attending to such priestly duties as were appropriate at this hour. An acolyte was messing around with candles; Bernie waggled his bushy eyebrows at the robed figure. The chimpanzee inclined his furry pate toward the confessionals, and Bernie followed the inclination with his feet. As he approached the cubicles, an orang was just abandoning the left-hand side. Bernie steered to starboard. Inside the cozy little compartment, he plunked himself down as comfortably as could be managed. He heard the panel slide, revealing a rococo tracery of secondhand annunciator screening, and through it, a hunched-over shadow.

"How y'been doing?" Bernie asked.

"You're supposed to say, 'Bless me, for I have sinned.' "

"Me? Yeah, well, y'may have something there at that." He peeked again at his softly glowing watch and did that brief mental calculation he was long accustomed to performing. "It's only been a couple days for you. Subjectively I been out eighteen weeks this time, covering seventy-five years of th' rise an' fall of th' Soviet Empire. Sometimes, even for a veteran like me, it gets goddamned confusing."

There was a whispery rustling on the other side of the partition. "It is not considered seemly to take the Name of the Deity in vain—particularly in His own House. In fact, it is a mortal sin. Now do you have something to tell me, or may I return to my other—"

"Don't get excited! I just ain't usta all this mumbo-jumbo." Bernie began wishing he hadn't tossed his cigar away so casually.

"Perhaps you'd be more comfortable on a couch over at St. Sigmund's," the priest suggested with a trace of humor.

"Yeah? An' you can come along an' tell 'em why I started coming *here* in the first place. It's a good thing my great-great-grandfather the rabbi didn't live to see—"

"Bernie, you're digressing again. Now unless you get to the point . . ."

"Okay, okay! Keep your collar on! I *knew* I shoulda waited until 2400, but—what th' hell, there's somethin' I gotta tell *somebody,* an' I can trust *you* not t'pass it along to a Higher Authority, namely th' Temporal Academy Review Board." He paused, gathering his courage: "It's th' freenies—I think they're my fault."

In fact, I *know* they're my fault. Me, Bernard M-for-moron Gruenblum, boy Time Traveler. It's what I get for fooling around with Spacers.

Didn't know about that, did you? Very hush-hush it was, at least afterward. Usually I just ferry eggheads back an' forth through history, take 'em where they can spy on Julius Caesar or Julius LaRosa, or the guy who whipped up Orange Julius. I'm just a taxi-driver—punch in th' coordinates an' try t'make a landfall that won't get passed down by th' locals as a flying saucer or a Holy Manifestation—no offense.

But us Temporals aren't more'n a little wagging tail thumbtacked to th' big shaggy dog of the Ochskahrt Memorial Academy. Th' rest of th' beast is th' *Spacers*—cripes, their ships work on th' same basic principle as mine: they beat Einstein's speed limit by arriving where they wanna go a few days after they left; I get where I'm goin' *before* I left, sometimes by as much as a couple billion years. That's a damnsight more complicated an' delicate t'do right, so why do th' Spacers get all th' glory?

Personally, I'd never been out farther before than th' satellite we're sittin' on right now, but I sure-as-shootin' seen the elephant, as they say, an' a coupla thousand different species of dinosaur t'boot. Took a goddamned archaeoastronomer t'get me mixed up good an' fatal with th' Spacers.

Archaeoastronomy? It's a mouthful, all right, little junk, like those grains of half-melted sand y'find outside your doorstep when y'go up on th' surface, fused by some prehistoric solar hiccup. Big junk, too—the supernova that knocked off all those selfsame dinosaurs on Earth, an' enough antediluvian algae so th' seabottom still stinks of it.

But th' pointy-heads still don't have everything figured; on occasion somethin' throws 'em a curve—like maybe a little star that went kaplooie when it was still on th' main sequence? That's what got me in trouble: Yamaguchi W523, a wisp of expanding former solar system whose primary threw a rod while it was still in warranty. Th' bulge-brains wanted t'know why, so why did they pick on me?

Why do they *always* pick on me?

First thing—right out there in th' freight-yards not a mile an' a half from here—they cranked my little time-buggy up into a stinking Spacer's hold, great greasy steel hawsers scraping at her freshly waxed hull. You bet I supervised *that* procedure mighty close. Those thumbfingered garbage-skulls'd smash passenger-pigeon eggs just t'make a yolk. Then we blasted out several thousand light-years, an' it was three weeks of bad food an' worse company until they heaved us over th' side t'fend for ourselves.

Lemme tell you, it was eerie. I'm usta pilotin' a time-ship from Luna, where we're based, to Earth in any century y'wanna go. I've even conned a shuttle, courtesy of its crew, down t'Oklahoma City, where I hang my hat off-duty. But squattin' there in th' middle of *zilch* with nothin' more t'aim her prow at than a bunch of numbers on a read-out? Never again! I started in punchin' buttons an' tried t'ignore the excited babbling of the half-dozen scientificals stuffed in behind me. For lack of anything more constructive, I left the exterior pickups on during transit, an' before y'know it, th' gas-clouds shrank up like cigar smoke down a Hoover nozzle, an' there, once th' dust settled, was th' neatest little solar system anybody'd wanna live in—provided they didn't know its sun was constructed by th' lowest bidder.

Six major planets there were, most of 'em in th' low-rent district: ammonia giants an' little bits of rock, parboiled or freeze-dried. One fairly decent prospect, least it looked that way from space: oceans, clouds, and lotsa vegetation—if y'like putrid colors assembled in bad taste. I made some measurements, distributed some orbital gimcrackery for th' longbeards, then put her down where we could establish some kinda base camp.

We were back a thousand years before th' blow-up. Idea was, we'd park ourselves a few days, let the instruments in orbit feed data to th' computer—not *mine,* but one th' lab-coats'd crowded in an' gouged up my little buggy parqueting with. Then we'd skip ahead a couple dozen decades an' do th' same thing all over again. Sooner or later we'd get a pre-eruptive pattern of some kind (it was hoped sincerely by yours truly) an' we'd leave real quick.

Novas make nasty neighbors.

Any luck, an' th' Spacers'd even remember t'pick us up—if somebody else tied their highly polished shoelaces for 'em an' wiped the drool off their nobly cleft chins.

Well, all that scientific palaver I left to th' diploma-domes. This was gonna be my most boring mission ever. One small compensation for us Temporals is that we get t'visit some mighty interesting neighborhoods, ordinarily: ancient, *decadent* Rome; ancient, *decadent* New York; an-cient, *decadent* Oxnard—th' town that made th' twenty-second century *sizzle.* You get th' picture.

So what was I doin' out here on a mudball with *almost* bearable temperatures, *scarcely* breathable air, *monumen-tally* bilious scenery, an' a sky lookin' like something th' cat threw up?

Like I said, it's what I get for messin' with Spacers.

Just t'give you an idea: on this planet, th' deer hunters'd hafta wear *green* t' stand out. Like an explosion in a Sherwin-Williams factory. Vegetation ranged from yechy yellow through odorous orange to putrid pink; what passed for grass looked like it'd been *passed,* all right—straight through the G.I. tract of some hallucinating Herford.

Goes without sayin', we didn't eat or drink anything in-digenous, an' wore filters over our mugs whenever we went outdoors. That "we" is purely editorial, 'cause th' hyper-lobes just huddled over their precious dials an' gauges, guz-zling java an' dry rations. I mooched around outside, grate-ful even for that much t'do, though I was glad, for once, that I could pack my old Colt .45 in the open. It's against Academy regs t'carry lethal weapons in the Earth's past—

might mess up th' present, get it? But those Aztecs an' suchlike really know how t'hurt a guy, so I just sorta discreetly tuck it into a variety of ridiculous an' uncomfortable nooks an' crannies, hopin' I can whip it out fast enough to avoid bein' added to a megatherium's menu someday.

No such trouble here. This joint was scheduled to be vaporized any millennium now—not a molecule left sticking to another, an' ionized salt sown on th' ruins. Got in about as much practice shootin' as my ammo supply'd allow, even rummaged an old Milt Sparks competition rig outa th' slopchest an' strapped it around my coveralls, feelin' like Wyatt Earp.

Which brings me back to th' scenery. Th' fauna were about as disgusting as th' flora—several dozen colors that'd likely be *illegal* back on Earth—blended in with th' nuts an' berries real well. Nothin' very big, an' nothin' I'd wanna skin out an' hang on th' wall back home. Probably break my lease, even in Oklahoma City. Most of th' local talent consisted of little boulder-shaped molluscoids skittering around on about a zillion legs an' peekin' through a single, faceted eyeball up on the end of a thick, carroty stalk.

That's right, th' freenies.

Only you gotta understand: they weren't all Proxmire University grads back then; they weren't even barbarians or savages.

They were animals.

Bright animals, right 'nough. I hadn't anything else on my dance-card, so I started in rigging up little mazes from plastic partitions in ship's stores, even built a few nonlethal traps t'see if they could learn to avoid 'em. Which they did, after a while. About th' level of baboons, I figured, not nearly as clever as your altar-boys an' congregation even before their microprocessors get implanted.

Now these traps an' mazes had t'have bait. At first I watched t'see what their favorite natural munchy was—a squarish, warty purple thing that'd make an ugly-fruit look wholesome as a ripe Delicious. Pretty quick I got tired of hiking over the surrealistic countryside, an' searched through th' garbage-masher, instead. Don't usually get t'clean my ship out in mid-mission like that—who knows what the Carthaginians could do with a worn-out flashlight battery or a box of prophylactics?—but this time I was gonna bring 'er back as tidy as I took 'er out.

Sure enough, th' freenies found somethin' they'd practically bore through th' hull t'get at. Give you a hint:

". . . from the Turkish *quaveh,* an alkaloid stimulant and diuretic; may be synthesized from uric acid . . ."

You got it. They also went for old teabags an' th' dregs of various soft-drinks. Caffeine—*I* before *E,* except after *F*—in any form we had it. Struck me as sort of cute, so when we warped outa there, headin' for th' next milestone in th' self-destructive progress of that cosmic pimple shinin' overhead, in addition to th' garbage heap, I left off as much other good-stuff as I could spare without leavin' ourselves short. Lotta surprising things got caffeine, includin' several brands of orange juice—for that mornin' pick-me-up Mother Nature never thought of.

At our next stop, two hundred years later down th' track, they asked me for more.

In English.

Not too articulately, mind you. Ain't that much vocabulary to be learned from reefer packages an' cornflake boxes. But they made themselves understood. Another hundred years an' they were crankin' out their *own* narcotics, like it says, outa uric acid.

But I was *still* their goddamned patron saint. Whenever we materialized, there were crowds an' speeches, an' th' most nauseatin'-sounding bands this side of Guy Lombardo. Still can't pass one of 'em in th' street without he wants t'shinny up m'leg an' kiss me on all four cheeks. *Blechh!*

Well, you know what happened after that. I'd made th' mistake of shooting videos—I just thought it was so goddamned cunning how th' little buggers'd work through a hundred yards of complicated maze just for a teaspoon of coffee grounds. Made my second mistake back here, handin' th' tapes over to the Academy's exobiologists. One turned out t'be a bleeding heart, an' before you could say "gopherwood," they launched a trillion-credit transgalactic, transtemporal rescue mission t'save the nuclear-powered civilization those freenies had erected in just a thousand lousy years since I first introduced caffeine into their planetary ecology. They weren't quite far enough along t'build their own escape ships, but they didn't miss it by more'n a decade.

I hope th' little bastards like Ganymede—it's just like their own planet, only even *more* nauseating. Give 'em a couple years an' plenty of coffee, they'll fix it up just fine. Meanwhile, they don't take up too much room here in Luna.

Isn't really that strange—caffeine raises *human* intelligence, too. Just measurably. The freenies were teetering on some kinda evolutionary razor-edge, an' a good, strong cup of joe shoved 'em over. I don't think they're really *brighter* than we are—intelligence is a qualitative sort of thing, not quantitative. They just have short generations, about seventeen sexes, and pass along what they've learned via something like our RNA. Lotta smarts get concentrated that way; their kids are born knowin' how t'read an' write—an' who their goddamned favorite human bein' is—long as they get plenty of health-giving Coke (builds strong freenies twelve different ways!). Shit.

Maybe they'll rescue *us* someday.

The priest stirred on the other side of the confessional. "I knew all about the discovery and rescue, of course. It was the story of the century everywhere. But was your involvement really that involuntary and cynical? How *very* disillusioning. Or perhaps you're merely pulling my leg."

"A priest? You gotta be kidding. Anyway, the Academy doesn't want anybody t'know about th' caffeine thing, any more'n they want ancient folks knowing about time travel. Hell, if people found out that a brand-new competing species could be shut down completely just by denying them a nice glass tea! And *nobody* knows it was me who started it, see? That's the way *I* want it. An Invasion from Outer Space, an' *I* had t'be th' caterer!"

They were both silent, then Bernie continued. "So maybe I've just started th' possible destruction of my own species. What kinda penance does *that* call for—Hail Marys expressed in exponents?"

"Well, I'm not sure." The priest thought for a moment, then said, "But it seems to me you may have done both our races a favor, Bernie. As you say, freenies just might rescue humanity from something awful someday, who can tell? It isn't very different from any immigrant situation: everybody thinks it's a disaster at first: higher taxes, losing jobs to strangers; it never occurs to them they're also gaining millions of new *customers*.

"The freenies have looked over human culture and already come up with a hundred new inventions, medicines, production techniques—we've both leaped forward several centuries just in the past few years. In turn, humans looked at freenie culture and derived a new ethical system, several fascinating games, and a cure for the common cold. It always happens when peoples bump into one another gently."

Bernie considered that. Was it possible he was actually a benefactor to *both* civilizations? The thought was even more revolting than—

"As for penance, Bernie, let's get out of this confessional and we'll figure something out, what do you say?"

Bernie complied, waiting for the priest as he gazed across the church, a place in many ways far more alien to him than the planet of the freenies. The acolytes busied themselves calibrating coils on the heads of a scattered collection of worshippers. No wonder the old priest hated what his avocation had become, but you go where your customers are. Religion was in its final decline among humans, and no one except the simians was interested any more.

Because they were *programmed* to be, at least once a day.

He watched the sacrament of Holy Induction begin, the charging of internal batteries which powered the implanted microprocessors that gave the chimps, gorillas, and orangs that little extra mental boost caffeine seemed to supply for the freenies. Well, as he had told the old priest—without much gratitude on the old man's part, it seemed—it coulda been worse. It coulda been banana-flavored communion wafers.

Behind him, the new priest said, "I believe several cups of coffee and a nice thick steak on your credit account ought to do it, Bernie." She smiled and loosened her collar a bit, then gave her luxuriant golden mane a shake. "And afterward, your place or mine, darling?"   ☆

Pelangus

Rick Raphael

They drowned three rustlers during the night at Coral Bar
Ranch after catching them redhanded hauling fifty yearlings through a hole in the fence. By midmorning almost
everyone on the Plateau knew of the incident.

Mike Elliot and Quent Markham, who had been inside
pen four all night rigging a branding-and-counting chute,
didn't get the word until Merrill Clark finned up about
noontime with the news.

Clark, Seacrest Ranch's senior marine biologist, was
making his last circuit at the 390-fathom line when he
spotted the strobe the two line riders had rigged to attract
the herd of young stock into the branding chute. Merrill
tied his saucer to the red plastic latticework of the pen,
then pulled on his eyeshields and lifted the hatch plate in
the floor of the saucer. He slipped his feet into the racked
fins alongside the hatch, slid his hand around his exposed
neck to clear his gill slits of the work suit, and slipped into
the water. Breathing easily through the membrane implanted in his neck, he swam to the latticework walls and
squeezed between the rough strands.

He reached the opening of the chute and flashed his
wrist beam at the distant work saucers where Elliot and
Markham were nudging the last strays toward the enticing
strobe lights at the far end. As the last nearly hundred-
pound fish slipped through the chute, Elliot's voice boomed
over his outside speaker.

"Shut the gate, willya please, Merrill, and turn off the
brander. Just save us the trip."

Clark nodded, and when both tasks were done, flippered
under the motionless saucer and emerged inside the lighted
work sub. He pushed his eyeshields back and resumed normal heliox breathing as his gills closed, then pulled himself

up so sit on the edge of the open hatch with his legs dangling in the violet-blue ocean.

"All through for the day?" he asked Elliot as Quentin Markham finished the last of his tally sheets.

Mike nodded. "Yep, but it looks like we're short about forty head. Quent and me will have to run the whole damned pen wall tomorrow and find the break."

"Heard the news?" Merrill inquired. "Coral Bar nailed three people last night sneaking yearlings out in a transporter."

"What happened?" Markham asked.

"The rustlers tried to drop the tug and make a run for it, but that new sonabuoy system Coral Bar installed last month worked pretty well. Twelve cars showed up inside of two minutes. They just boxed the rustlers in and punched them out."

"Any idea who they were?"

"They claimed they were Bahamas Seamount hands who made a mistake on the corral color—thought they were in their own pens, they claimed. But Bahamas said that was plain bullshit. Never heard of them. So the Coral Bar hands punched them out . . . One of them was a woman."

A moment's silence descended as that bit of information was considered. "Shit," Markham finally muttered. "Don't get enough women down here as it is. Shouldn't go around wasting 'em like that. Seems like this is the third or fourth set of rustlers we've had to drown this year."

"So what do you do with them when you catch them?" Clark asked. "Send for the sheriff or the U.S. Marshal?"

Markham snorted. "Yeah, that's it. Send for the *Yew Ess* Marshal!"

Merrill sighed and pulled his eyeshields down. "On top of that, I got word at the office that the Bahamas flotilla has picked up the signature of a couple of attack subs, possibly Chinese. And our damned isotherms are still bad. Say—you guys finished here? I'll help you close up and then we can all head for the ranch."

Since neither fence rider was an *aquaticus*, Merrill unhooked the laser–counter unit from the chute and handed it up through the pressure hatch to save the others from suiting-up for the job. "You guys drive on out and I'll close the gate behind you," he said. "I'm tied up beside the gate."

He slipped out of the work saucer and swam for the outer wall as Mike turned on the saucer lights. The brilliance outlined the access gate for work vessels. Clark unlatched the gate and held it open until the saucer had slid through, then locked it shut behind him and reentered his own vehicle. Moments later both saucers were threading their way up a two-hundred-foot-high corridor between two of the Seacrest Ranch pelangus pens, following the rising floor of Blake's Plateau on the secondary Continental Shelf to field ranch headquarters.

One hundred and fifty miles to the east lay the true edge of the Shelf, the 100-fathom line, and another seventy-five miles farther east the gentle slope rose out of the abundant sea to the shoreline of the southeastern Atlantic states.

Seacrest Ranch's triple-ping sonar beat steadily through the little work sub, so Merrill flipped his gang bar controls to HOME and let the system do the piloting.

From time to time, he glanced out the viewport at the other work sub just a few feet to his right. Merrill reached for the interboat talker. "You fellows happen to look at the feeder density today?"

"Nope. Too busy trying to get those squirmy bastards into the tube."

"Do me a favor," Clark said. "When you go back to check on the fence hole, run a feed density check for each quadrant."

"No sweat," Quent answered. "Troubles, Merrill?"

"When isn't there trouble down here? We're getting a steady isothermic shift that's moving the plankton base and diatom fields out of the pen areas. Going to have to do something about that real soon."

Forty-five minutes later, 150 fathoms higher, and five pressures fewer, the sharp, tapering side of Johnson's Seamount rose before the two saucers. Strings of lighted warning beacons scaled the almost vertical walls. Merrill could just make out the sound of mercury shifting to the after ballast tanks as the saucers nosed up sharply nearly three hundred feet, then shifted into level-neutral and hung expectantly at the edge of the underwater garages like work horses waiting to get into the barn. They eased through the maze of anchor beams and guide lights to their regular stalls. Merrill blew tanks and the saucer rose until it nudged the underside of the garage floor. A light flashed green on his board and the door of the stall slid open. The saucer bobbed up in the brilliantly lighted building and four metallic arms extruded to raise the sub clear of the water. The hatch closed and he dropped from his vehicle to the floor of the garage, work charts and lunchbox in hand. A pair of mechanics walked toward him past a dozen other saucers hanging in racks.

"Hi, Merrill," one of them called. "Everything okay?"

"Fine." Merrill grinned. He slapped the side of the dripping little vessel. "Walk him 'til he's cool, curry 'im good, and feed him a bushel of seaweed. He's done a good day's work."

The two mechanics grinned back as Merrill moved quickly toward the door of the big garage, picking his way through the clutter of equipment and working men.

Sprawled for a hundred acres across the level plain of the flattopped seamount were the working headquarters for Seacrest Ranch. Anchored to the granite and basalt of the seamount itself, the big complex comfortably quartered one hundred and twenty men and women who worked the ranch, including fourteen *Homo aquaticus,* all native-born Seacresters who extracted oxygen from seawater through surgically implanted gills. For the remaining "Cresters" helium-rich air was maintained at forty-five pressures.

Cresters and the other ranchers of Blake's Plateau nurtured, raised, and sold the pelangus, potentially more valuable to mankind than the abundant rare metals lining the ocean deeps or the oil that lay untapped miles beneath the sea floor. Oil and metal are for making things that people use; pelangus are things that people eat. Man was returning to the sea that had nurtured and spawned him. But not without a fight.

The oil rigs with their spills and fires and pollution and piracies started it, but it was the development of the mutant pelangus that shaped the war of social and economic interests.

Its name was an amalgam of 'pelagic'—of, pertaining to, or living in the open oceans and seas—and 'black angus,' one of the finest breeds of cattle ever developed. Pelangus was the chimera of a mutant strain and a tailored genetic chain, neither fish nor fatted calf, but something akin to both—an undersea, controllable meat machine, a cow with gills. It was fitting that the genetic program and its subsequent development stemmed from research begun at the University of Florida, in a state so close to and dependent upon the sea that some swore U.S. Highway 1 rose and fell with the tide. Though the development of pelangus occurred at a time when the land was no longer able to produce sufficient beef, pork, and poultry to feed its people, when overbuilding, pollution, leached land, and high production costs all had contributed to the productivity decline, cattlemen, farmers, processors and distributors looked at the pelangus as the greatest economic threat in the history of the world. And they lost no time in trying to legislate the pelangus into extinction.

Merrill Clark hesitated for a moment outside the door to the foreman's office to glance for the final time at his calculations, then shook his head and walked in.

Apart from his notable position as working boss of the largest of the Continental Shelf's marine spreads, Andrew Jackson McFadden had another honor to his credit. Forty-four years earlier he had been the first child born below the sea. It hadn't been planned that way. Mary McFadden had been packed for three weeks before the baby was due and had a room reserved at Jacksonville's Memorial Hospital on shore, but the pains heralding Andy's arrival had come as Hurricane Cora ripped piers and buildings from Florida's eastern seacoast. So, in a tiny ranch dispensary 306 feet below the storm-tossed waters, Andrew Jackson McFadden had first drawn breath. It was the same mixture of oxygen and helium he had been breathing almost daily ever since.

He looked up and shoved papers aside as Merrill entered.

"You must be a mind-reader." He smiled. "I've been meaning to call you all day. Have a seat. Things any better?"

Merrill sank into a chair across from the foreman and shook his head. He fished out his graph rolls and laid them on the desk.

"Still bad, Andy. We don't know why, but we suspect a seismic disturbance and following undersea waveform are giving us an isothermic shift. The waveform is just shoving the base plankton and diatom layers away from the feeder pens."

McFadden studied the graph and ran his fingers through thinning red hair.

"So we move the feeder pens," he said.

"I wish it were that easy," Clark said. "We're not sure how much the gradients will vary and shift over the next couple of months or longer and when and where they'll stabilize. They might settle right back into their old forms.

"Meanwhile, that doesn't solve the feeding problem. We're still getting the usual biota drifting down into the pens, but you know that isn't a hundredth of what fat stock needs to keep it fat. We need the plankton."

"I know," McFadden replied wearily. "So what's your answer, Merrill?"

"Force-feeder system throughout the pens. We harvest and haul until we see where this is leading us."

"Now you're talking equipment and money," McFadden said, holding up a hand. "Hold up a few minutes until I get Jerry Swinney in engineering and Carl Pasco out of accounting. They might as well get the good news right from the top."

Both men joined McFadden and Clark shortly and heard Merrill outline the problem.

"We can design, probably even build the equipment," Swinney said, "but it's going to be damned expensive."

"And money is the one thing we have trouble raising down here," Pasco added. "It's very tough in the market right now."

When the best figures had been projected, McFadden shoved back his calculator and shook his head slowly. "My God, two and a half million," he muttered, "and that's just for operations. What is this going to mean to all the ranches down here?"

"It could mean wipeout," Carl Pasco replied. "It's a case of damned if you do and damned if you don't. You may sink all this into the equipment and find out that everything is back to normal in two months. Or you could wait two months and find out that it's too late. We have to invest or go under, and either way, we might still blow up."

McFadden drummed his fingers on the desk and stared blankly at the far wall, lost in thought. "What we need to do as a matter of good business practice," he finally said, "is to borrow as much as we can and spread the risk around."

"And just where do you expect to find that kind of loot?" Pasco asked. "Working Wall Street with a tin cup? Andy, I just got through telling you, things are tough up there on the dirt. Money is tight."

"I understand," McFadden said. "But there is one source of that kind of money, enough to pull all of us through this crisis."

Pasco's eyebrows rose.

"That's right, Carl," McFadden said evenly. "Washington. The federal government."

"Are you out of your mind?" Jerry Swinney yelled. "We aren't even a part of the United States! We don't belong to anybody. What the hell are you thinking about . . . trying to get foreign aid?"

"Nope," McFadden said smoothly, "not foreign aid, but a federal business loan. This time we move the bill through Congress so fast that they won't know what's hit them. We are going to become the Territory of Marina, just like that bill that's been sitting in Congress for ten years calls us. And we'll do it now."

He reached for his communicator. "You three be ready in four hours to head for Upper Shelf and corporate offices. Plan on being gone a couple of days, because I have a hunch we'll wind up in Starfish sometime tomorrow. Talk this over with your people and either have their ideas firmly in mind or bring them along.

"We are going to boycott those son-of-a-bitches into giving us our rightful protection."

It was after midnight, however, when McFadden's team assembled in the garage. During the preceding hours the ranch foreman had been on the communicator almost constantly, talking first with Seacrest's general manager, Ron Seward, at the Upper Shelf headquarters, then to dozens of foremen and managers of the other major ranches north and south of Seacrest on the Plateau that ran from the Bahamas to its bottleneck end off Wilmington, North Carolina. While McFadden made his calls, Seward contacted ranches, industrial operators, and weed farmers on Upper Shelf. The men piled into the ranch's subbus, and as it slid out of the parking pool, they began decompressing for the three-hour trip to the Upper Shelf. During the trip up, McFadden agreed to contact Sea Farm Cooperative's John

Burnett to ask that he represent the weed farmers at the coming meeting.

When they trooped into Ron Seward's office, he was still talking on the communicator. He waved to them and then pointed at sandwiches and coffee. They settled themselves around his desk and waited.

At the end of his conversation, he stood and walked to the coffee urn, talking the entire time. "It's all ready to go. When we get through here in a few minutes, you fellows catch some shut-eye for a couple of hours. We leave about nine. The Territorial Constitutional Convention reconvenes in Starfish at ten in the morning, but I've already gotten hold of some of our more dependable dirtside suppliers and put in rush orders for delivery within seventy-two hours. Told them we're having thermoshifts and everyone's working around the clock. That's no real lie anyway, according to Merrill's report."

He sipped the hot coffee and waited for McFadden to speak.

"I don't think we're going to have any problem with the ranches, Ron," the redhead said. "We've all had just about enough. The last thing anyone wants is to become a United Nations protectorate. But unless we can get Congress to act right now, that's what's going to happen—either that or find ourselves in the middle of a shooting war. The Chinese want our breeding stock and our lab equipment. But if the U.S. tries to stop the takeover, calling it a threat to national security, the war is on. Once the UN acts, the U.S. can't prevent our becoming a protectorate, since it isn't a Security Council matter. Nope, we go for the works in Washington or we go out of business, Ron. It's down to that."

The general manager nodded his head in agreement. "I've been listening to variations on that theme all night from the Upper Shelf people," he said. "Only the oil and mineral companies are laying back because they think they can squeeze out an exemption. They think because they're multinationals that they can handle this just like they handle any foreign-rights problem.

"Well, we'll know pretty damn quickly if it's going to work. The word is out to every ranch on the Plateau. Not another head of stock leaves the pens until this is over. But we don't want to make that public for a couple of days yet.

Give our supply people time to get some stockpile on the way down to us before the shit hits the fan. Find a rack and get some sleep."

The violet-blue of the lower-shelf waters gave way to the clear blue-greens of the upper ConShelf as the Seacrest convoy threaded its way into the parking pool of Starfish, the Shelf's largest community and the supply center for all the ranches of the southern shelf. The Seacrest vehicles locked into vacant dockside slots, and Seward and McFadden led their delegation to the ramp to the tram terminal.

Vessel supply shops, repair facilities, and equipment stores lined the ramps leading to the port's double-pressure lock doors. Everything in Starfish—including the city itself— was privately owned, and money was the passport to entry. Whatever you obtained in Starfish—from the air you breathed to the water you drank—you paid for to one or more of a hundred private enterprises. Though the majority of installations on Blake's Plateau lay outside the vague shelf limits generally agreed upon by coastal nations, the matter of who really owned the seabeds had been in standing committee of the United States for more than a half century without resolution.

Starfish's largest corporation, Aquaports, Inc., had taken the small original cluster of submarine shelters and gradually expanded them into a city. Aquaports, Inc., leased space and facilities of Starfish, and the company's board of directors was the closest thing to a governmental body available. But there were no courts recognized by any nation or the UN, no law enforcement or armed forces. Since life below the ocean's surface required common effort, there was surprisingly little personal crime in either Starfish or its northern-shelf sister city, Aquadia. But rustling and piracy, the only real crimes against property and person, were increasing, and the vigilante action of the ranchers grew out of a need for mutual protection. Frontier justice prevailed for frontier living. Catch 'em and drown 'em.

The aquanautic population had been seeking Territorial status from the United States for more than a decade. A Territorial Convention had been convened, a constitution drafted and agreed upon, and a petition made to Congress. A bill had been drawn to annex them as the Territory of Marina. For ten years, through five sessions of Congress, the bill had languished, opposed by the entrenched cattle, hog, and sheep growers, the meat packers, the farmers, and their allies, the teamsters who hauled the land-grown meat to market.

Because the Plateau was denied U.S. Territorial status, it became a foreign supplier, and a protective tariff had been pushed through Congress that forced the price of pelangus up more than a dollar a pound above the price it took to raise it, ship it to shore processors, and transship it to market. Not satisfied with that, the same foes forced a new series of quasilegal export taxes and restrictions on supplies needed by the Shelf residents, helium being the most expensive and prohibitive.

Despite the inflated cost of pelangus, its popularity with the housewife and the nutritionist continued to rise. It accounted for more than a third of the national meat supply in the United States, and its market share was growing with each year. Only small shipments were made elsewhere, notably to Canada and the British Isles.

The Seacrest men joined the throngs hurrying to the community center auditorium in the heart of Starfish. It was already two-thirds filled when they arrived. McFadden, as permanent chairman of the convention, moved to the podium and looked at the chrono. At the instant of 1000 hours his gavel descended. "I declare this emergency session of the Territorial Constitution Convention of Marina in session." There was a burst of applause and whistling.

"You may not be so enthusiastic after you've heard of the problems that bring us here today. The first order of business must be an explanation of the crisis situation affecting us all. I want you to listen to Merrill Clark, Seacrest's senior biologist and the man who brought this to my attention. I'm sure that many of you already are aware of the thermal shifts. We're laying our cards on the table, even to the extent of what financial effect this is going to have on Seacrest economy. I hope all of you will follow suit in pooling information and ideas, for I assure you we will all be affected. Merrill."

It took the biologist and Seacrest's engineer, Jerry Swinney, less than half an hour to sketch the isothermic drift, its probable effects, and the proposal for the feeding machines.

After Clark and Swinney stepped down, McFadden took the podium again. "I know you all have technical questions, but I ask that you hold them until we are through with this plenary session. Then we'll break up into specialist groups to work out details.

"You've heard the problem and a possible solution. I can state right now that the problem isn't going to change or go away in the immediate future. As to the possible solution—force-feeding machines—that may or may not be the answer. We'll have an engineering group working on this starting the instant this session ends. But whatever the details, one thing is absolute—it's going to cost us a fortune. For some of us, it may mean bankruptcy. And as if the isothermic shift isn't enough, we have an upsurge in rustling.

"I'm almost tempted to let the dumb sons-of-bitches take the whole damn herd. They deserve the headaches."

He paused to let them laugh and to give himself time to choose his next words carefully.

"There has been a meeting of your executive committee in the past twenty-four hours, and we have come up with a possible solution and suggestion. Before I present it I want you to understand that should we adopt this measure, not one word about what we have decided upon must leak to any source before we release it officially. A single, premature word can destroy us—financially and literally."

The only sounds in the big room were the rustle of papers and an occasional cough.

"And a final note of caution. The cure may be worse than the disease. Having said that, I want Carl Pasco to outline the suggested courses of action to you."

Carl moved to the podium and looked out over the rows of expectant faces.

"To paraphrase an old saying," Carl said grimly, "when you can't beat 'em, join 'em." He paused. "Then beat 'em," he shouted.

The audience exploded into a roar of yells and cheers.

Carl waited for the pandemonium to subside.

"We have waited ten long and fruitless years to be recognized for what we are," he declared, "good and loyal American citizens. I say ten years is too long. I say the time has come for us to demand our rightful status as citizens of the United States of America, and for the services and protection that go with citizenship. We are an economic and geographic entity of our country. Why shouldn't we be a political entity of it?

"We are faced with a natural disaster that in any state or Territory would automatically send federal aid rushing in. We are beset by thieves and are without legal protection. We are attacked by foreign forces and left defenseless. We are vulnerable to seizure and enslavement or even death by a foreign power.

"There is a bill once again gathering dust in both houses of Congress that would grant us Territorial status. Do you know how long it would take to get that passed by Congress and signed by the President if Congress and the American people were so moved? Less than forty-eight hours!" Carl paused to catch his breath.

A low, angry growl rose from the delegates.

"But it takes something to stir them to that kind of action, and we of the executive committee feel we know the answer to that problem, and, once given Territorial status, we will have the source of emergency funds we need to tide us over this thermal shift crisis and provide us stability to *really* develop Blake's Plateau into the greatest financial and natural resource in our nation.

"I ask your action on a suggested resolution . . ." He paused for effect. "That as of twelve o'clock noon, this date, not another head of pelangus be shipped shoreward from any facility on the Plateau until this Plateau formally becomes the United States Territory of Marina."

He stepped back from the microphone as pandemonium erupted.

McFadden let them go for a full ten minutes before gaveling for order. It took him another ten to get the delegates back to their seats.

When it was quiet enough to be heard, Carl went on.

"Before I ask for a motion, much less a vote," he cautioned, "I want you to once again consider what you are demanding and what you will be getting for what you give up.

"You will get American citizenship, but you'll also get American taxes. You'll be rid of the high tariffs, but you'll be subject to a hundred federal agencies, each with different regulations. You'll get a chance to pick a President, but you won't have a voice in Congress and you may not even have the right to choose your own resident Commissioner or Governor. But your children and *their* children will also be born American.

"During the next few days, when the full effect of the embargo takes hold, we can expect reprisals. We are caught in a love-hate situation, with the dirtside meat people hating us and calling our pelangus inferior foreign meat designed to put Americans out of work and out of health. We must pool our resources for a public relations campaign to counter that. Once the American people see the cost of meat rise out of sight as pelangus goes off the market, they will be ready for the message that we can and will sell it to them cheaper than any other meat source in the world. But first they may try to starve us or even bomb us into submission. We must be prepared to act quickly to meet every emergency. Now, do I hear a motion in support of a total embargo on pelangus until we are granted Territorial status?"

By five that afternoon, the Convention had recessed on the call of the chairman, and the delegates were heading home to prepare for the siege.

The four-man carryall moved slowly into the docking slip at Wilmington. A uniformed attendant walked toward it, eyeing the red insignia of Aquaports.

Carl cut the engine as Paul Smith undogged the hatch. Smith, Martin Wainwright, and Ted Steiner, like Pasco, were all in their early thirties. Smith was corporate counsel for Aquaports, Wainwright the farm co-op economist, and Steiner a marine chemist for an Aquadia firm. The four constituted the Territorial blitzing front four in Washington.

Smith took the luggage handed up to him and set it on the dock.

"Going to be in town long, gents?" the attendant asked, charge book in hand.

"We'll take the slip for a month," Pasco said, reaching for his credit plate.

The attendant took the plate and scribbled on his pad, then briefly held the charge plate against the paper, tore off the receipt, and handed it to Carl, together with the credit plate.

Pasco glanced at the receipt and then roared. "Three

hundred dollars! The most we've ever paid for a carryall slip here is five bucks a day!"

The attendant shrugged. "I don't make the rules, mister, I just do what I'm told. My new rental rate card says ten bucks a day for any subcar not carrying American registration—and that you ain't got."

Carl jammed the receipt into his pocket and picked up his bags. "Come on, let's get the hell out of here before they charge us for parking our feet on their damned dock."

The quartet moved to the customs and immigration shed. With nothing to declare they were waved through customs to immigration.

"How long do you plan to be in our country?" the inspector asked.

"Look," Smith said, "this is our country too, mister. We're not foreigners."

"You don't live in the United States," the immigration man said. "Under the Second-Generation Rule of '05, *none* of you is an American; you don't pay taxes to this country, and as far as we're concerned, you're not Americans. Now, I repeat, how long do you plan to remain in the United States?"

"About a month."

"Very good. I'll issue you thirty-day travel permits. Remember, they are good only for that length of time. Should you need to remain longer or have a medical emergency, report to the nearest immigration office and make arrangements for an extension. Failure to report an overstay will subject you to arrest and deportation. Remember, you are subject to all the laws of this country while you are visiting here.

"Enjoy your stay in our country." He handed over the blue temporary permits.

"This is the last time," Carl said through gritted teeth as they walked out of the shed. "I swear it is. The next time I come through here, that snotty bastard will be saluting."

By the end of the following day, Shelf Research Institute had rented office space in downtown Washington, D.C., and the four scattered to put their battle plans into action. Smith, Steiner, and Pasco were closeted at 5 P.M. with the current sponsor of the Territorial bill, New York Congressman Jack Haskins.

* * *

Merrill Clark was finishing the last of a series of feeding tests when McFadden entered the lab. The ranch foreman watched as Clark worked with a hundred-foot-long control tank in which a dozen 500-pound pelangus were swimming. Clark triggered a cylinder fastened to the side of the tank, and through the big quartz viewing window McFadden watched an inky blob squirt into the waters and slowly spread and gain in size. At first the fish ignored it. Then the two pelangus nearest the approaching edge of the food cloud whip-turned and knifed into the murkiness, mouths opening and closing in great gulps as they consumed the concentrated fodder. Five seconds later, all twelve were feeding greedily.

Clark had been watching and timing them. He turned to face McFadden.

"That's fine if they happen to be around the tanks when the feed is expelled," he said. "But if they were downtank, the cloud might disperse right out through the netting before they could find it. Now watch this."

He turned to an identical tank. Clark waited until the fish had drifted almost to the far end of the pool and then simultaneously triggered a battery of strobe lights and the feeder release. A ten-second delay was programmed between the time the strobes started flashing and the food was shot into the tank. The instant the food cloud began emerging from the nozzle of the feeder, twelve more pelangus were bumping each other for position, waiting for the food. Clark grinned. "It took me just three days of starving those fish and two days of brief feedings accompanied by light signals to teach them that light now means food."

McFadden smiled, clapped Merrill on the arm. "Great work, boy, just great—"

The annunciator on the wall blared. "Andy. Andy McFadden."

"In the bio lab," Andy called out.

"Better get back to the office on the double. There's been a raid on Coral Bar and a helluva fight—and they've caught one of the raider subs!"

The foreman was already sprinting for the door, closely followed by Clark.

A large number of off-duty pen riders and men from all departments who had heard the bulletin over the ranch-wide system were crowded around the door of the foreman's office as he bulled his way through. Simpson, the assistant foreman, was sitting on Kathy's desk, phone to his ear.

"He's talking with Ed Billings at Coral Bar right now," Kathy said to McFadden as he swung around her desk.

"Wait a minute, Ed," Simpson said. "Andy's here now." He thrust the headset at the foreman.

"Ed," McFadden called, "what's happened?"

"We need help, and we need it fast, Andy. Three of our pen riders found a wall punched in. Instead of calling for help, they decided to play hero. They rigged a triple-weave trap net across the opening and then sat back and waited to see what would happen. They saw, all right.

"A fast, small transporter came charging out through the hole, hit the net, and fouled itself. One of 'my boys headed back for the ranch, but the raider was calling for help too. A pair of killer subs knocked the pen riders off and were trying to free the transporter when I got there. I guess they thought I was Navy, because they took off when they spotted us coming. But I don't think they'll stay bluffed too long. We've got their transporter sealed into our garage and we're pretty sure the vehicle itself is not armed. But I'm in no position to fight off professionals all by myself if the killers come to the rescue."

"Ed, hang on," McFadden yelled, "we're on the way. I'm going to put Simpson back on the phone; you tell him what you think we need, and he'll keep me posted."

The ranch foreman returned the receiver to his assistant. He turned and began snapping orders.

"Kathy, get word to all pen riders to stay clear of any strange vehicles—report their presence but stay away. That's an order.

"Clark, get your shark-bomb inventory aboard a transporter and take eight men with stun guns and whatever else you can find in arms. I'll meet you at the garage."

McFadden searched the crowd. "Swinney," he yelled.

"Here, Andy," the engineer called from the edge of the group.

"Get all the people you can spare from your section and take what vehicles we've got other than Clark's transporter and my carryall."

The foreman spotted the field ranch medical director. "Doc, you're in charge of this base while we're gone. Get every man, woman, and child into lung gear. All off-duty personnel not already assigned to jobs report to their quarters and stay there. That goes for families as well. Everyone else in lung gear at their duty stations. In case you get hit while we're away, order immediate evacuation to the surface.

"All right, move!"

As the men raced to their assignments, McFadden grabbed the hydrophone circuits and punched up the Jacksonville dirtside operator.

When she answered, McFadden yelled, "Defense emergency. Get me Jacksonville Naval Station duty officer."

There was a faint gasp at the other end of the underwater circuit, then a series of clicks. A man's voice sounded.

"This is Commander Anderson."

"This is Andrew McFadden, foreman of Seacrest Ranch. Coral Bar Ranch is under attack by what we're sure are Chinese raider subs. We're possibly next in line, but we're going to help them. Can you assist immediately?"

"Stand by one," the crisp voice replied. As McFadden waited he could hear the duty officer calling orders. "Coral Bar. Enemy sub attack. All patrol vessels immediate area respond. Order Bahamas Patrol to flank speed."

The officer came back to Andy. "We're on the way, McFadden."

"One more thing," the ranch foreman said. "I've ordered surface evacuation of my people in the event the raiders hit our base here. Can you have surface vessels stand by at Seacrest Breather Station Two, please?"

"They'll be there," the Navy man replied. "Good luck."

The Shelf might not be part of the U.S.A. to the politicians, but the Navy took a different view.

McFadden dropped the phone and raced for the base garage. The last of the engineering department team was swinging a piece of equipment down the hatch as he ran into the shed. Swinney was already in the foreman's carryall with two of his men as McFadden dropped down the hatch, then sealed it. A minute later, Seacrest's expeditionary force slid under the water and gunned for Coral Bar Ranch.

McFadden glanced over at the instrument panel. Swinney already had full sweep search sonar in action. Andy thumbed his mike. "This is McFadden. All Seacrest vehicles on full sonar search," he ordered. "Clark, prepare your shark toys for seeding. Clump them in units of twenty! The Chinese subs have sturdy hulls."

Twenty minutes later Swinney called out, "Coral Bar coming up."

McFadden checked the sonar. Only the usual and expected marine life echoes were recording.

A confirmation check with Coral Bar via Seacrest relay reported no sign of returning raiders.

McFadden picked up his mike. "Merrill, take a ninety-four-degree heading for four minutes, then turn on one eight two again and start seeding in a broad semicircle and with what depth variation you can manage around Coral Bar—say, to about two hundred fifty degrees, then come on into the ranch."

"On the way," Clark replied from his transporter. McFadden watched its echo on the sonar as it turned out of the Seacrest convoy.

Eight minutes later, the remaining Seacrest vehicles surfaced in the Coral Bar garage. Ed Billings was waiting as McFadden climbed out of the carryall. The Coral Bar foreman was grim-faced. "Thanks for coming, Andy. Although God only knows what we can really do if they decide to take us."

Around them Seacrest and Coral Bar men were unloading gear from the vehicles. At the far side of the shed, a battery of lights coldly illuminated a strange vehicle. A small circle of Coral Bar hands surrounded the sealed vehicle, which was wrapped in a shroud of twisted net.

McFadden gestured at it with his head.

Billings nodded. "They haven't made any attempt to open hatches. Frankly, until you got here, I've been a little leery of forcing it open. I don't think there could be more than a dozen men aboard that thing, but I don't know how they're armed."

The two foremen walked over to the raider vehicle. Andy studied the vessel for a couple of minutes. "You tried to talk to 'em, Ed?" he asked.

"I tried," the other man replied, "but they don't answer."

Swinney had followed his chief. McFadden turned to the engineer. "Got a can opener with you, Jerry?"

"As a matter of fact, yes," Swinney answered. The Seacrest engineer ran back to his team and returned with them and a small laser unit. A tap was run to the Coral Bar nuclear power plant line, and five minutes later Jerry turned to the two men. "Want me to burn 'er open?"

"Hold it a minute," McFadden said. He turned to Billings. "Got any plastic blasting goo?"

"There's plenty of it in the explosives locker at the back of the shed."

Minutes later, a bundle of explosive was rigged in a sling over the entry hatch of the foreign transporter and the laser unit aimed at the sealed port.

Andy reached over and magnoclamped the output transducer of a resonating communicator against the hull of the vessel. He took a mike in hand.

"I hope that someone in there understands English because it may save your lives. We are going to burn you open. The instant your hatch is cut, an explosive charge will drop into your hull. You have one minute before we start cutting."

Forty seconds elapsed before the hatch swung out. An Oriental face appeared in the opening, hands raised over its head. The Chinese stepped out onto the dock, followed by five others. Angry Coral Bar hands moved in on them.

"Hold it," Billings ordered. "Take them over against the back wall and tie 'em up. If their chums decide to come after them, this is the place they'll come, and I want them to find their dead bodies if they finally manage to break in here."

As he finished talking, a vessel slowly surfaced in the pool and every man swung around in alarm. Swinney grabbed the laser unit and was aiming it—suddenly he relaxed. It was Merrill Clark's transporter. The bright yellow Seacrest vehicle slid up to the docking slip and Clark emerged.

"Seeds all planted, Andy," he called as his men were debarking.

"Drag out the keyboard for the shark bombs and take it over to the sonar panel." McFadden pointed to the portable console that Coral Bar men had set up in the garage. Even as he was giving the order, the man at the console shouted.

"Three echoes approaching at one hundred two degrees. No IFF."

The foreman ran for the console.

"I called for Navy help before I left," Andy gasped as he ran. "It might be them."

"No reply to ID request."

"Clark," McFadden shouted, peering over the operator's shoulder at the sonar position scope, "get that keyboard over here in a hurry."

Clark ran up with the keyboard slung from his shoulder. He glanced quickly at the semicircle of dots showing on the console between the approaching blips and the ranch.

"That southernmost sub looks like a cinch," he murmured, fingers moving across his control box like an accordian player's.

"Remember," McFadden warned, "shark bombs don't pack much of a wallop. Make damn sure he's right on top of the clump before you kick it. Five feet away might just as well be five miles."

Clark nodded silently, his eyes glued on the scope. The three blips were now almost into the semicircle.

"What the hell are those?" Billings whispered urgently to McFadden, pointing to the motionless dots.

"Shark bombs," McFadden replied. "If we get lucky, it might slow the bastards down until the Navy gets here."

The three Chinese subs were now entering the shark-bomb ring. Clark held his breath and rested a finger lightly on button twelve. As the southern sub seemed to merge with the bomb, Clark still waited. Then, almost imperceptibly, the tiny dot that was blending with the bigger blip moved. Clark's finger stabbed. Ten seconds later the water in the parking pool rippled slightly; on the scope, dot and blip vanished.

"Got him," Clark yelled.

The other two blips were turning 180 degrees and heading back to the continental slope.

The yells of the men echoed through the big shed. Billings looked over at the five Chinese, squatting against the far wall.

"That's the first payment on the loss of my two men," he spat.

The sonar now showed two departing subs at the outer range and still going. The echo of the shattered sub reappeared, slowly drifting toward the bottom.

The annunciator blared. "Ed, take the phones."

Billings picked up the headset. "Go ahead," he said.

"Hello, Coral Bar," a voice sounded. "This is flotilla commander, Bahamas Patrol. We are closing on your location at thirty knots on a heading of one hundred ninety-three deegres. What is the situation at this time?"

"This is Billings, Coral Bar foreman. We have just repulsed an attack by three subs, presumed Chinese. We got one. Approach area with caution. Those bastards are still out there. We have seeded clusters of shark bombs around our base."

"Affirmative, Coral Bar," came the reply. "Our commander wants to know if you have made positive identification of the attacking subs."

"Notify your commander," Billings bellowed, "that we have not made any identification of the *vehicles*. But you can also tell him that we've got five of the meanest Cantonese-speaking sea slime he's every seen, tied up here in our garage. But for all I know, they could be from Hutchinson, Kansas."

"Acknowledged, Coral Bar. We will be closing."

The sonar man nudged Billings and pointed to the scope. A group of ten blips had appeared at the outer range marks, approaching on a 193 bearing.

"What's the size of your flotilla, Navy?" Billings asked.

"We have ten vessels."

"Okay," Billings said, "we have you on our scopes."

The sonar man yelled, "Here comes one of the bastards."

On the scope, the blip of a vessel appeared, moving fast on a heading slightly off-angle from Coral Bar headquarters.

"Navy," Billings yelled, "one of them is coming in again, moving like a shark with a torch on its tail. Bearing oh seven one, heading two seven three."

"Stand by your box," McFadden warned Clark.

They watched the sub streaking toward the ranch. At six thousand yards, it suddenly turned sharply and sped back on its original course. A minute later the rumbling "boom" of a tremendous underwater explosion shivered the building, and the parking pool rose in a surge that sent transporters crashing against one another and the docks. It hurled the smaller single-seater patrol subcars out of the water to crash down on the landings. Water cascaded over the garage area.

"The bastards!" Billings screamed. "The dirty, no-good, lousy sons-of-bitches have bombed my pens!"

Purple with rage, he stormed across the slippery floor of the shed, stumbling over equipment in his haste. He charged into the five Chinese tied against the wall and smashed the back of his hand across the face of the first one he could reach. The Oriental careened to the floor and Billings drew back his arm for another blow. McFadden and two Coral Bar hands seized his arm and restrained the enraged foreman.

A few minutes later the flotilla commander's gig surfaced in the pool, and a dozen armed sailors, led by a young lieutenant, swung onto the docks.

"I'm Lieutenant Nelson," he introduced himself. "It looks like the raiders spotted our approach and decided not to wait around. We picked them up on our search gear, heading for deep water. We've got a couple of snappers chasing them, but I haven't much hope of catching them. Looks like the fight's over before we got started." He surveyed the dripping garage.

The five Chinese prisoners were turned over to the Navy patrol. Lieutenant Nelson had them frisked, then detailed two men to act as prize crew for the captured sub. "We'll be maintaining a patrol off the Shelf from now on," he said as he climbed into the gig. "That will probably discourage further raids, but if anything does show up or slip past us, give a yell and we'll get here as fast as we can." He waved a hand, jumped below, and dogged the hatch. The gig slid beneath the surface.

Billings turned to McFadden. "No point in going to look at the pen damage yet. That sediment won't clear out for hours. But I guess I won't be needing the feeders now, Andy."

"Wait until you see how bad it is," McFadden told him, "before you start crying. You and I didn't get these outfits going by quitting every time something backfired."

The Seacrest men helped their neighbors get the worst of the damage cleared away and then climbed into their own vessels to return home. Because one of Seacrest's engineering two-seaters had a smashed hull from the bomb impact, it was left behind for Coral Bar mechanics to repair. The two men the car had carried jammed into the biology transporter.

Back at Seacrest, a message to call Carl Pasco was waiting for McFadden. The foreman slumped wearily into the chair behind his desk and placed the call to Shelf Research Institute offices in Washington. When Pasco was on the line, McFadden said "Encode" and flipped a switch. In Washington, Pasco did the same. Now any interception of the call would be so much gibberish to an eavesdropper.

"Andy," Pasco said quickly, "what the hell has happened, and tell me fast. The videocasts have had nothing but meaningless bulletins every ten minutes for the last two hours."

McFadden sketched the events for Pasco.

"You say the Navy has the Chinese in custody now?" Pasco inquired. "Where are they taking them, Andy?"

"Dunno. I assume to Jacksonville. It never occurred to me to ask."

"I'll try and find out right away," Carl said. "I've got to go now, Andy, and get on the wire to Marty. He's built the UN contacts for us, and I want our team to get at them before the Chinese do. I'll call you back later."

". . . this unprovoked attack by a band of savage, lawless, and stateless barbarians on the unarmed training vessels of young cadet merchant submariners," the envoy of the People's Republic of China intoned into his mouthpiece as he stood at his seat in the tiered hall of the General Assembly, "is bad enough. These barbaric outlaws should be wiped from the bottom of the ocean waters that they pollute. But the affair was made even more reprehensible when armed aggressor underwater forces of a member nation of this body, flagrantly and without warning, opened fire on our defenseless cadets, causing the loss of five of our vessels and the lives of more than two hundred of our young hopes for the future. And this deed of cowardice, the People's Republic of China contends, is an act of outright piracy, since this killer pack aggressor force was outside the recognized boundaries of any nation and in internationally free waters."

"They lost one sub," the American undersecretary whispered to his UN Ambassador, "and it was blown up by our rancher friends with a very appropriate weapon—a shark bomb."

The Ambassador repressed a grin.

In the gallery, Martin Wainwright was listening intently to the colorless translation of the Chinese envoy's tirade.

"The People's Republic of China demands that the barbaric outlaws and the imperialistic pirates of the United States of America who aided in this unwarranted and savage attack be subject to the severest reprisals of this body. And my government has informed me that it will demand monetary retribution from the imperialist government of the United States in the amount of five hundred million dollars, the bulk of which will go to the grieving widows and children of those gallant submariners struck down by this deed, the remainder a token payment to the People's government for the loss of our training vessels."

There was a stir of excitement in the great hall as the Chinese sat down. The delegates waited tensely for the United States to reply.

The American delegate rose slowly to his feet. He looked around the crowded chambers and waited for silence. When even the breathing was hushed, he uttered two syllables.

"Hogwash!" said the American Ambassador to the United Nations.

In the gallery, Martin grinned broadly and whipped off his translator headset, then hurried out to the nearest visiphone.

Pasco was out of the Institute offices when Martin called. The receptionist put Ted Steiner on the screen.

Wainwright quickly reviewed the current situation at the United Nations.

"How soon will our bill be ready, Ted?" he asked. "I want to push it as fast as possible 'cause I'm afraid this thing may get the UN moving toward the establishment of a protectorate—and *then* we'll have a helluva time pulling ourselves out of that sticky net back to the U.S. of A."

"Carl's over on the Hill now," Ted said. "The bill will be voted in the Senate a week from Monday. And we've got Haskins from New York and O'Connor of Tennessee pushing for a House vote at the same time."

"See if you can't get them onto the floor sooner than that," Martin urged. "This thing is going to be sticky for our people here, and right now the State Department would love to see us bundled off to the UN, particularly since we seized those five Red bandits."

Steiner frowned. "I don't know if we can swing it, Marty," he replied, "but we'll try. I'll see if I can get in touch with Carl, and in the meantime, you keep the stall going as much as possible up there."

While Ted and Martin were winding up their conversation, Carl was closeted with five Republican congressmen from the New England states.

"I could start off with the traditional blarney," Carl said smilingly, "about how you gentlemen represent constituencies that bred the famed American seafarers of the eighteenth and nineteenth centuries, and that you've got your roots in the sea. But I don't have to resort to that kind of meaningless oratory, because it isn't your roots that are in the sea any more, gentlemen—it's your bellies."

He paused and surveyed the group.

"You all come from high-density population districts in the middle-income brackets, and I'd venture to say that each of you came to Washington from a family in that category," Pasco continued. "You know damned well how tough it is for a working man to feed and house his family adequately today in the face of rising prices. Right now the American per capita consumption of meat products is one hundred thirty pounds per year—less than it was a century ago—and yet we claim to live in the greatest, most progressive society in the history of mankind.

"Now I know that there are a multitude of meat substitutes on the market, but if you've ever eaten synthetic steak, you know there is no substitute for real meat."

Carl noted with secret satisfaction the slight curling of lips at the mention of synthetic foods.

"I also know that you've all been eating pelangus steaks, roasts, and flakes for years. You know that is a red fish-meat, juicier than beef, tenderer than chicken, more flavorful than pork, and contains more all-round nutrition than the other three put together.

"Right now your wives are buying pelangus at the market for about $1.30 a pound, and they're buying their so-calld meats for anything from ninety cents to a dollar and a half or more a pound for prime beef. Now there is no such thing as a choice or a good grade of pelangus. There is only one grade—that's prime, gentlemen, or it wouldn't pass the buyer inspection.

"Your wives are paying $1.30 a pound, gentlemen, for a major food products that we would like to sell to them at *thirty* cents a pound. That's what is physically costs us to produce and market pelangus, gentlemen. And by 'produce and market,' I mean just that. This covers our overhead, depreciation, market fluctuation, capital improvements, salaries, dividends to our stockholders, processing, marketing, and retailer markup—the works!"

He paused dramatically.

"But do you know why we don't sell pelangus at thirty cents a pound instead of $1.30? Because the other dollar is imposed upon us in special tariffs instigated by the cattle and farm lobby that doesn't want you and your people to have a cheap, delicious, wholesome, and plentiful meat that would depress the cost of their automated meat factories and cut off the flow of dollars to their pockets—dollars, gentlemen, that are coming from you and your constituents!

"It is for this reason that we whose parents migrated into the sea to produce food for our nation are now asking that we be accorded the rights and privileges of American citizens and that we no longer be treated like foreign invaders in our own land. Gentleman, ninety cents of every dollar made by the residents of the Continental Shelf of the United States of America comes back to the mainland. Gentlemen, we are Americans and we want to be treated as such and, further, to be protected from outrages such as the attack by the Communist Chinese that took the lives of innocent ranch hands yesterday on Blake's Plateau. I ask your support of the Haskins-O'Connor bill when it is presented to the House of Representatives. I'd be happy to answer any questions you might have."

Carl sat back in his chair and fished out his pipe.

The representative of Boston's Forty-third District spoke up. "You said that the average per capita meat consumption is one hundred thirty pounds, Mr. Pasco. How much of that would you estimate is so-called red meat and how much is pelangus?"

"I'm not estimating," Carl replied. "I'm citing the latest figures of the U.S. Census Bureau and the American Consumers Association. We supply thirty percent of the nation's meat supply *right now* and are capable of increasing that figure to more than fifty percent in five years—and at the same thirty cents a pound—once we are relieved of this unjust tariff burden."

"You realize, of course," the congressman said, "that you are trading off the tariff for the price of federal taxes and restrictions, don't you?"

"We come out way ahead on that score, Congressman."

"Well, it just seems to me that we are going to be annexing and providing Territorial status to a very small group of people and not a hell of a lot of land, either."

Carl smiled. "That precedent was set some time ago. Thirteen years after Congress paid for Seward's Folly, the purchase of Alaska, the 1880 census counted only four hundred thirty nonnatives in the entire Territory. We acquired the Territories of Midway and Wake Islands in the Pacific prior to World War Two without a single soul in permanent residence. By comparison, Congressman, Marina is a veritable metropolis."

Since most of the planning and action leading up to the imposition of the actual embargo occurred toward the end of the week, realization that it was happening didn't begin until the start of the following week. Some ranches had stock en route to the market when the embargo was begun, so the East Coast meat processors had the usual supplies on hand for a couple of days. It wasn't until the appearance of the market reports for the close of business on Monday afternoon that buyers realized something was seriously amiss.

Over a half century at the three major ports of entry, great packing and processing plants and stockyards had been created for the abundant and popular pelangus flesh. Livestock sales were reported daily for Jacksonville, Savannah, and Charleston. Since the seasons had no meaning on the subsea ranches, a constant flow of live pelangus was delivered daily to the huge holding pens at each of the three ports. Because the price was the same at all three yards, deepwater ranchers had no need to watch the livestock market reports.

But suddenly the number of pelangus delivered daily did vary, and the red-meat growers and packers could hold off their marketing deliveries to coincide with low pelangus sales.

That Tuesday afternoon, Jacksonville, Savannah, and Charleston livestock markets showed not a single head of pelangus delivered or sold for the day.

While frantic yard buyers jammed the hydrophone lines to Plateau ranchers, the first thought of red-meat growers was that some happy disaster might have beset the undersea growers. That night, great forty- and sixty-ton cargo carriers rolled out from access roads throughout the West and Midwestern meat-growing regions on the continental thruways, loaded with cattle and hogs bound for the market. The failure of the pelangus market might last only a couple of days, but the time to sell was now, when the competition was nil.

At eight Tuesday night, the junior yard buyer for Ocean Sea Meats, the nation's largest pelangus packing and processing industry, reported to his superior. "I've been talking and had a couple of our other buyers talking to every damned one of our suppliers, and every one gave us the same story. They say there's something wrong with their herds and they're holding 'em off the market until it clears up."

"What the hell is wrong with the herds?" the senior buyer snapped.

"None of 'em would say just what it was."

"I know what that 'something' is. Those bastards are just trying to hold us up for a higher price." The senior buyer drummed his fingers angrily on his desk top. "See if you can get a line on what Reynolds Packing and the others are doing in Savannah, and then see what you can find out about Charleston. If those smart-ass ranchers think they can put the squeeze on us, they've got another thing coming. I'll see to it that they don't sell one damned head on this coast until they come crawling back to us. And they won't even get the price they got yesterday."

At the end of the week, the senior buyer boarded a subcar and headed down the Shelf anticline toward Starfish, where he had called all of the company's regular suppliers to a meeting. After two days of waiting in the Starfish hotel for someone to call, the buyer stormed back to the parking pool and whipped his car downward toward the nearest of the many ranches in the vicinity.

The general manager of Sea Canyon Ranch let the buyer

simmer in his outer office for a half hour before calling him in.

By this time, the first real inkling of the fears that had been in the back of the buyer's mind for two days was evident on his face as he bustled into the sea rancher's office.

"Cliff," he cried anxiously, forcing a smile to his lips, "what are you trying to do to us, boy? What's going on down here?"

The ranch manager sat back in his chair and eyed the buyer coolly.

"Nothing's the matter, Pritchard," he replied, "nothing at all—at least, not down here."

Pritchard frowned. "You know what I mean. Don't play cute with me, Cliff," he pleaded. "We've been buddies too long. I mean how come no deliveries? You know damned well that you can't keep this up. All you're doing is hurting yourselves. I don't want to see you do that, boy. We've been friends over the years. And friends got to stick together. Maybe you don't like the way Reynolds or some of those other sharp outfits operate, but Ocean Sea has always given you a good deal."

"Have you talked to any of the other ranchers?" the general manager asked.

The buyer shook his head. "I sent word for all of 'em to meet me in Starfish," he said, "but nobody showed up. So I thought I'd better get out and see what was the matter. And I thought of you first of all. Like I said, we've been buddies over the years and I know you'd tell me the straight story."

The rancher leaned forward. "You're right, Pritchard, I will give you the straight story. And just to show you how much I appreciate all you've done for me and my fellow ranchers over the years, I'm going to save you a lot of time, because I know to a big man like you time is money, and you've always been one to try and save time—at our expense. I'm going to save you the trouble of going any further, because what I'm going to tell you right now is the identical story you will get from every rancher on the Plateau. But if you don't believe me, then you just go right ahead and check me out.

"If you haven't figured it out by now, Pritchard, I'll spell it out for you. We aren't selling you one damned fish, and when I say 'we,' I mean every rancher on the Plateau."

The buyer's eyes widened in frightened surprise. "But why, Cliff? Why do this to *us*? We've always treated you right at Ocean Sea."

The rancher stood up behind the desk and leaned forward angrily.

"Yes, you've been our friend, you miserable bastard. You've cut and managed the prices you've given us for years, until we couldn't even meet payrolls. And you've sat back and applauded every time the red-meat boys had another tariff slapped on us because you could shave another cent while adding the tariff markup to the price you paid us. And all the time, you treated us like foreign dirt.

"Now you listen good, Pritchard, because I'm only going to say this once, and then I'm going to kick your fat little butt right back to the dirt you wallow in. You go back and tell your real buddies, those other bastards in Jacksonville, Savannah, and Charleston, that the Plateau ranchers will not sell another head of pelangus until we are a Territory of the United States of America and all tariffs are removed. Then we'll sell you our meat-fish at twenty cents a pound and tell the whole nation how much you are paying us for it so that you don't try to keep the prices up where they are now. So if you want to keep your goddamned plants open, you'd better get your people pushing for our bill in Congress—instead of against it. Because you aren't getting anything to pack until the day that bill is signed. Now get out!"

The buyer scrambled to his feet and ran angrily to the door.

"You'll never last it out," he snarled. "You'll starve to death before we let you fishheads tell us how to run our business."

"Pritchard!" the rancher snapped. The tone stopped the buyer in his tracks. "How many men do you employ in your plant?"

"More than a thousand," the buyer replied, off-guard.

"I have a hundred and fifty," the rancher said. "We can eat our own herds. What are you going to feed your men?"

National publicity also brought the first countermeasures. Although Plateau ranches and farms had been combing the Gulf markets for all available helium in preparation for a long siege, helium is a rare metal and the supplies on hand were dismally short. Attempts were made by small, seemingly private groups to pick up additional stores in the gas-producing Gulf states, but news of the embargo broke as they were buying, and their deepwater transporters had taken on only four loads at dockside when supplies from the interior suddenly stopped.

So did all other shipments of items purchased from inland sources. Calls to plants and supply houses quickly revealed the trouble—the International Union of Transport Workers, the same group that controlled beef and pork distribution, had ordered its members to refuse goods marked for Plateau delivery. In a public statement, the powerful head of the union told the press, "These people, who pay no taxes to this great nation of ours, are now attempting to force us to pay ransom prices for their inferior, foreign-made, foreign-bred products, while selling those same products to the Asian Communist Bloc at below cost. The loyal workers of the International Union of Transport Workers refuse to further aid this enemy of our great nation."

Unfortunately for union solidarity, four days after the helium shipments stopped, a team of the Plateau's nuclear physicists was able to transform a little-used lab experiment in the production of helium into pilot-plant production through an ingenious acid–uranium-ore method. Plateau mining operations had been discarding uranium ores for years while coring for more desirable rare metals. Now the dump slopes of every dig became a potential source of life for the Plateau.

With helium supplies assured, the Plateau was secure indefinitely from everything except armed attack.

Within two weeks a hungry nation had consumed all pelangus in the markets and was exhausting wholesaler stocks. Then storehouses packed with irradiated pelangus meat began to empty. The price rose from $1.30 a pound to just above three dollars. And then there was no more. Red-meat and poultry products followed the spiraling pelangus prices up—and stayed there.

"Carl," Martin said from his New York office, "something's come up which may help us, but it can also be dangerous. I've just been approached through the usual diplomatic maze with an offer to purchase our entire pelangus and weed stock. And there's a strong hint that we would be able to unload everything else we produce on the Plateau to the same sources from now on."

"Any idea where the offer comes from?" Carl asked, signaling Ted to pick up the connecting visiphone at the other desk.

"I'm pretty sure of the source, but that's not all. Almost at the same moment, we found out that the General Assembly's committee on protectorate administration was meeting with members of the World Food Organization and that a major source of surplus meat products that could be tapped by UN action was seriously being considered."

"This could be the clincher," Carl said. "Where did the purchase bid come from?"

"The People's Republic of China," Wainwright replied. "Apparently they had no success—as we knew they wouldn't—in breaking our genetic code on the pelangus. And, though the purchase offer was couched in honeyed diplomatic terms, a strong undertone said, 'What can't be bought can be bagged.' "

While Pasco was concluding his conversation with Wainwright, Steiner was on the phone with a key source in the State Department.

A few moments later, Pasco and Wainwright left the building for a conference on the Hill.

Coincidentally, the Third and Fifth Submarine Fleets of the United States Navy—one patroling the mid-Atlantic and the other the South Pacific—were changing courses and racing to new stations at flank speed. A coded message from Washington reached both fleet commanders a few moments later. By dawn of the following morning the Fifth would be in screening position deep beneath the storm-swept surface of the South Atlantic, its main task force straddling the seas between Africa and South America. Reconnaissance forces from the Fifth spread from both the Cape of Good Hope and Cape Horn.

Farther north, the small Bahamas flotilla that patrolled the waters along the continental slope was reduced to the role of a corporal's guard, for lying out from the Bahamas flotilla was the full strength of the Third Submarine Fleet. The on-station signals from both fleets were flashed to ComNav in the final moments of the conference on the

Hill and filtered through reliable sources to the red-eyed Steiner as he prepared to leave Paul Smith's office. Haskins had been ordered to bed at two o'clock in order to be ready for the coming House debate, and a battery of transcribers was completing precise reports for his perusal before the House convened.

While the United States Navy guarded against raids upon Plateau food supplies, the Plateau's residents found their rear unprotected from mainland reprisals. Because of the action of the Transport Workers union, shipments earmarked for Plateau destinations had ceased, but some items could be purchased at the ports where Plateau residents had been shopping for decades.

Shortly before the shops opened for business on the morning of the impending Washington debates, a four-passenger carryall from a weed farm close to Aquadia surfaced in Savannah harbor and moved to the metered parking slips.

Three men and a woman climbed out of the vehicle and walked slowly up the jetty to the customs house. "No gear with us," one of the farmers called out cheerfully to the customs agents lounging in the entrance. "Just a shopping trip for the little lady." He smiled indulgently at his wife.

The quartet started past the counter.

"Hold it!" one of the agents barked. "Who told you you could just barge on past like that, Conshee?"

The trio of men swung about angrily. The woman stepped back.

"I said we had no gear," repeated the farmer who had first spoken.

"I heard you," the customs man snarled, "but nobody said you could just walk into our country."

"Now hold it just a min—"

"Shut up and strip," the customs agent ordered. "You want into this country, you get searched just like any other foreigner. I wouldn't doubt but that you've got narcotics in your possession. Now strip, like I said."

"The hell we will," one of the farmers growled, moving forward menacingly.

"You'll strip," the customs man said smoothly, reaching under the counter and swinging a stun gun into sight, "and then you're under arrest for threatening a federal officer and refusing to obey a lawful demand. Now out of those clothes!"

Sullenly, the trio of Plateau men began unsealing the seams of their light coveralls.

"You too." The customs agent waved the gun at the woman.

"She will not!" the first farmer roared, lunging toward the counter. The gun swung quickly.

"You make one more move like that," the agent said menacingly, "and I'll hit you so hard with this thing that it'll scramble your brains."

"It's all right, Tom," the woman said, slipping out of her coveralls. She stood nude in front of the agent. "Satisfied, sea slug?" she spat disdainfully.

A small crowd of men gathered at the exit from the shed. Soon they were hooting and whistling obscenely. The trio of farmers stood naked while two customs men inspected the nude woman. They gave the three men a cursory glance, then allowed the quartet to don their coveralls.

"Now," the man with the stun gun said, "walk ahead of me to the far door and don't try anything." He pointed to the far end of the shed, where the crowd was loitering.

They walked slowly toward the door, the three men automatically moving to flank and protect the woman. The mob at the door was mostly dock hands and laid-off packing-house workers, and an ugly murmur arose from them as the four approached.

"Here's some of those foreign bastards that took our jobs away," someone in the crowd snarled. "Let's give 'em something to remember us by."

The mob moved into the shed.

"Now wait a minute," the customs agent with the gun called out, "you got no right in here. These people are under arrest and in my custody."

The mob continued to move forward.

"You in love with the bastards?" a voice jeered.

"No," the now-frightened agent gulped, "but I'm responsib—"

"Fish-lover," another voice screamed from the mob.

"Get the bastards!"

The mob surged forward and the customs agents backed away fearfully to watch from a safe distance.

*   *   *

"The undersea industries have been accused falsely of withholding their goods from the market in an effort to starve the nation and to jack up their own prices. They have also been accused falsely of withholding their produce in order to sell it to nations whose policies and ideologies conflict with the democratic principles of this nation," Haskins began from the floor.

"Lies, gentlemen.

"Granted Territorial status, which will eliminate onerous and illegal tariff barriers, the residents of this area are prepared to put pelangus, their major food product, back on the market at *one-fourth* the previous price and to guarantee that or a *lower* cost by submitting to both an audit and a price control by the United States Department of Agriculture. This, gentlemen, is not the act of a selfish, greedy industry seeking to force prices up.

"As for the second lie, the statement is so patently obvious that it really needs no rebuttal. Not only have the residents of this area consistently refused to deal with other nations, they have been subject to piracy by at least one totalitarian nation rumor accuses them of dealing with."

The call receptor in Haskins ear buzzed suddenly.

O'Connor's voice whispered tinnily in his ear. "Yield to me, Jack. I've just received word of new aggression."

"Mr. Speaker," Haskins said, "I now yield for five minutes to Mr. O'Connor." The Speaker confirmed.

"Mr. Speaker," the lanky Tennessee legislator began, rising, "and gentlemen, I have just received word that certain powers are considering invasion of the area under consideration by this body, for the purpose of seizing the very products that we are discussing. Such an act, close to the shores of our country, should be considered an act of aggression. I have been informed that major elements of our Navy have been deployed to meet this threat. Gentlemen, I submit this constitutes *de facto* recognition of the Territorial status of the very area that is now petitioning us for such status.

"Further, I have been informed that the United Nations is seriously considering to mandate protective status over this undersea area, a situation which would be intolerable to the interest of this nation.

"Gentlemen, we are arguing parliamentary procedures

while those who would bring injury to our country are acting."

O'Connor sat down, looking at Haskins, who had remained on his feet during the brief period that he yielded
the floor.

"Mr. Speaker, and gentlemen," Haskins took up the debate anew, "it should be obvious that we can no longer play
politics or be the pawns in anyone's financial chess game.
This issue must be faced immediately, and I urge your ayes
in demanding this bill to the House floor forthwith. Thank
you, Mr. Speaker." He resumed his seat as a flood of lights
hit the board.

The Speaker again recognized the chairman of the agriculture committee.

The Nebraska congressman looked slowly around the
House and up to the gallery before he spoke. Then his
words were slow and spaced out.

"Mr. Speaker, gentlemen," he began heavily, "I find it
difficult to formulate the words I need at this moment, for
my mind and heart are sorely beset by the charges leveled
by the gentleman from New York and the information just
delivered by the gentleman from Tennessee. As if this were
not burden enough, I have received information of my own
just seconds ago which both saddens and sickens me."

He paused, and his heavy sigh was audible throughout
the chamber.

"I have just been informed that mob violence in the port
of Savannah, Georgia, has taken the life of a resident of
Blake's Plateau and has brought grievous bodily injury to
three other residents, including the wife of the dead man."

There was an instant of stunned silence, and then a wave
of sound swept the House and gallery.

Ten blocks away, in Paul Smith's office, Steiner was
screaming into one visiphone to the Institute while Pasco
was trying to reach Seward on the Plateau. Smith was on a
third circuit to the Savannah city authorities.

Carl got through to Seward. "We've just gotten the
news," Seward said. "The dead man is a weed farmer
named Tom Quincy. His brother and another man are in
critical condition in a Savannah hospital, and Quincy's wife
was raped and beaten.

"This tears it, Carl. I've just talked with John Burnett,

and the entire weed cooperative is arming and getting ready to head into Savannah and take the city apart."

"For God's sake, Ron," Carl yelled, "try and keep 'em from going. We're right on the thin edge of winning this thing, and a revolt is the last thing we need. Get hold of Burnett and try to stall them for an hour or so. I'll call you back as quickly as I can."

He broke off the connection and punched up the Senate offices. A quick explanation to an aide and Tim Perkins's face appeared. "Senator, see if you can get to the President immediately," Carl said rapidly. "You've heard the word from Savannah?"

Perkins nodded somberly.

"A force of armed weed farmers is gathering, and they're going to try and take Savannah!" Carl exclaimed. "Explain the situation to the President and see if he will agree to get on closed circuit and speak to them—tell 'em the guilty parties will be arrested and executed, whatever, but have him dissuade them from moving on Savannah."

"I'll call you right back," Perkins said, breaking the connection.

Carl slumped in his chair, his face a mask of despair. Steiner was still talking urgently with staff members at the Institute. Smith finished his conversation and turned to Pasco. "They've already seized the ringleaders of the mob, Carl, and are trying to round up the rest of them. But the chief of police says he's having trouble with the packing-house men who are being fed a line by some outsiders. I have a hunch this is the work of our friends from the West."

Carl's phone signaled. Perkins was on the line.

"The President will talk with your people any time you say," the Connecticut senator said.

"Hold on, please, Senator," Carl replied, reaching for another phone. Moments later he had Seward again. "I've got Senator Perkins on the other circuit, Ron, and he's arranged for the President to speak to the farmers. See if you can get a circuit set up fast, then notify Burnett."

"Burnett said they were all to meet at Aquadia and dive from there," Seward said. "I'll set it up for the community center there in one hour from now."

Carl turned back to the other visiphone.

"Did you hear that?" he asked.

"I've already informed the White House," Perkins replied. "Let me know what else I can do."

"You might try prayer," Carl said.

By three o'clock that afternoon, House Bill 5680 had passed by unanimous vote and was sent to the Senate for concurrence.

HB 5680 moved through the Senate under similar emergency suspension of the rules and was voted upon and passed—but not unanimously. It went to the President for signature.

Even before final passage, transporters were moving into position at scores of upper water holding pens at most Plateau ranches, preparing to hook onto the long cargo slugs that were now filling with fat, darting pelangus. The open end of the plastic cargo slugs had been slipped over the neck of the pens. Ranch hands in single-seater subcars were inside the pens, and when the cargo slug was secure, they began nudging the big meat-fish out of the pen and into the slug. A hundred head went into each slug and the pen was snapped shut. The towing clamps sealed the end of the slug and the transporter took it in tow. The vessels turned shoreward and upward for the slow, two-day haul to market.

Other cargo slugs were being loaded with processed seaweed, minerals, and all of the natural and man-made inventory of the Plateau. There was a quiet but jubilant air of approaching victory evident along the entire Shelf.

After President John Heyburn had finished signing the document that officially created the Territory of Marina and had distributed all the pens used in the signing, he returned to his desk.

"I have one more duty to perform," he said. "Mr. Andrew Jackson McFadden, will you please step forward?"

A puzzled look crossed Andy's face as he moved forward from behind the desk and stood beside the President.

"By the powers invested in me this date by the Congress of the United States of America," the President said, "it gives me great pleasure, sir, to appoint you to the office of Governor of the Territory of Marina, to serve thereas from this date forth and for an indeterminate time at the pleasure of the President of the United States."

Stunned, McFadden took the President's proffered hand.

Six weeks later the Territory went through *pro forma* elections for its own legislature and for officials to represent it in Washington. Carl Pasco, who had remained in Washington, D.C., to maintain liaison with Congress until the elections were held, had voted by absentee ballot. Late that night, Governor McFadden called him with the results.

". . . and, of course, Marty Wainwright was elected as our nonvoting delegate to Congress."

"That's great," Carl said. "Now we can get a truly official office going here."

"You haven't heard it all," McFadden said. "I found out that it was you and Paul and Marty who got me stuck with this job. I couldn't get even with you until after the elections, however. Now it's my turn. Listen carefully, you sneaky little creep. By the powers invested in me by the Constitution of the Territory of Marina, I hereby appoint Carl Pasco to the office of Resident Commissioner for a term of six years."

Carl could hear McFadden chuckling as he hung up before Pasco could reply.

Carl and Martin Wainwright went home for the Christmas holidays.

The wind was still blowing and ice coated the docks and superstructures of the surface vessels on January second, when Carl's bright blue official subcar surfaced in Wilmington harbor, where he and his three companions had first debarked on the crusade to Washington.

The two men walked up the dock and entered the customs house. The agent on duty had made a fast binocular check as the blue vehicle entered the slip. Now he smiled and waved the two men past. "Cold day, eh, Commissioner?" he observed pleasantly.

At the far end of the shed, the same U.S. Immigration Service officer who had checked them in months before waited for them. He too waved them on.

Carl stopped and faced the man.

"Aren't you going to ask us what our nationality is?" he inquired.

"I know you're both American citizens, sir," the man replied stiffly.

Carl eyed the officer coolly for a moment, then nodded and turned to leave.

The officer stiffened. "Have a good day, Commissioner," he said as he rendered a snappy salute.

Carl and Marty walked out of the warm shed into the full force of the wintry gale. Both were grinning happily as they lowered their heads and bulled into the chill, clean air of their homeland. "I told you that son-of-a-bitch would salute the next time he saw me," Carl chortled. ☆

The Mystery of the Duplicate Diamonds

Paul A. Carter

Three miles from downtown, among the fast-food places, car washes, and hardware stores, a little road angled into the highway from the left. At the point of the angle was a scraggly patch of tall dead grass. A low brick wall separated this beer-can-strewn scrap of lawn from a potholed parking area. On the side facing the highway, a neon sign blinked BLUE DIAMOND JEWELERS over a dark-stained, Swiss-chalet-style storefront. However, from the entering side street anyone could see that the wooden façade masked a dusty iron quonset hut.

Hal Jorberg watched for his chance, shot across three traffic lanes with inches to spare, and pulled up alongside the brick barrier. A moment later, but with considerably less noise, an old Chrysler slipped in from the side road and parked in the space between Jorberg's maroon Mustang and the Renault that already stood next to the quonset's end wall. The Chrysler's door swung open, spilling out two lovely long legs.

Hal took quick inventory. Short, well-kept dark hair. Tailored jacket, subdued in color and probably expensive. Strong cheekbones, giving the face an attractive contrast of curves and planes. Dark blue eyes that, he suddenly knew, had just caught him staring.

He played the gambit of a tentative smile.

"What's the matter," the woman asked in a voice that would have been delightful if it hadn't carried a cutting edge, "are you just back from Siberia, or something?"

Jorberg's smile turned crooked. Her words reminded him of the small velvet-covered box in his jacket pocket. "Uh—yeah, kind of."

"Well, times have changed." She walked past him, opening the shop's front door with a jangle of its warning bell. He followed her in, feeling a bit of a fool.

The clerk behind the counter assumed that they had come in together, and beamed. "Yes, folks?"

"I'd like to sell this ring," the woman said.

That's my line, Hal thought, as he fished out the little box. Woodenly, he repeated her exact words: "I'd like to sell this ring."

The boxes were identical. So were the rings; each had seven tiny diamonds set in a floral pattern. "Purchased here, I see," said the clerk, taking off his jeweler's glasses and putting on a regular pair to hunt through his cardboard box full of invoices. "Ah, yes, M's" (he slurred the "s" so it could have been either "Ms." or "Miss"). "M's Madison. Was the ring not satisfactory, M's Madison?"

Hal groaned inwardly. *Madison. Why does she have to have the same last name as*—

"Perfectly satisfactory," the woman replied. Her tone implied that the man who had given her the ring had been something less than satisfactory.

"I see," the clerk said politely, thumbing through the slips of paper in the box on the counter. "And Mr., uh, Jorberg?" He pronounced the "J" like "Y."

The woman shot a quick, startled look at Hal. "I don't believe this!" Then she took a long, gulping breath. "Look. I've never seen you before in my life, and it's none of my business. But—" Her voice caught. "I just broke up with a guy named Hal Jorberg." She pronounced it like "J."

The man felt a faint chill of wonder. "But that's *my* name. And *I* just broke up with someone, too. And her last name is just like yours. Madison. Moira Madison."

The woman sounded possessive and indignant. "That's *my* first name!" Then the absurd coincidence got to her, and she laughed. It was a warm, chuckly, heartbreaking laugh. Hal couldn't help it; he joined in. The store clerk permitted himself a benign smile.

"It's ridiculous," said Moira. "The Hal Jorberg I—was going to marry—" Her smile faded. "He's about six four, two hundred and forty pounds. Too fat and doesn't exercise, otherwise he'd be a regular blond beast. Not like you at all. And he definitely doesn't drive a Mustang." Jorberg didn't know if he had been complimented or put down.

Rationalizing, macho fashion, he assumed the former.

"My Moira," he started to say, then corrected himself. "The Moira Madison I was engaged to doesn't drive at all. She's darker than you, not as tall, and—" he allowed himself an appraising look—"hasn't got a figure as good as yours. She lives in a two-decker on Elm Street."

"That's where *I* live!" Moira exclaimed. "What on earth. Listen, do you live out on Ridgway Drive?"

"Well, yeah, I do. Eleven seventy-two." Hal fumbled out his driver's license; Moira, more efficiently, already had hers on the counter.

First and middle names. Dates and places of birth. Current addresses. Signatures. Everything checked.

"Well, I'll be damned." He looked at this Moira Madison again, and back to the color photo I.D. Hers matched the woman beside him, not the woman he had left in wrath just an hour ago. His card showed no blond beast; it duplicated his own craggy features and sandy, thinning hair. "Look, uh, let's go have a drink, or something, and try to figure this out."

"Coffee, thanks," she answered sharply, "and I don't play games. But yes, I do want to know what's going on. There's a diner just down the block."

"Pardon me," the clerk broke in. "Do you wish to keep the rings?"

"Oh." Hal's frozen brain was beginning to thaw. "Could I—could we see those order forms, please?"

The clerk spread the papers on the counter. "Here we are. This one was bought on March twenty-first by Mr. Harold Yorberg. One-third down. The balance remaining, as you can see, is—"

"I paid cash!" Jorberg shouted, as if accusing the little man of fraud.

The woman's foot trod warningly on Hal's toe. "Perhaps the *other* Hal Jorberg paid in installments," she said smoothly. "Let's see. This ring was paid for by check from Harold Jorberg, made out to—to me, and endorsed over to Blue Diamond Jewelers."

"We don't normally take two-party checks—" the clerk began.

"But that's not the way *he* did it at all!" she interrupted. "He went down to the bank, got out the cash, and told me to come in here and pick out the ring I wanted. Right then is when I began to have doubts about marrying him." She turned to Hal. "Come on, I think I want that cup of coffee now."

Hal picked up his ring box and put it in his pocket. Moira also put hers away. The little bell over the door tinkled as they departed. "Shall we drive?" Hal suggested, reaching for the door on the passenger side of his car.

"No, thanks. I've seen the way you drive." With that she was off, moving away with a hiker's energy-saving stride. A bit sheepishly, Jorberg followed her, once again relishing those excellent legs.

He caught up with her at the first cross street and offered to take her arm. "Watch the traffic," she warned, jerking away. A crumbling sidewalk led them past an auto parts place, and then they were climbing up four steps to the door at one end of a steam-windowed old red diner. She was inside before he could open the door for her. Mildly irritated, he joined her in one of the hard-backed wooden booths.

"What'll it be?" a dark-mustached counterman called out over a babble of customers' voices without moving toward them.

"Coffee. Black," Hal answered, then turned to Moira. "What do you take in yours?"

"Everything." She dug into her handbag. Automatically Hal got out his lighter—he himself did not smoke—and extended it to her. Then he saw that what she was getting out was not a pack of cigarettes but a pipe. *His* Moira would never have done that.

"Oh," was all he could think of to say as he put away the lighter. She was striking a wooden kitchen match on the underside of the table. The gesture, he thought, just didn't go with those clothes.

The counterman brought over their coffee in big mugs, slopping some of it. Moira got her pipe going and took a long draft of the khaki-colored brew. "There. Now, have you any idea what's going on?"

"Let's see." Jorberg began ticking points off on his fingers, a gesture Moira—the other Moira—had always disliked. "One: we—the Hal you know, and I— were born at the same place and the same time, and live at the same address. Two: the same is true for you and the Moira *I* know. Three: the other Hal seems to have paid for two rings—one by that second-party check, for yours, and a third down on the other, which went into that jewelry store's records as part payment on mine. Four: nevertheless, I *know* I paid the same store cash, in full—"

"And so do I," Moira interrupted his lecture. She frowned, reminded of something. "What kind of bills did the bank give you?"

"Why—hundreds, a fifty, a couple of tens, and a bunch of twos. Somebody had cleaned that teller out of smaller bills."

She took a long, shuddering pull on the pipe. "That's just what Hal—the big, blond Hal, not you—gave me. I particularly remember the twos."

Jorberg took a large swallow of bitter black coffee. "Alternative universes," he said, half to himself.

"Alternative what?"

"Other worlds, some of them very unlike ours. Others exactly like this one, except for some minor detail—such as who two ordinary people really are. It's an old idea in science fiction."

"I don't read science fiction." From her tone he judged that she did not approve of science fiction.

There was an awkward silence. Moira broke it by pulling out a paper napkin and spreading it between them on the table. "Let's see if any of this adds up," she said, digging out a felt-tipped pen. She began to print, in neat block letters:

HAL, A (YOU): PAID CASH IN FULL. MOIRA, A: GAVE RING
    BACK (TO YOU).
HAL, B (NOT YOU): DREW FROM BANK, GAVE CASH TO
    MOIRA, B (ME).

"But, you see," she said as she wrote, "there has to be another one—"

HAL, C: PAID ONE-THIRD DOWN. GAVE RING TO MOIRA, C
    (?)
ALSO WROTE CHECK MADE OUT TO—(MOIRA, C?)
    (MOIRA, D?)

She crossed the last line out, started to write HAL, D— then wadded up the napkin, flung it away, and knuckled her temples in silent frustration. After a time Hal spoke:

"We're going to have to go back and talk to that clerk again. Maybe he knows something we don't."

She nodded, drained her cup, and stood up. "No, wait a minute," There was a pay phone in a half-booth down by the cash register. Moira lifted the battered phone book on its chain up to the counter and began to turn pages.

The man came over and stood beside her. "It's here," she said, pointing. "Madison, M., at my address, and it's the same number."

"Let me see that." Hal turned from the "M's" back to the "J's" and ran his thumb down the page. "Yes, and here's mine."

"Well—" she laughed, a little nervously, "shall we call ourselves up and see what happens?"

I'm not sure I dare to, Jorberg thought. However, from his own notions about proper male roles it was up to him to go first. He got out a coin, dropped it in, and dialed the familiar number.

He got a busy signal.

"Well, *somebody's* using my place," he announced, cradling the phone. The coin rattled down into the return slot.

"Let me see that!" Moira exclaimed.

"Why, it's nothing special. Just a regular Nixon quarter."

She looked at him aghast. "A *Nixon*—!" Then, with determination, she led him back to their booth. "Now. Sit down, order us more coffee, and tell me what happened to Tricky Dick that got him on United States coins."

"I thought everybody kn— Oh. All right. Richard Nixon was elected president for two terms. Midway between his first and second terms he uncovered what *he* said was a conspiracy, masterminded by Fidel Castro, and smashed it. You know about Castro?" She nodded. "The Democratic National Committee was implicated, and the national chairman went to jail, but a hung jury let McGovern go." Moira looked blank, not recognizing the name. "Personally, I thought the conspiracy was a hoax, but the public bought it, and Nixon became a hero. Then he became a martyr. Late in his second term the Taiwan Chinese invaded the China mainland. They couldn't make a go of it, of course, so we went in after them. President Nixon flew into Quemoy to inspect the battle front, and a short-range missile fired from a shore battery took out Air Force One. The Navy rescued the troops in a Dunkirk operation, the new president took the blame for the invasion's failure, and Congress put Nixon on the twenty-five-cent piece."

Moira shuddered. "Then it's not just us."

"What do you mean?"

She pulled a quarter out of her purse. "Look at this. Robert F. Kennedy. Elected president in 1968, re-elected in '72. So far as I know, Richard Nixon was *never* president. John Kennedy defeated him in '60, and eight years later so did Bobby. John was assassinated in Dallas, Robert in Peking. The Chinese blamed it on the Gang of Four."

Now it was Hal's turn to look blank. He had never heard of the Gang of Four. "It looks like our next stop is a library."

"Not yet," Moira said, knocking out her pipe. "Go try that phone call again."

He did. This time the phone rejected his Nixon quarter. They tried one of her Kennedys. It stuck.

"Hell," said Jorberg. "Let's just go on over there."

They paid for the coffee; she insisted on Dutch treat. The counterman accepted, without comment, her George Washington dollar bill and his Alexander Hamilton ten. Curious, Moira looked at her change. "Let's see. Lincoln on the penny, okay. Roosevelt on the dime—"

"But it's the wrong Roosevelt! Nixon replaced him with Teddy."

"—and *John* Kennedy on the half. That checks."

"No, it doesn't. Congress dropped him, too, for Douglas MacArthur. Another byproduct of the China War."

Her face relaxed into a half-smile. "Then if there's anything to this alternate worlds business, we must be in my universe, not yours."

"No." He turned over the quarter the counterman had just given him. It was dated 1981, and it showed the traditional profile of Washington.

Moira picked up one of the other coins from Hal's pile. "*Mmph*—look at this one. No name, but it sure looks like Susan B. Anthony, and it wasn't coined in my world. I don't have any dollar coins with me, but ours is cartwheel-sized and shows Martin Luther King." Finally, conscious that they were stalling, she suggested that they go over and find out who was using the phone.

"All right. But on the way let's stop in at that jewelry store."

They walked back through the mid-afternoon chill to the Blue Diamond. This time when he took her arm she made no objection.

The door swung open, agitating its little bell. The clerk looked up at them. "Back already?"

"Listen. Think hard," said Hal. "Did anybody recently come in here and buy one of these rings for cash? The exact amount, including a bunch of two-dollar bills?"

"Oh, no, sir. I'd remember anything like that."

"What about me?" Moira demanded.

"No. Quite apart from the cash transaction, I would have remembered *you*." The little man allowed himself to look at her with appreciation. Then, resuming his clerk-mask, he leafed through his order file for the record of the second-party check. "Come to think of it, the lady who gave me this did not look like you at all, M's. Darker, she was, and, if I may say so, rather intense."

"Did she look like this?" Hal slapped his wallet down on the counter, displaying a snapshot he had not yet gotten around to throwing away.

The clerk peered closely at the picture. "No, sir. She did not."

"May we use your phone?" Moira asked. "It's a local call." As Hal reached for the receiver she shook her head and took it herself. "I've got an idea."

She dialed, listened—and looked startled. Recovering her poise, she spoke in a professional tone: "Is this the Jorberg residence? This is Blue Diamond Jewelers calling. I am sorry to trouble you, but did you recently purchase a diamond engagement ring from us? And do you recall the financial arrangements? Oh . . . yes, I'll speak to him." She listened a minute. "Thank you, sorry to have bothered you," she said, then hung up gently. "Well." A long pause. "*Well!*"

"What's up?" Hal asked.

Ignoring him, Moira turned to the clerk: "Did you also sell a wedding ring to Mr. Jorberg?"

"As a matter of fact, we did. And it was the same arrangement. One-third down."

Why in hell didn't you say so before? Hal fumed mentally.

Wide-eyed, Moira looked at Hal. "A *woman* answered that phone. When I made my pitch she said, 'Wait a minute, I'll let you talk to my husband.' Then a man came on the line and said, 'This is Harold Yorberg.' No, it wasn't my blond beast, and I'll bet my last Kennedy quarter she wasn't your Lady Macbeth, either. It looks as if in this universe Hal Jorberg, or rather Yorberg, and Moira Madison got married."

"Q.E.D.," said Hal.

"Now let's check out the other one. You call her, this time."

Why me? Hal protested inwardly, but he picked up the phone and dialed the number. He thought he recognized the sound of the instrument in (his?) Moira's apartment. It rang and rang and rang.

"No answer," he announced unnecessarily.

Curiosity seemed to get the better of the thus far non-committal clerk. "Pardon me. May I inquire what this is all about?"

"Mistaken identity," Hal answered rather brusquely. "Come on, Moira, let's go over to your place." She frowned at the implicit intimacy, but turned to leave without comment.

The clerk followed them to the door. "Goodbye, and, er, good luck."

As usual Hal tried to take charge of the situation. "My car or yours?"

Moira caught her breath. "I don't think we're going to have the choice."

Hal looked at where she was pointing. The Chrysler and the Renault were still there. The Mustang was gone.

"God-damned teenage car thieves! I'm going to call the police."

Moira shook her head. "I don't think that's what happened at all. Look—Lady Macbeth gave you back your ring. You drove here in a huff, and in the process you managed to drive through into another universe. Somehow while you were running around over here, your car made it back into the world where it belongs."

An icy puff of air blew a bit of newspaper over the brick wall. Hal moved toward Moira's car. "No, that doesn't work. Judging from the happy couple now nesting at 1172 Ridgway Drive, *neither* you nor I belong in this world. So how come this heap—" he slapped the Chrysler's ancient, but well-polished, hood—"is still here?"

"It's not a heap. It's got a good engine, and I service it myself," Moira retorted. She opened the car door and slipped lithely in. "We've got one more clue to follow. So let's follow it."

Hal stood on the driver's side, waiting for her to slide over. She didn't get the signal. "Would you like me to drive?" he finally asked.

"*No*, dammit! Go around and get in."

Mentally hauling down his flag, Hal complied. Moira smoothly backed the big old gas guzzler out and moved off into the traffic with easy competence.

When they stopped at a red light, Hal broke the silence. "Hey! I just thought of something. How do we know this Yorberg married a Moira Madison? The woman you talked to could have been someone else."

Moira shook her head. "No. He married a Moira, all right. I know it."

Hal tried kidding. "Woman's intuition?"

"Mind your manners!" she snapped, tromping on the gas pedal as the light changed. It knocked the breath out of him.

"Uh! Sorry. Still, it *could* have been someone else."

The woman shot him a withering sidelong look. "Over the phone in the background I heard him ask, 'Who's that, Moira?' "

"Oh." Conversation ceased until they were across town and heading into an old residential area dating from the days of trolley cars. Unlike most places to which realtors give rustic names, Elm Street actually possessed a row of elms. Moira's flat was the upper story of an ugly-comfortable frame house with gable ends. A gravel drive-way led around the back to a two-car garage. Moira climbed out and pulled the sliding door.

As it rumbled upward she silently articulated an impolite word. The garage was crammed. Stoves, rockers, refrigerators, kitchen chairs, an aluminum boat with oars, a stuffed elk's head, oil paintings in chipped plaster-gilt frames, rugs, skis and ski poles, sacks of potatoes. "Well," Moira said at last, "this is certainly not *my* 224B Elm. When I moved in, the garage was just as full, but my landlady cleared out this half so I could put my car inside."

"Maybe we ought to talk to your landlady," Hal suggested.

"Let's not," she replied, then led the way to the outside back stairs. At the top Hal started to knock. Moira waved him aside. Her key fitted the lock in 224B's back door. She pushed it open quietly, and they stepped inside.

The kitchen looked newer than the house: modern, functional, and meticulously picked up. Moira checked one of the cupboards. "Well, this Moira Madison buys the same kind of groceries I do, anyway." She opened a closet door, revealing a double row of mason jars. "And this checks. My landlady is always giving me stuff she cans. Tomatoes, applesauce, beets. I *hate* home-canned tomatoes."

Hal followed her into a small, formal dining room, set up with places for four. She tapped on the leaded-glass front of a handsome china closet. "Mm. She has expensive tastes. *I* don't have any Wedgwood." They passed into a hall leading toward the front of the house. "If this were my place," said Moira, "this would be my bedroom." Her tone implied he shouldn't get any ideas.

They stepped over the threshold, and all bantering stopped.

Hal hadn't thought she was the kind of woman who would scream.

The body lay half out of the bedclothes, with its head and shoulders on the floor. A broken lamp lay beside the bed stand. Blood matted the roots of the long, curling midnight-black hair.

Darker than you, the clerk had said, *and rather intense . . .*

On the third finger of the flaccid left hand glowed a handsome engagement ring with seven diamonds.

In one bound Hal was around the bed and reaching for the phone, but Moira's sharp cry stopped him. "Just what do you think you are doing?"

He was dumbfounded. "Calling the police, of course."

"Like *hell* you are! You're always wanting to call the police. Put down that phone, wipe off your prints, don't touch anything else, and come to the kitchen with me."

He tagged along after her like a little kid. "But why—"

"*Shut up!*"

When they reached the kitchen, Moira took some scrap paper out of a drawer, sat down at the table, and began to sketch. "Here, make us some coffee while I try to work this out. Over there, on the counter. Just plug it in." Her brows were drawn down in furious concentration.

Hal Jorberg silently put out the cream, sugar, cups, and saucers. As he sat beside her his thoughts were whirling like a Fourth of July pinwheel.

Moira looked up from her scribblings and saw the distress in his face. "I *have* been a bit rough on you," she admitted softly, leaning across the corner of the table for a brief, sweet kiss. Then she rapped on the table with the eraser end of her pencil. "This is the way I've worked it out so far."

On the paper she had ruled three columns, labeled "Nixon," "Kennedy," and "Susan B. Anthony." Arrows ran from one to another. "Look here," she explained. "we'll call you Hal One. In your world, you bought a ring for cash and gave it to Moira, whom we'll also call One."

"You can continue to call her Lady Macbeth," Hal murmured.

Ignoring the interruption, she went on. "Moira One gave you back the ring, and you hightailed it over to the Blue Diamond to try to get some of your money back. In the process you somehow crossed over here, into column three."

"Obviously."

"Hush. Now. We'll call the blond beast Hal Two. *He* got out a bundle of money and gave it to me, so we'll call me Moira Two. I bought the ring. Then we broke up, I headed for the Blue Diamond to sell the ring for as much cash as I could get, and I also ended up over here in column three." She paused. Hal said nothing.

"Okay. In the column three world, we have Hal Three and Moira Three. He makes a down payment on a ring, and on that shaky financial basis they get married. Since column three is *this* world, that purchase shows up on the books at the Blue Diamond."

"Check."

"But this is where it gets sticky. There ought not to be any other Hals or Moiras. There isn't room for them, in the three worlds we've found out about so far. Three universes, three Moiras, three Hals—yes, I've bought your science-fictional explanation, it's the only one that makes any sense. But there *has* to be a fourth couple, or there couldn't be that other, two-party check to the Blue Diamond, or—" Moira's calm voice wavered—"that poor girl back in there."

"And, circumstantially, she's got to be a Moira. She was wearing the same diamond ring."

Moira looked miserable. "Yes. Christ, yes."

"Couldn't there be a fourth universe, home base for a Hal Four and a Moira Four?"

"No, I don't think so. Otherwise these two checks wouldn't both have ended up in this universe at the same jewelry store. Remember, the man didn't have a record of your purchase or mine for cash, so those invoices must have stayed behind us in—Nixonland and Kennedyland."

Hal wasn't satisfied. "Still too many loose ends. Who killed her? Maybe Hal Four. But maybe not. This is a fairly tough part of town she—and you—picked to live in, so it could have been an ordinary thief who flew out of control."

"An ordinary thief wouldn't have left the ring. No, there's something that doesn't fit, and frankly, I'm getting scared."

"You?" He meant it as a compliment, and she took it with a wry smile.

"Not an ordinary thief," she repeated. "But not Hal Four, either."

"Who else?"

"That's what scares me. There's a principle of sufficiency involved. *Three* worlds, *four* Moiras. When you were a kid, did you ever play a game called Going to Jerusalem?"

"We called it Musical Chairs."

"Okay, so you never went to Baptist Sunday school. Anyhow, they take away one chair, and the music stops, and everybody scrambles, and one kid has to drop out of the game."

"Good God!"

"Yes. Good God. Somebody is trying to balance the books of the universe, and they're halfway toward making it come out even."

"*Very well put, M's Madison.*" The voice was horrible in its familiar blandness. They whirled toward the hall door. The jewelry clerk stood there in his unobtrusively tailored dark gray suit. One hand rested inside the coat pocket.

"I owe you an explanation," he began apologetically. "There is a mathematical concept known as Goedel's Theorem—"

"Oh!" Moria exclaimed, beginning to comprehend. Hal, as yet, did not. Even in the tension of the moment he was able to grumble at himself: *Is this wonderwoman a math major, too?*

"I regret the absence of a blackboard," said the clerk, dropping into a lecturer's tone. "There are various non-mathematical ways of expressing Goedel's great insight, none of them very clear. One way is to say that no self-consistent logical system can be constructed which fully accounts for itself. There will always be unaccounted phenomena left over.

"Were we dealing with but one universe, this would create difficulties enough. When two or more universes are involved, the interplay of these leftover phenomena endangers the fabric of Reality itself—"

Hal started to edge closer. The concealed hand in the suit pocket waved him back. Smoothly, politely, the clerk went on. "Let me put it this way. Universes One, Two, and Three exist in a relationship resembling that which exists in music between harmonics and their dominant tone. Anything in violation of that relationship, such as four Harold Jorbergs or four Moira Madisons in a plenum that has room for only three, is discordant. Such discord can ruin the 'music' utterly. Unattended, with these disharmonies running wild within it, the Cosmos itself might cease to exist.

"There is no way—*none*—by which such discords with Reality can be foreseen or prevented. According to Goedel's Theorem as I comprehend it, they just happen. Once found, they can only be 'tuned out,' so to speak, by hand."

His tone became rounder, grander. "I have balanced the Moira Madison account. It is time now to deal with the surplus of Harold Jorbergs. M's Madison, if you will kindly step to one side—"

Moira moved, straight at him, with a loud martial-arts *ki-yai*! Instinctively he quailed. Then one splendid leg lashed out in a karate kick, and her hands went in, one! two!

The clerk collapsed in a heap, and all at once seemed too small for his clothes. Jorberg knelt beside him. "You overdid that," he said, shaken. "He's going to be out for quite awhile."

"I meant to." Her face was like stone. "If *she* had known how to do that, she'd still be alive." Moira stood with her back flat against the wall, taking deep breaths, trying hard not to break or cry.

Gingerly, Hal pulled the concealed hand out of the pocket and separated it from a tiny antique single-shot derringer. He patted the now-rumpled suit, pulled out an ornate billfold, and opened it. Inside were the usual driver's license, insurance I.D., Social Security, credit cards—and one other item.

A counter check on a local bank, made out by Harold Jorberg to Moira Madison, and endorsed over to Blue Diamond Jewelers.

"Look at this, Moira." Numbly, she stumbled over, then sank to her knees by the clerk's side. She looked at the slip of paper, only half seeing it. Then its signal got through. Her eyes widened.

There had been an attempt to disguise the handwritings. Nevertheless, both signatures—Hal's and Moria's—were the work of the same person.

Moira picked up one of the department store charge cards and held it alongside the check endorsements. "Why, there never was a Hal Four. This crazy little creep forged a check to his own store."

"Then *why*—?" Hal gestured back toward the bedroom.

"Oh, the clerk lures her up here by some pretense—God knows why men do these things, or why women fall for them! Then he sets up the payment mystery so we'll come and investigate, and he follows us from the store. The idea was to cover himself by pinning the murder on you. The motive would seem obvious; you were jilted. Then it would seem you had an attack of the remorses. So the coroner rules you a suicide, and Mr. Friendly here is in the clear. He had it all figured out, and *he* wasn't going to be the kid who lost his place when the music stopped—"

There was a knock at the kitchen door.

They froze, wordless.

An elderly voice quavered through the door. "Is anything the matter in there? I thought I heard a noise."

"My landlady," Moira whispered, suppressing a giggle of

relief. "No, Mrs. Foster, everything's fine," she called. "I'm rehearsing a part in a play."

"Oh. Well, if you're sure everything is all right—"

"Yes, perfectly."

"Would you like some raspberry jell? I just made some."

"Later, Mrs. Foster. Later."

"All right. I'll be back in a little while." Slippered feet shuffled away and creaked down the back steps.

"*Now* can I call the police?" Hal asked.

Moira cut him off tensely. "No time. She'll be back in five minutes." She seized Hal's hand and tugged him into the hall. "We'd better go out the front way . . ." The sentence strangled into silence.

Hal looked through the bedroom door.

The bed looked as if someone had hastily jumped out of it, perhaps having overslept, knocking down a lamp and breaking it. But there was no body, and no blood. And, of course, no ring.

Moira darted back into the kitchen and suppressed a sharp cry. The fallen jewelry clerk was no longer there.

"Three Hals," Hal summed up. "Three Moiras. And, since that check was never intended to be cashed, three sales. The books are closed."

Faintly, on the other side of the house, they heard the sputtering cough of a car starting.

"No, they're not closed yet," said Moira, quickly retracing her steps along the hall and motioning to Hal. "That's not my car; it must be the one he drove here from the store." Hal at once remembered the Renault in the Blue Diamond's parking lot. "Come on, *move!* That crazy man's getting away!"

But halfway down the stairs they stopped. Under the stairs, Mrs. Foster was on the telephone.

"Hello, Mrs. Yorberg? I was just up in your old apartment—and somebody's been in there."

Moira's hand closed tightly on Hal's.

"Yes. At first I thought it was you. Sure sounded like you. I got suspicious when she wouldn't take some of my preserves. I know how you used to like my raspberry."

Moira couldn't help a wry smile. "Anyway," she murmured into Hal's ear, "it sure beats her tomatoes."

"So I unlocked the apartment with my own key—hope

you don't mind—and went in. There was hot coffee on the counter, and the bed's not made."

Moira tugged at Hal. They continued to inch their way down.

"Yes, Mrs. Yorberg. I'll call them right away. Goodbye." The old lady hung up, and immediately dialed another number. "Hello? Hello, police headquarters?"

Moira eased the front door open. Elm Street seemed deserted. They sprinted along the driveway toward her car.

It was not there.

They crouched in the shadows behind the garage. "Well, we'll never catch him now," Hal said. "Are you *sure* that wasn't your car he drove away in?"

She shook her head emphatically. "Remember, only one universe per customer. Maybe the Moira who used to live here sold her car when she got married, or maybe she and that Hal took it with them to the house on Ridgeway. Either way, it's still running around this town. So there's no room in this world for *my* car—and it went back. Just like yours."

"Then how come we're still here?"

"That's what doesn't make any sense," she admitted.

"Should I go down the street and call us a cab?"

"No, you dummy! Not with Mrs. Foster calling out the Marines, and especially not with our homicidal bookkeeper cruising the streets. We're going to walk, and we're going to start by using this back alley for a few blocks."

"Walk where?" Hal demanded.

"To the only place in three worlds where everything comes together. We're going to have to go back to that crummy jewelry store."

Hal felt the handle of the ridiculous little weapon he had taken from the clerk. Although it had the same shape as the gun Booth used on Lincoln, it didn't much reassure him. "That clerk," Hal muttered. "Do you suppose he's really Hal Four after all?"

"No, he's not. I'm sure of it. I can't imagine *any* variation on Harold Jorberg committing murder. Not even the blond beast, the big clunker—and certainly not you."

"Gosh, thanks."

"Don't you see, Hal," she pressed on, ignoring the sarcasm, "there *was* a Moira Four, but there was *not* a Hal Four. That is the real Goedel anomaly. The Cosmos could shuffle four couples across four alternate worlds, singly or together, without any real violation of cause and effect, and with full conservation of matter and energy. But the extra Moira is—was—one of those 'wild' phenomena no logic could have predicted. For every Moira there has to be a Hal." She stopped, aware of certain personal implications in what she was saying. Without another word they started down the alley.

They walked, and they talked, and they stopped a couple of times for coffee, taking care not to compound the paradox by passing the wrong world's coins. They told each other about the world of the two President Kennedys and the world of the China War. They told each other about themselves—what they liked to eat and drink, what they cared for, what they were afraid of—and it grew dark and very cold.

They came at last to the triangular island between two converging streets where, earlier on that crowded afternoon, they had first met. The building was dark, and the tiny parking lot was empty.

"So. He didn't come back here after all," said Hal, mildly pleased that he had finally scored a point off Moira.

She brushed past him, much as she had at their first encounter, and pushed at the door. It opened easily.

"Whoever heard of leaving a jewelry store unlocked at night?" Hal wondered aloud. Then he realized that the neon sign had not merely been turned off; it was not there at all.

Moira's hand found the light switch. Fluorescents flickered on. The store had been cleaned out; the display cases were empty. Hal rushed around the counter and shoved the door that led to the back. It flew open.

The iron roof of the quonset arched overhead, bare and unadorned. A few torn packing boxes and shards of broken glass lay on the cement floor. Otherwise, nothing.

"Our bird has flown," said Hal. His voice echoed hollowly in the empty room.

"No, not flown. Damped out. He got caught in his own effort to tinker with the universe. It's as if he had never existed. I'll bet we'd find that Blue Diamond Jewelers isn't even in the yellow pages now."

"Then there is some justice in the Cosmos."

"Justice! Tell that to Moira Four."

Anyhow, Hal reflected as they departed, in this present world Moira Three and Hal Three would receive no dunning letters about their partly-paid-for rings.

Moira walked over to the low brick barrier, stooped, and picked up a discarded newspaper, absently smoothing its crumpled folds. Then her eyes widened. "Hal, look!"

His heart jumped at the headline:

JOINT U.S.-FRENCH EXPEDITION PLANNED FOR MARS

"Well, that never would have happened in my universe," he said at last. "France broke off relations with us because of the China War."

"But it *is* happening in mine! The French admired both Kennedy brothers, and after Bobby's death Jackie spent a term as our envoy in Paris. Don't you see it yet, Hal? Here—right here, where we parked our cars this afternoon—must be where the three universes come together."

"Then we can go back."

"Yes." Her face clouded. "We can go . . . home. And that's what the script calls for us to do. If I walk out of here the way I came in—" she pointed up the side street— "and you run across the other road and go back the way *you* came, everything should be just as it was."

"Yeah," he said bitterly. "I take my ring back to Lady Macbeth, you put yours on and make up with the blond beast, and everybody lives happily ever after. Very neat! Q.E.D.!"

"But we can't," she breathed.

"Why not?"

"Because of the *money*, you fool! That's the one Goedel paradox that dreadful little man couldn't tidy up. Banks in two different universes have records of paying out exactly the same amount of cash—which both of us remember spending." She lifted her strong hands and slowly, deliberately, placed them on his shoulders. "Each of us is stuck with a memory connected with the other's world—and personally, I wouldn't have it any other way." Then, to Hal's infinite astonishment and delight, Moira kissed him, slowly and very thoroughly.

"What'll it be?" Hal asked when they finally came up for air. "This way, to my world? That way, to yours? Or stay right here?"

"Uh-uh. Can't stay here. Have to leave this universe to

those newlyweds. Besides, I just can't face their Mrs. Foster."

A police siren wailed in the distance, reminding them that in this universe they were also fugitives from the law. "How about your world, then? It would be good to live on an Earth where they're serious about going to Mars."

"My world has problems, Hal. America on my Earth is going to be a dynastic monarchy in a few years. And your America sounds like a hypocritical police state. Let's—" she led him over to the barrier—"let's go *this* way!"

Hand in hand, they took a running jump over the brick wall. Spurned by Hal's foot, a Coke can clattered over the curb. Three bounding strides through the dry yellow grass, and they were at the very point of the angle. One more step, and they were in a new world.

The Two Tzaddiks

Ira Herman

We have a saying in Mishnim: Even in heaven you can stub your toe.

And you can almost forget you're not in heaven in our beautiful little colony! You should see our village. It nestles in green hills like a gemstone. Our houses string together like pearls: peaked cottages with stained glass windows; imperial mansions of carved oak; whitewashed, sensible two-story dwellings with balconies on every side. And in the summer when the corn has eared and tasseled, you can stand on such a balcony and look out over field after field dotted with yellow tassels like stars in a night sky.

And what corn we grow. You cannot get corn like this on Earth!

When the first Chasids came to space colonies, they brought holy men, *tzaddiks*. Climbing aboard *Ark II* with horses and ducks, they preserved their way of life by escaping Earth and bringing the old ways with them.

Where a tzaddik settled, a pious community grew around him. Where a tzaddik died or moved on, the community dissipated.

How lucky we are that in Mishnim we have not one but two tzaddiks to lead us! To know one such man in a lifetime is a blessing, but to know two, ah, now that is something. How alike and yet how different they are!

Tzaddik Tzadeka is a very saintly man. He is tall and thin, with fingers like slender white twigs. His yellow beard goes to a point. Tzaddik Tzadeka's nose takes three twists before reaching his lower lip. And what a scholar! Possibly the greatest of all time on the Talmud.

Tzaddik Farachachdela, too, is a very holy man, but he is short and thick in stature. His beard is white and parts in the middle. Farachachdela is so pleasant! When you see

him on the streets of Mishnim, he will not pass without
offering sunflower seeds or a piece of dried fruit and saying, "Bless you, Lord be with you. All God's creatures are
one today!"

When you see Farachachdela's walk, you are reminded
of the slow gait of a horse. Tzaddik Tzadeka hardly walks
at all. When he does, he leans on a cane and limps painfully.

And what friends are these two tzaddiks! They even
live in adjoining houses. In early days they used to accom-
pany each other everywhere. Israel ben ha-Levi, the black-
smith's brother, says that the Almighty had bound them
together with a rope. Where one went, the other followed.
Always you hear Farachachdela say, "What a blessing it is
to have a man like Tzadeka. His qualities are more precious than gold!" Tzadeka calls Farachachdela "a spiritual
man—a saint."

But these two friends do not agree on everything. A discussion arose between them in the basement of the synagogue, and it ended in an argument. It had something to
do with how Mishnim faces the Moon, the calendar, and the
coming Shavuos. Shouting started. Tzadeka smacked his
cane against a chair and limped out of the synagogue. Farachachdela flew into a fury, calling to Tzadeka that he was
"as stiff as a board."

No one, not Nezin or Zlotkin, not Israel ben ha-Levi,
who had known them the longest, had ever heard the two
tzaddiks quarrel before. A shadow was thrown over the
light and gay spirit of Mishnim. That evening, dissension
racked every household. Never since leaving Earth had
such unhappiness been known. Rishbam ben Jachi and his
wife, Rivke, had a terrible fight, during which they threw
cabbages and oranges and broke all the windows in their
house. Even in heaven you can stub your toe.

Outside the colony, huge planar mirrors discreetly
shifted, slanting beams of sunlight onto tree-covered val-
leys. Light splashed through branches of a plum tree and
into the bedroom windows of Tzaddik Farachachdela, illu-
minating the framed pictures of Rabbi Hillel and Mohan-
das Gandhi. Some of it shone on the face of the sleeping
tzaddik. He blinked twice and sat up in bed. Through the
windows Farachachdela could see yellow heads of sunflow-

ers and ripe tomatoes in his garden. Mauve and pink on the hillsides, fruit trees bloomed in clusters where, years back, he had set them out.

What a wonderful day, and how blessed our life! Farachachdela thought. He got out of bed and stepped into leather sandals. Today, after feeding the animals, I'll weed the radishes, dig last year's potatoes, and plant five more rows of corn! He paused at the window, slipping on his nankeen housecoat. He squinted, unable to see pipes against the arching metal ceiling. No rain programmed today.

Farachachdela chanted morning prayers. Then he went to the bathroom and put in his teeth, which had been soaking all night in a glass of salt water. He walked into the kitchen and had breakfast: a dark spice cake, three different cheeses, and a slice of white melon with goat's milk. Washing the dishes, he noticed something unusual. At the end of the wooden passageway connecting his house with Tzaddik Tzadeka's, the door was closed. Through this door Farachachdela could always see Tzadeka at this time of the morning, seated at his desk poring over some old tome or book of the Talmud. But the door was closed. He remembered their argument. Farachachdela stopped, the dishrag still in his hands, and said, "What was it? We were having a discussion about the calendar, and he starts calling me names, seriously, in front of everyone!"

Farachachdela visualized Mishnim orbiting between Earth and the Moon, nearly in its second quarter. *And we're about to celebrate Shavuos!* he thought. *It's wrong, completely!*

Farachachdela put off feeding the animals and working in his garden. He changed into leather boots and, still in fringed housecoat, went out for a walk.

Even the main street, thronging with barterers and ladies, did not cheer him. He found Meyer Nezin, a chicken under one arm, sunning himself in the butcher's doorway. Nezin's round face lit with delight.

"Dear Tzaddik! How wonderful it is to see you looking so well—and on such a day!"

Nezin is an excellent speaker, but during his orations a fine spray issues from his mouth. Farachachdela was glad that the size of Nezin's stomach prevented him from standing too close.

"Blessings upon you, Nezin," Farachachdela sighed. "It's a troubled time for the colony, I'm afraid."

Nezin's bulging eyes followed the movements of passersby. "Ah, it's nothing. A little argument—nothing! You'll go to borrow candles or take bread, you'll start talking and laughing over something, and it will fade into unimportance," Nezin said with a wave of his hand.

"But it is important, Meyer. We're celebrating the holidays, even the Sabbath, at the wrong times. We must change the calendar—and at once!"

Nezin's eyes bulged nearly out of his head. "Change the calendar? Why? No one has brought up such a subject before."

"Meyer, don't you see? We have preserved our way of life, even escaping our mother planet to do so. And this was good. It was meant to be, for the observance of the law is more than just ritual for Chasids, it is the fabric of life! And what is at the center of the law? The Sabbath and the holidays. But what good are such observances by mistake—at the wrong times?"

"The wrong times how? Why change them?"

Nezin's body was like a balloon, squeezing air out.

Farachachdela gazed above the foothills to the endcap of the colony and at the blue ceiling. Cottony clouds drifted below it. "The key point is this. The Talmud instructs that our months be based on the phases of the Moon, and for nearly four thousand years we have followed this teaching. But, Meyer, listen. We are observing a calendar based on the phases of the Moon *as seen from Earth*. From Mishnim, the phases are different from the ones they see there. The Talmud says to follow the phases of the Moon. It does not say that 'this applies to Earth' or 'this applies to space colonies'; it just says—do it! But we are not. We are ignoring the words of the Talmud. Is the Moon no longer the Moon?"

Nezin shifted the chicken under his other arm. "And if they studied the Talmud on Mars, would they have a different calendar there, too?"

"Of course," Farachachdela declared triumphantly. "From every position, every different angle to the Moon, a new calendar. On Earth it may be Shavuos, on Mars it may be Purim, and in Mishnim it may be Yom Kippur all at the same time. It depends on position in relation to the Moon."

With his free hand Nezin took out a linen cloth and blew his nose thoughtfully.

"We must switch over—and tonight!" Farachachdela bellowed. But he could see that Nezin was accepting none of it. He tried one more time. "Meyer, the whole Chasidic movement was founded by a freethinker, a revolutionary. Rabbi Israel ben Eliezer, the miracle worker himself, would agree!"

Nezin grunted. "And when we reach the stars, what then?"

"Who knows?" Farachachdela held his palms up. "That's a long way off. Maybe by then we'll have a new revelation, a new law. But for now we have our Talmud, and we should follow it!"

"Such matters are for tzaddiks to decide," Nezin said. "You should settle it with Tzadeka and be friends again. If tzaddiks cannot agree, how are we, normal men, expected to?"

Farachachdela left the butcher's doorway and walked down the street. He eyed the curved azure ceiling and pondered the improbability of a meteoroid impact. A signal would go off and a monitoring ship would be here in less than a day to repair the damage, he thought. A signal would go off inside the colony, too, blasting at intervals, telling everyone to hurry to the temple. The warning signal sounded like the honking of a huge goose.

After passing Israel ben ha-Levi without returning his greeting, Farachachdela decided to go back, to take care of his animals and work in his garden.

At this late hour Tzadeka was still asleep. He had gotten up at six or seven to go to the bathroom, but he had been so weak and his left foot hurt him so much that he had shut the door to the passageway connecting his house with Farachachdela's and gone back to bed.

Downstairs, Gavrila had been awake for three hours and was on her fourth cup of tea. After reheating the tzaddik's breakfast twice, she resolved to deliver the meal whether he was asleep or not and get on with her daily chores. Gavrila is a sturdily built, attractive young girl who goes about in overalls or thin cotton dresses.

She drew a sweater across her shoulders, picked up Tzadeka's tray, and started up the stairs, thinking, He comes in without a word, and half the night I'm kept awake by the sound of his pacing, with that limp, above me.

Tzadeka limped across the room, putting on a long black housecoat. When he opened the door, he thought Gavrila studied him critically for a moment. She handed him the tray without smiling or saying anything and went back down the stairs.

Tzadeka prayed, though it was no longer morning. Then, with cane, he went to the bathroom to look at his nose in the mirror.

How could it grow so long, be so flexible? Tzadeka tormented, studying his nose in the mirror. I've lived with it for many years and still I can't get used to it! If it could only stop here, at the halfway mark, or even here, at two-thirds. Tzadeka covered the end of his nose with his fingers to see what it would look like at the halfway mark, and at two-thirds. No, that would not be too bad. But as it is, how ugly it makes the rest of my features look. What was it? I should get my nose out of books? How rude it was for Farachachdela to call attention to it!

Tzadeka is sensitive about his long proboscis and does not appreciate references to it in conversation. This one, coming from Farachachdela and in front of the assembled elders of Mishnim, had stung particularly.

Tzadeka went into the study, his left foot throbbing. I stay up half the night reinjuring my foot because of him. If not for the toe, he thought.

Tzadeka remembered the time when he had been reaching for a copy of Asher ben Jachiel's *Responsa*. Something had broken, and the entire shelf had come down on his left big toe, crushing it completely. Two bones in the foot had been broken. Even a doctor from Earth had not been able to set the fragile bones so as to heal without leaving a lingering pain.

He sat at his mahogany desk and tried to read, but his concentration was uneven. He was too upset by the quarrel with Farachachdela. "Not only losing his hearing but his mind as well," he said. "If I try to understand him, I will lose mine also." Tzadeka might have sat, beard in hand, for an hour, but he heard a voice, Gavrila's, and then footsteps on the stairs.

Without waiting for a knock he opened the door. Tzadeka's narrow face narrowed further into a long-toothed smile.

"Mordechai, just the man I want to see—an angel sent—yes, an angel!" Tzadeka said humbly, backing away to let in his friend.

Taller than Tzadeka, Mordechai Zlotkin looks even more like a scarecrow. His face is like a stork's.

"I came to see how you were," Zlotkin said, stepping inside. "Someone said you had trouble, that you might be upset. I told him, 'For Tzadeka this is a once-in-a-lifetime occasion. Not to be missed!' "

Tzadeka laughed self-consciously. "It's nothing—absolutely. A bit of foolishness that will pass over. Come, you'll sit and have something. A few apricots, some wine?"

Zlotkin relaxed into the oak rocking chair, shaking his head. Tzadeka turned his own chair to face him.

"And what a day," Zlotkin said with a flourish. "To breathe air like this is to recover youth!"

"And so near Shavuos, too," Tzadeka said.

"Yes—near Shavuos." Zlotkin shifted uncomfortably, creaking the rockers.

Tzadeka went on, quoting from the Talmud to explain that if Shavuos falls on a certain day, it is a special Shavuos, a more joyous and spiritual one than comes again in a generation. He pointed out that the coming Shavuos would fall on the very day, making it doubly sacred.

The more Zlotkin listened, the more he felt as if he had eaten something rotten for dinner. He twisted in his chair as Tzadeka spoke. Finally he said, "Shavuos on Earth."

All the joy drained from Tzadeka's face. "Shavuos on Earth, and Shavuos everywhere!"

Zlotkin held up a finger. "Not Shavuos everywhere." He was about to say, "Maybe Reb Farachachdela is right, maybe we should refigure the calendar. Is the Moon no longer the Moon?" But before he could say it, Tzadeka stopped him, banging his cane.

"This has been brought up before," Tzadeka nearly shouted. "Nine hundred years ago, Al Hasi ben Yehudin, writing a decision of the Sanhedrin, said that if the Moon should be hidden from view, by clouds or whatever, or should in any way be different for a prolonged period, our time should follow that of the Holy Land. The question came up a second time when Moishe—"

"Interpretations," Zlotkin interrupted, parting his hands. "Opinions. Maybe Farachachdela is right. Is the Moon no longer the Moon?"

Tzadeka rose shakily with his cane, tears welling in his sunken eyes. "So—you fall in with him, too. You're taking his side in this, after all?"

"What side? He has merely brought up the idea that the phases are different, and maybe we should refigure our calendar according. That perhaps we should consider . . ."

"How quickly you would throw it all away! Four thousand years. It's the reason we left Earth!"

On the word *Earth* Tzadeka's voice was like something scraping glass.

Zlotkin rose, trying to smile. "It's merely a question, something to talk out. You'll agree, then you'll say the blessing over wine and drink it up together."

"Never!" Tzadeka trembled. "To change the Sabbath— the holidays—you're tampering with things that only—"

"You're upset," Zlotkin cut in, walking to the door. He placed a hand on the knob. "I'll come back when you're feeling better."

"No," Tzadeka said. But it was too late. Zlotkin had already shut the door and started down the steps.

Tzadeka picked up his white scarf and wound it nervously around his neck. Then he proceeded to do something that, for him, was very unusual. He went out to take a walk in his backyard, along the dung-colored path that Gavrila had worn by carrying laundry to the clothesline.

Tzaddik Farachachdela had, by this time, changed back into his sandals and was walking on the spongy black dirt in his garden. He paused, took off his vest, and hung it on the arm of a sunflower. Warmth invigorated his shoulders and back.

Proudly he gazed at the rows of corn he had planted, now like green fences; at the clusters of white and yellow blossoms at his feet; and beyond, at pepper plants and squashes venturing onto hillsides. He paced to a row of tall radishes, stooped, and started weeding them with his hands.

At the end of the row stood a weed that was taller than the rest. It was leafy, an almost domesticated-looking plant. It took all Farachachdela's strength to pull it up. The weed possessed a long fleshy root. Like a cross between a wild carrot and a radish, Farachachdela thought. For a moment he considered the half-rotted, bug-eaten root as possible food for his two goats, Esma and Esmarelda. But the more he looked, the more it seemed the most disgusting thing he had ever seen. In revulsion he said, "Looks like something you might feed a pig." He pitched the weed out of his garden. He threw it with such zeal that it cleared the fence and went into the next yard.

Farachachdela had thrown weeds over the fence before, but this time was different. This time, Tzaddik Tzadeka, who had not yet reached the clothesline, happened to be walking just on the other side of the fence.

Tzadeka turned, hearing only the word *pig*, and was met full in the face with the weed and clumps of dirt clinging to its root. Cane flying, he collapsed. By the time he had picked himself up and removed the dirt from his mouth and eyes, he was furious.

Beyond the fence he saw Farachachdela, who had finished the radishes and stood beaming.

Tzadeka's heart pounded. "*You* are the pig!" he screeched.

"What?" said Farachachdela, coming over and raising his voice. "What did you say?"

"A pig," Tzadeka said. "I called you a pig."

"Ha, ha," Farachachdela laughed. "It's surprising to me, with a nose like yours, you do not oink!"

Farachachdela meant this to be a joke by which he showed his willingness to forget their quarrel, but Tzadeka went into a rage.

"I spit on your head, Farachachdela! I declare that from this point I shall no longer know you!"

"Such tragedy," Farachachdela said. "I won't have a neighbor who calls me names."

"I will never set foot in your house again!"

"Nor I in yours," Farachachdela shouted, getting angry for the first time. "That will be fine with me. From now on, I will not speak to you, Tzadeka!"

Farachachdela made an insulting gesture and started walking to his house.

"Agreed!" Tzadeka called, hobbling away still combing dirt from his yellow beard.

Farachachdela turned to ask, "What was it, how have I wronged you, Tzadeka?" But Tzadeka had reentered his house, and the door slammed behind him.

This scene had a single spectator, Rudkin, a skinny boy of seven who had been watching from behind the trunk of an apple tree on Tzadeka's side of the fence. When the door slammed, Rudkin took to his heels as fast as he could.

The news of the incident shot through the community like a thunderbolt. Rudkin ran home and told his mother, Rena, who told it to her husband, Rael. He passed it on to Mordechai Zlotkin. It might have gone no farther, except that Rena ran into Rishbam ben Jachai, who knew most of the story already, so she answered his questions. Soon all Mishnim was buzzing. Late that night, a meeting was held at Zlotkin's house.

"They're both acting like children," Nezin said. "To call him a pig is disgraceful! But on the calendar thing, Tzadeka is right!"

Israel ben ha-Levi had a jug of peach wine in one hand and a drawing in the other. The drawing depicted the relative positions of Earth, the Moon, and Mishnim. He ran from person to person, showing it to illustrate the two viewpoints. "From here you see a half Moon, and from here you see a quarter, a different month!" he repeated each time.

"A change should come from the Almighty, not from us," said Rishbam ben Jachai. "If we tinker with our observance of the Sabbath and holidays—who knows?—it might be another golden calf."

"There were those who said we never should have left Earth," Mordechai Zlotkin protested.

"Perhaps we shouldn't have!" someone cried.

"It's very confusing. If we change, how will we know when to observe the Sabbath?" Nezin demanded.

"Perhaps we should honor both times of the Sabbath," Zlotkin suggested.

"Two Sabbaths?"

Zlotkin shrugged. "What else can we do until it is decided which is right?"

They voted to attempt a reconciliation between the two tzaddiks. The next day, a meal would be prepared at the synagogue. Nezin would see that Tzadeka attended, and Zlotkin would take the responsibility for Farachachdela, even though both tzaddiks might have to be misled into thinking the other would not be coming.

Twelve women cooked and scrubbed for hours in the synagogue's kitchen. By evening a magnificent meal had been set on the table: roasted turkeys stuffed with cabbage balls inside of which were bits of sausages or corned beef, plates of pickled herring and sturgeon caviar, chopped liver, hard rolls with poppy seeds, potato cakes, and at least ten different kinds of pastries.

Nezin and Zlotkin were the first to arrive, followed by Israel ben ha-Levi. Before long, the room was filled with elders, ladies, and children of every description. No one ate because the tzaddiks were not present and the blessings had not been said. The aromas drifting from the table were almost unbearable. Small boys swarmed around one end, threatening to snatch cookies.

Cheeks quivering, Nezin said to Zlotkin, "Have you had these little red sausages? Wonderful heated up. They pop and explode in your mouth! Gavrila makes them with spiced fat."

Zlotkin nodded. "Perhaps we're asking too much in seating them together." He indicated the two chairs across from each other at the center of the table.

"How else to break the ice?" Nezin said. "I've already passed the word. When Farachachdela comes in, Israel ben ha-Levi and the others will see that he sits in this chair. You and I will guide Tzadeka to that one."

The crowd turned as Tzadeka came in, assisted by Gavrila. Tzadeka used two canes now, instead of one. His foot was wrapped in a heavy linen bandage. He took off his black coat and wide-brimmed hat and greeted Nezin.

A few seconds later, Farachachdela entered through the side doorway. People massed around, maneuvering them to their chairs. Farachachdela glared at Mordechai Zlotkin. Tzadeka pinned Nezin with icy gray eyes. They had been lied to. Everything froze.

"Can you not greet your lifelong brother?" Zlotkin asked them, holding out his hands. "Let us say the blessings together!"

Nezin quickly filled cups with wine. Zlotkin served
bread from a glistening braided loaf. The two rabbis said
the blessings together, the others joining in. By the time all
said, "Amen," the tension in the air had been broken. Zlotkin and Nezin pulled chairs out. This was taken as a signal,
and everyone sat and began eating. The tzaddiks were directly across from each other at the center of the long table.

"Here they are," Zlotkin whispered to Nezin, "two lead-
ers of a space colony, and they won't even speak to each
other."

"So it will be all right?" Farachachdela said at last, jerking his nose at Tzadeka's foot.

Tzadeka, chewing a piece of herring, looked up. "Lieberman says it will heal. No bone damage, so the pain I have
now should pass." He slid a herring bone off the end of his
tongue. "There's always something to be thankful for."

"Lieberman?"

"You know him, the doctor from Earth, the one with
sagging ears."

"Oh, yes, very good, very good man," Farachachdela
said, looking at his plate. "Does Gavrila take good care of
you now?"

Tzadeka ran a crooked forefinger down his nose. What
was it all about? he wondered. He might have been clumsy,
but he *meant* no harm.

"Gavrila comes every five minutes to check on me,"
Tzadeka replied. "She drives me crazy with her checking."

Farachachdela focused tobacco-colored eyes on the other
tzaddik. "You know, of course, that I meant you no harm,
that never in a hundred years would I wish you any physical injury, Tzaddik Tzadeka."

Tzadeka shifted in his chair with his canes. "I know
that."

Everyone began nudging and smiling in anticipation.
Farachachdela started feeling in his pocket for his leather
pouch of dried fruit and was about to say, "May you be
blessed." Tzadeka was going to say, "Let's toast and forget
the whole thing." But he said instead, "And the calendar,
are you willing to forget that foolishness?"

Farachachdela's mouth tightened. "I have been observing the phases of the Moon through a telescope, and I have

refigured the calendar accordingly. This is not Thursday evening, it's Monday morning. On *Earth* it's Thursday, but here, at a different angle to the Moon, it's Monday."

All at the table looked to Tzadeka for a reply, but he kept silent.

"I have already begun observing by the new calendar," Farachachdela announced.

Tzadeka turned to Nezin. "It's as if he doesn't hear a word. Ignoring the greatest tzaddiks, he looks up at the ceiling and gets an inspiration."

"The whole thing's ridiculous," Nezin whispered.

"It's you who cannot hear," Farachachdela shot back. "Hear the commandment of the Lord! Perhaps too much of you has been put into your nose to the detriment of your ears, Tzadeka. The Scripture is clear. No interpretation is needed. We must change the clocks."

Tzadeka restrained himself to saying, "Depart from tradition? Change our observance of the Sabbath? Surely at the very least, the matter requires deeper consideration than one can give who stays in a garden. Perhaps, Reb Farachachdela, you should spend more hours in a study going over the law than out in the fields with the goats and the swine."

Farachachdela's eyes blazed. "Look up, Tzadeka! Raise your eyes from interpretations—get your snout out of the mud!"

"Enough!" Mordechai Zlotkin said, holding up his hand. "It is better to go out at once than to hear such talk between tzaddiks! The matter is easily settled by calm discussion!"

At this point a small dog ran into the room, chased by Rena's daughter, Risna, a girl of five in a red-and-white-checkered dress. The dog scampered under the table, and it was some time before it and Risna could be untangled from the legs of the men seated there. She ran out, spanking the mutt vigorously.

Zlotkin held out a hand to each tzaddik. "It is foolishness to argue, to call each other names. Go to him, embrace your brother tzaddik! Extinguish the flames of enmity between you. It is forgotten! The quarrel is over! Ask for God's forgiveness as you forgive."

Everyone was stunned. Tzadeka even began to rise. "And the calendar?" he asked.

"We will settle that after dinner," Nezin put in. "For now, embrace and forget the past."

Tzadeka said, "After we've talked, we'll embrace. We need to come to a decision. Then once more we will live in peace in Mishnim."

"Tzadeka is right," Farachachdela said. "We can forgive, but we cannot agree without discussion." Farachachdela's face softened. "If two old friends cannot agree, who can? What was it about, really?"

Tzadeka looked away, embarrassed. "Perhaps it was silly to argue." Everyone watched closely. "It was stupid, really. The whole thing, just because I called you a pig."

It all went to hell.

If Tzadeka had said *goose* or *dog*, or if he had even said *pig*, but said it in private, a reconciliation might still have been effected. But with the utterance of that word in front of the whole community, Farachachdela's small nose turned as red as one of Gavrila's sausages. Beads of sweat popped out on his forehead. His lips quivering, he screamed at Tzadeka, "May you wake up in the night and bang your foot—to get infected—and may it not kill you, but may it cause you so much pain that you end up killing yourself!"

Mouths gaped in horror.

"Reb Farachachdela!" Nezin called out.

"It's a sin," someone whispered.

"The Lord forgive you for uttering such an oath!" Zlotkin cried.

"I mean it!" Farachachdela shouted. "I do not take it back!"

Tzadeka stood up with his canes, tipping his chair backward. He made a noise in his throat like an animal and spat on the floor. "From now on, there are two Mishnims!" he shrieked.

Farachachdela had also risen to his feet, and both tzaddiks were being held apart by the horrified men of Mishnim. To make matters worse, Risna and her dog ran back into the room, this time accompanied by her brother, Rudkin. Tzadeka lost his balance and fell backward onto the dog, which bit him on the arm.

The room presented a striking picture: elders crowding around Tzadeka; Farachachdela on the other side of the table screaming, "Pig, pig"; women and children staring in disbelief; and in one corner the boy Rudkin, sitting quietly with his shoes and socks off, picking at his toes.

A week passed, during which the community underwent a transformation. Two schedules of services were conducted at the synagogue: one following Tzadeka's time, the old calendar and the Jewish calendar of Earth; the other going by Farachachdela's time, according to the phases of the Moon as seen from Mishnim. People attempted to observe both schedules of services, but this soon became a hardship. Choices were made. The community split into two halves: those observing Tzadeka's time and those observing Farachachdela's. It was a fairly even split. Zlotkin went with Farachachdela, Nezin with Tzadeka. Rishbam ben Jachai stopped going to services altogether.

One day, coming down the steps of the synagogue, Nezin met Zlotkin, who was on his way into town to do some shopping.

"I'm beginning to have doubts. Maybe Farachachdela is right," Nezin said. "Perhaps we should go by the new calculations."

Zlotkin raised an eyebrow. "Who can tell? After all, the Lord did not make space colonies to provide different angles to the Moon—mortals did. What if the phases of the Moon as seen from Earth are merely God's trick to have us observe at the right times?"

"It's very confusing. If only we could get them to agree."

Zlotkin threw up his hands. "Tzadeka says he would rather make friends with the devil! Farachachdela flies into a rage every time Tzadeka's name is mentioned."

"And the Shavuos dance," Nezin asked, "will you be coming?"

"I suppose I'll come," Zlotkin sighed. "What trouble can you get into for going to a dance?" He pulled a splinter from the synagogue stair railing and snapped it in his fingers. "Tzadeka might come, but there's no way we could have them both."

"If one thinks the other is coming, of course not," Nezin said, a sly glint in his round eyes. "But there is a way."

"Not again! It's like spitting in the face of God to lie to a tzaddik!"

Nezin touched a fat finger to Zlotkin's chest. "This time go to Tzadeka, and I'll go see Farachachdela."

"I couldn't—it's not possible."

But Nezin was very convincing, saying, "It's a lie, but
it's a holy lie, to right a misunderstanding," and other
things, and Zlotkin was finally persuaded to go on this
"fool's errand."

The synagogue basement was festooned with colored paper streamers. Chairs were stacked in rows in the corners.
The long table, covered with a white cloth, was laid with
bowls of fruit and pecans and salted walnuts.

People mingled and talked on the dance floor, the older
ones in traditional dark clothing, the young people in scarfs
or brightly colored hats. Farachachdela's entire Sunday
School class was there, twenty-two thirteen-year-old boys in
all. You could tell them by their blue lapel buttons. Nezin
and Zlotkin leaned against a counter, talking. Israel ben
ha-Levi exchanged sips of peach wine with Zvi Isachar, a
man who has an identical wart on either side of his nose.
Rishbam ben Jachai and his wife, Rivke, were talking to
Rena and Rael. Lilly and Mona, Shira's daughters, skipped
rope in one corner, clapping. The room was a milieu of
talking, eating, singing, laughing.

Tzaddik Farachachdela, in work clothes (he wears
these even while leading the service), was sitting at one
end of the long table. The gaiety in the room shone in his
lustrous eyes, and he tapped his palm on the table in time
with Lilly and Mona's clapping.

Moments later Gavrila entered the room with Tzadeka.
Tzadeka exchanged greetings with his friends, then he was
halted by a stillness in the room. Farachachdela stood.

Tzadeka limped to Zlotkin, pointing with one cane.
"What is this, a change of plans? Or you lied!"

"I lied," Zlotkin said without shame. "It's a terrible thing
to lie to a tzaddik, but it had to be done. We agreed! How
else to bring two friends together?"

Farachachdela turned to Nezin. "Meyer, how many
times has it been written, no good comes from telling a
lie?"

Each tzaddik spoke as if the other were not present.
They refused to look at each other.

On impulse, Mordechai Zlotkin took Nezin's hand and
began to sing in Hebrew. Slowly, hands joined and men
and women chanted in euphony. The sound grew in vol-

ume and energy, a sound of infectious joy. Arms coupled into a great writhing, swaying snake of dancing men, women, and children.

They formed into a circle. The step was one, two, to the right then jump, doing a partial turn. After a while even Farachachdela danced, his square frame bouncing with the agility of youth.

Ha-Levi broke into a smile. "How good it is to see an old man dance like that," he said to Zlotkin.

"Look at Nezin," Zlotkin said. "How he dances—despite his stomach!"

"He draws wind from it. In dancing or talking, you get Nezin started and your arm could fall off."

"A man who cannot see his feet," Zlotkin said, whirling away.

Tzadeka watched the circle-dance from his chair. He joined in the singing a little, showing his yellowed teeth. He began to clap his hands and bob back and forth in rhythm. The circle expanded. Farachachdela came around in it, jumped to the side, and landed squarely on Tzadeka's left big toe, the one that was already injured.

Tzadeka fell, gasping. Zvi Isachar rushed forward, knocking glasses off the table. Nezin tore his sleeve. A crowd formed around the fallen tzaddik.

Zlotkin and ha-Levi examined the foot. They picked him up and carried him outside, Tzadeka hissing, "A plague! He's like a plague!" between grimaces.

Zlotkin climbed into his carriage and whipped up the horses. He and ha-Levi lifted Tzadeka into it. The coach lurched away with Tzadeka in the back, moaning.

Inside the basement, Farachachdela waved his hands wildly. "The best thing now is for everybody to go home. An unfortunate accident, unfortunate!"

Parents gathered up toys, children, and articles of clothing. Horse-drawn vehicles began pulling away from the synagogue. Soon it was empty except for a single white duck, pecking at the paper streamers that had been torn down in places.

A winter came to Mishnim, a winter unattended by snow or harsh winds or cold temperatures. Peach and pear trees were still covered with delicate blossoms. Butterflies still cavorted over green meadows. This was a different kind of winter, a winter of the human spirit, the spirit of a community broken in half, of lives torn asunder by endless haggling and mischief.

For weeks (time becoming confused under two calendars) the two old friends refused to speak to each other. Then, one day, as Farachachdela was hoeing dead corn out of his garden, something extraordinary happened.

He felt it more than saw it. A fiery streak sizzled through the atmosphere and hit the ground somewhere behind him. The honking-goose emergency signal blasted. Farachachdela dropped his hoe and searched the sky. He could barely see a tiny black hole in the ceiling. "A meteorite! The colony's been struck!" he exclaimed.

Tzaddik Tzadeka, who had been reading the *Otsar Rabati* in his study, saw it out of the corner of his eye. Something burning fell from the sky and struck the ground several fields off. At the sound of the warning signal, he put down the book and hopped across the room to get his coat. He knew what the signal meant. He had heard it in tests, years before, when the emergency procedures had been announced.

Farachachdela hurried around the side of his house to the front yard. There he saw Nezin, Zlotkin, and Rishbam ben Jachai. Across the way, Tzadeka appeared with both canes.

"What is it, what does it mean?" Nezin called out.

"Nothing to worry about," Farachachdela answered. "This is the first time it's happened—but precautions have been taken."

"A meteor, it's put a hole in the ceiling!" Rishbam ben Jachai cried.

"Correct," Farachachdela said calmly, "and our atmosphere is starting to escape through it."

Already Nezin began choking.

The warning signal sounded again.

"There is nothing to worry about?" Zlotkin asked.

"Nothing. Repairs will be made, but we must get everyone to the synagogue. It's pressurized with emergency atmosphere."

Whole families poured out of houses, parents shouting to their children.

"To the temple! To the temple!" Farachachdela called to them. "But don't run—you'll use up your air."

A confused mass rushed to the synagogue. There were
people Farachachdela hadn't seen for months: Yudel
Chaim and his family, old Pishalev in his wheelchair—
everyone. Free-spirited children ran alongside the crowd,
despite Farachachdela's instructions.

In no time the whole colony had gathered in the basement of the synagogue. All the husbands and wives of
Mishnim, the little children clutching pets, the wise old
men like graying birds, sat on opposite sides of the room,
Farachachdela on one side, Tzadeka on the other. The
doors were sealed, cutting off the outside. Even the
honking-goose signal could no longer be heard. Some of the
children started crying.

"We've been hit by a small meteroid, but we are safe,"
Farachachdela began, getting up. "Our emergency atmosphere is stored here—not to mention we're in the temple,
which is like being held in the palm of the Lord Himself!"

The children stopped crying immediately.

"Outside, the air pressure will drop a little," Farachachdela continued. "Not much—about the same as if we
climbed a mountain on Earth. A ship has already picked
up the signal. In a few hours it will repair the damage and
the atmosphere will be restored to normal."

Tzadeka watched from a wicker chair on the opposite
side of the room.

Farachachdela held his hands in a graceful gesture. "We
have a reasonable time. The rules for this situation are
based on the need to conserve air supply. Take it easy, no
hard work, no fires. Rest, rest—" Farachachdela waved at
them to rest.

Zlotkin came up to him, smiling. He towered over Farachachdela and placed a hand on his shoulder. "This is just
like the Sabbath. Same rules, eh?"

Farachachdela smiled. "Like the Sabbath. Nothing to
worry about."

Everyone in the room seemed to relax. Even Tzadeka
laughed, and held out his hand as if to catch an imaginary
drop of water from the ceiling. But Farachachdela's blood
pressure flushed his face, and his eyes reddened. He
counted on his fingertips, and in a moment he said, "Outside, it's just after sundown. By the old calendar, it *is* the
Sabbath."

Tzadeka watched him carefully.

"It took a sign—a messenger from the heavens!" Fara-chachdela knocked himself in the head and did a little dance. Then he started to quake all over like a bowl of chicken fat. Tears rolled down his full cheeks and into his beard like diamonds melting.

"I was wrong . . ." he whimpered in Tzadeka's direction. "It *is* the Sabbath. Forgive me."

Tzadeka stood without his canes as Farachachdela approached him. "I, too, was wrong," Tzadeka insisted. "I was wrong to make such a point of it. We should have known, Farachachdela, that it is *how* the days are observed, not *when*." Tzadeka held his arm above them all. "As it is written, when two friends argue, both are wrong. But you were right in one thing. The Talmud says to follow the phases of the Moon, and we shall!"

The tzaddiks embraced. Around the room, people wept and hugged one another. Nezin, Zlotkin, and Rishbam ben Jachai said, "Amen!"

Farachachdela even nudged Tzadeka's sore toe a little, but Tzadeka only winced, laughing. "In heaven, too—in heaven, too—it happens!"

Within hours, a ship had docked and repaired the hole in the ceiling. From that day on, the two tzaddiks were reconciled. Peace was restored to the Chasidic world floating between Earth and the Moon. The colony went on the new calendar, according to the Talmud, and when candles burned on Sabbath nights, their flames were miniature stars, and in every house in Mishnim there was joy. ✡

Identity Crisis

James P. Hogan

"There he is!"

"Marty, Marty!"

"That's him!"

The group of young people who had been waiting around the main lobby of the Toronto Hilton converged in an excited flurry of brandished autograph books and pictures around the figure coming out of one of the elevators. Marty Hayes forced his five-foot-five body to stand firm in the face of the possible threat to his physical well-being and stared at them mournfully through his thick-rimmed spectacles with the hang-dog look that had made him famous. "Hey, easy does it, kids," he cautioned as he penned his name nervously across one of the books. "I can't stand being crowded. It plays hell with my claustrophobia."

"You don't have claustrophobia," a grinning, red-headed boy chided. "We know that's not for real."

"It's real," Marty said as he thrust a signed photograph back at a well-endowed blond girl who was gazing at him rapturously. "My young brother used to have to put together my easy-to-make presents for me. That was how my inferiority complex started. I've had a morbid fear of Father Christmas ever since."

"We enjoyed the show last night," another girl said as she passed him a pen. "Do you know when you'll be doing another week up here?"

"It depends on my doctor. He told me that I shouldn't take anything to excess, even moderation. I always had this feeling that too much health was bad for you."

"So when are you going back home to Los Angeles?" another inquired. "Will you be spending any extra time here now your run's through?"

"I have to go back tomorrow . . . I think. I'm not sure.

I get depressed if I try and plan too far ahead. My doctor said he thought I ought to rest because he thought I had a heart condition. When I asked if I could have a second opinion, he said maybe it was a hernia." As Marty signed the last of the autographs, he caught sight of the broad, rotund figure of his manager, Abe Fennerwitz, standing outside the door of the coffee shop, his tanned scalp reflecting the light between the two patches of wrinkly hair that surmounted his ears. Abe was wearing a tartan jacket and chewing the unlit butt of a cigar. Marty gave an almost imperceptible nod to the hotel security man who was hovering discreetly in the background near the elevators.

The security man moved forward and began ushering the fans firmly but good-naturedly back into the center of the lobby. "Okay, people—I guess we have to call it a day, huh? Mr. Hayes has a busy schedule this morning. It was nice seeing you all, but time's getting on."

"Thanks, Marty."

"It was nice talking to you."

"Come back to Canada soon."

Marty watched solemnly as they moved away through the main doors, then relaxed and strolled across the lobby to join Abe. "I only just woke up," he said. "Wow, a week like that takes it out of you. You had breakfast?"

Abe nodded. He waved in the direction of the main entrance. "You just get mugged?"

"They're okay. It's a pity you can't give 'em more time after they've hung around half the morning, but once they start they'll tie you up all day."

"As long as you're happy." Abe's brow creased into furrows, and his manner became more businesslike. "Look, Marty, we've got a problem with Karlson. I got a call from him personally about an hour ago. He's not gonna be able to make it here this afternoon to talk about the deal. He's got some family problems or something down in Texas, and he had to go there right away. He doesn't know how long it might take."

"Do you think he might have changed his mind or something?" Marty asked, sounding worried.

Abe shook his head. "Uh-uh. I think it's genuine enough. He was very upset and apologetic about it." He shrugged. "I guess we'll just have to set up a meeting again for some other time. He's due out on the West Coast sometime in the next two weeks. We can fix it for then. Don't worry about it. The deal will go through."

Marty sighed and tossed up his hands in resignation. "Oh, well, I suppose there's not much else we can do. So what else do we have fixed for today?"

"Nothing that I can't take care of on my own," Abe told him. "You've been burning it at both ends this week. It's time you put some credit back into your domestic account."

"What do you mean?" Marty asked.

Abe's expression brightened a shade, and he clapped Marty amiably on the shoulder. "Go get some breakfast, then go upstairs and pack your things, and then get the hell out of here. Take an extra day off and spend it with that pretty wife of yours. Have dinner out somewhere with her tonight and buy her some nice flowers from me. Charge 'em to the firm."

Marty frowned for a second and looked as if he were about to object, then thought better of it. "Well . . . if you're sure that's okay, Abe. I guess it would sure . . ." He began nodding enthusiastically as he warmed to the idea. "That'd be just great! So . . . I'll see you again when?"

"I'll be back in L.A. tomorrow as scheduled. I'll get in touch."

"As long as you're sure it wouldn't—"

"Shut up, Marty. Just get the hell outa here."

A little over two hours later, Marty Hayes was looking down at the green and yellow checkerboard pattern of Nebraska from a Noram Airlines hypersonic DC-16 streaking westward at one hundred fifty thousand feet; he was savoring the feeling of satisfaction and euphoria that comes with the knowledge that work is over for the time being, and the relaxation ahead has been well-earned. One of the drawbacks of being a celebrity was that whenever he traveled on business he had to go as himself, which meant having to endure the hassles of airports and taxicabs that had once been a bane in everyone's life. Whenever circumstances permitted, he preferred going Arabee, which took no time at all and required only a minimum of local moving around. But most of the time he was obliged to join the ranks of those who, for various reasons, either chose or were forced to use more traditional methods of travel. At least, he reflected philosophically, it meant that he was doing his bit to help keep the airlines in business.

If that was a drawback, it was minor compared to the pleasures that came with the success which life had bestowed in return. As a boy growing up on the West Side of New York, he had rapidly discovered his spastic lack of coordination in the gymnasium and on the athletic field, and that in class he could interchange French verbs with differential operators without altering the perceptible meaning of either. In all things practical he had proved an equally dismal failure, and it had seemed at times that Nature had selected him to be its visible, walking proof of the Second Law of Thermodynamics by increasing the entropy, suddenly and catastrophically, of everything he touched.

For many troubled years he had resented and fought against being laughed at, but later on the realization slowly dawned on him that people liked to laugh. It made them feel good. And when he laughed with them instead of being defensive, they liked having him around. He soon had lots of friends and went to lots of parties. People told him that he had talent. And so, eventually, humor had become his profession, and over the years he had cultivated and perfected his own unique brand. And then, two years previously, the girl of his dreams had appeared out of nowhere in the form of a reporter for a national women's magazine, sent on a special assignment to do a cover-story interview with him. For heaven-alone-knew what reason, she had fallen in love with him, and he and Alice were married five months later. Yes indeed, Marty Hayes thought to himself as he gazed contentedly down over the Midwest, after something of a precarious start, life hadn't treated him so badly at all.

Alice hadn't been at her office when he called just before leaving the hotel. The answering computer had advised him that she was out on an assignment and had not logged in a rerouting number. Marty fished his compad from his jacket pocket and tried calling her again, but received the same message. No doubt she was interviewing or something and didn't want calls coming in on her own unit, he presumed. He tried calling home but got the same response from the domestic computer there. Not to worry, he thought. He'd make it a surprise—a fitting prelude to a cozy dinner for two somewhere tonight. While he was still connected, he accessed the autochef and tapped in an instruction for a hot snack and some coffee to be ready when he arrived at home, then he cut the call, snapped shut the lid of the compad, and slipped the unit back into his pocket.

At the airport he was stopped by a couple who recognized him and asked for his autograph. They had been married that morning and were on their way to Japan for a honeymoon. The encounter put Marty in an even more romantic frame of mind, and he hummed happily to himself as an aircab carried him above the Los Angeles suburbs toward his home in Newport Beach.

Marty set his suitcase down in the hallway, unslung his jacket from his shoulder, and draped it across the back of the chair standing at the foot of the stairs. He straightened up and looked around. The house was neat and tidy, and didn't appear to be very occupied. "Alice, surprise!" he called, just to be sure. "I'm back. Is anybody home?" There was no response. He went through into the kitchen, where a message on the screen of the monitor panel told him that his snack was ready and waiting. The time was not yet two o'clock, which would give him perhaps four hours to program an afternoon of music and relax with a good book before Alice came home. Or maybe he would call up the recordings of his Toronto performances from the Datanet and review them in privacy. Either way his afternoon sounded good. He began whistling tunelessly to himself as he walked out of the kitchen and went upstairs to freshen up.

Just as he was about to turn on the cold-water faucet in the bathroom, his eyes wandered downward to the bottom of the sink. He stopped whistling abruptly and stared. Around the drain, evidently deposited as the water ran away when the sink was last emptied, was a faint ring of black granules. Marty frowned at the residue for a few seconds while his mind refused to take in what it meant. It looked suspiciously like the shavings from a man's beard. He licked his lips nervously and tried to tell himself that he was overreacting. Alice probably just washed something in the sink, he decided. It wasn't what it looked like. But already his hand was moving to open the door of the wall-closet. He gulped hard and stood there, stunned. On the lowermost of the glass shelves inside, standing in a small cluster away from all the other, familiar things, were a safety razor, a can of foam, and a bottle of after-shave lotion. They weren't his.

"It's her brother from San Francisco," he muttered aloud to himself. "He showed up unexpectedly again. Or maybe one of the guys from back East is in town." But even as his mouth was mumbling its rationalizations, his feet were rushing him out into the passageway and along to the door of the guest-room. He flung it open and tore in. There was nothing—no bags by the bed or in the closet, no clothes in any of the drawers, and no clean linen beneath the counterpane. He came back out into the passageway, marched stiffly along to the door of the master bedroom, grasped the handle firmly, and entered.

A yawning pit opened up somewhere deep down in his stomach. The bed hadn't been made. It looked as if a whole football team had run amok in it. A man's blazer—dark brown with distinctive brass buttons and a lion's-head pin in the lapel—was thrown untidily across one of the chairs, and there was a crumpled white shirt underneath it on the seat. Draped over the blazer was a necktie with yellow and brown diagonal stripes, and a triangular motif offset to one side near the tip. A man's leather traveling bag stood by one of the walls behind a pair of tan leather shoes. And there were a few short, dark hairs on the pillows; Alice's was long and fair.

Five minutes later, dazed and bewildered, Marty came back downstairs, went into the kitchen, and consigned his snack directly from the autochef to the incinerator. Then he headed for the living room to pour a long, stiff drink with shaking hands, then slumped down into an armchair to read again the information that he had copied onto a scrap of paper from the hotel registration slip in the inside pocket of the brown blazer. It was from the Sheraton in Glendale, and confirmed that a Mr. Frank Vicenzo had a reservation from Friday the sixteenth, which was today, to Saturday the twenty-fourth. His room number was 494. There had been some other pieces of paper with various notes and phone numbers written on them, but they had meant nothing to Marty.

He downed half of his drink in one gulp and gnawed at his knuckle in an attempt to stop his body from shivering while he forced himself to think. His initial shock was giving way to anger, and he found himself growing impatient to confront them and mentally rehearsing what he would do. He would not humiliate himself in front of another man by allowing his hurt to show. A display of rage and indignation to see the expressions on their faces as they walked in . . . but what if Vicenzo were sneering and unrepentant or Alice unmoved? Perhaps he would show contempt by walking out in silent dignity and leave them to their shame. They might laugh at him instead. Slowly the cold, sickening realization came over him that he couldn't handle the situation . . . at least not here, today, like this. He needed more time to think it through, and they could come back at any minute. He had to talk to somebody to clear his head. After a few minutes of agonized pacing back and forth across the room, he picked up the compad from the coffee table and hammered in Abe's personal call-code. A few seconds went by. Then the miniature screen came to life to reveal Abe's features.

"Yeah?" Abe's expression changed abruptly to one of recognition. "Marty, what gives? Hey, you look worried. Something up?"

"Lots . . ." Marty was surprised to hear his voice choking from somewhere near the back of his throat. "Abe, I've got problems. I need to talk to you."

Abe's face became serious. "What?"

"I can't go into it right now. Can you get back to L.A. tonight?"

"Tonight?" Abe frowned. "Well, I did have plans for seeing a coupla guys for dinner, but I could put it off. If it's really that—"

"It is. I wouldn't ask you if it wasn't important. I'm going to check into . . ." Marty thought for a moment. ". . . the Palm Ridge in Santa Monica tonight. Can you get an early evening flight and meet me there?" Abe never went Arabee.

"The Palm Ridge?" Abe looked surprised and confused. "You're supposed to be home tonight. What in hell—"

"I can't explain now. It's all a mess. Look, I've got to go. Can you be there?"

Abe hesitated, digested the urgency in Marty's voice, and nodded. "Okay. I'll try and make it there around eight. Are you sure you can't tell me what this is all about?"

"Not now," Marty told him. "Thanks a lot, Abe. I'll talk to you later."

Marty cut the connection and used the compad again to call an aircab. After that he rinsed and dried his glass, replaced it below the bar, and returned to the hallway just as the falling whine of an engine-note from outside told him that his cab had arrived. He slung his jacket over his shoulder, picked up his suitcase, and let himself out the front door.

"Hell, I don't know what to say," Abe murmured awkwardly across a booth in the cocktail lounge of the Palm Ridge Hotel later that night. "Alice? . . ." He made a helpless gesture. "I'd never have believed it. It's easy to talk when it isn't you, so I'm not gonna say a goddamn thing. It happens. Most people survive. What else is there to say?"

"So what happens now?" Marty asked miserably.

Abe took a swig of beer and wiped his mouth with the back of his hand. "I'm not sure, but I think you were right to get out when you did. Sure, you could have stuck around and made a scene, but from a long-term point of view that wouldn't have been so smart. This way they don't know that you know, and it gives you time to get organized. Are you going to want out?"

The reality had by this time percolated through, and Marty could only nod morosely at his drink. "I wouldn't even want to live there any more, Abe," he said. "I had that house built for her, just the way she wanted . . . You know that." He shook his head disbelievingly. "In my own house. It doesn't make sense. If something was wrong, why didn't she talk about it? She always came across like she was on top of the world."

"It happens," Abe said again with a sigh. "Nothing's gonna change it." He studied his thumbnail for a second and used it to prise a piece of pretzel from his tooth. "What you have to do is snap out of feeling too sorry for yourself and start thinking about the practical side." Marty looked up but said nothing. Abe bunched his lips for a second, then spread his hands and explained. "I hate to say this, Marty, but you have to face facts. You're worth a lot of dollars these days, and in this kind of situation you could get burned bad no matter who's right or who's wrong. If you don't act smart, you could wind up getting ripped off on top of everything else."

"What are you saying?"

Abe looked solemn. "I know this is asking a lot, but I don't want you to do anything until we've got some hard facts and I've had a chance to talk to the lawyers. We have to know who this bum is, where he's from, how long he's been around, and all kinds of things like that. Right now it's your word against hers, and a compromise settlement could cost you an arm and both legs. For all we know, they might be fixing to set you up for just something like that." He paused while Marty grimaced at the thought, then went on. "Stay here tonight, go home tomorrow, and act natural, just as if nothing happened. It's tough, but you don't wanna let any of your hand show just yet. First thing on Monday I'll talk to the lawyers, and we'll see then how we play it from there. Believe me, I've seen this kind of situation before, and what I'm saying is for the best. Will you do that?"

Marty clenched his teeth, drew a long breath, and nodded resignedly. "Order us some more drinks, Abe," he said.

It was three A.M. when Marty eventually stumbled along to his room and fell into bed fully anesthetized. Even so he had a lousy night and woke up feeling lousier. He didn't call Alice to say what time he'd be back, and instructed his compad to reroute any incoming calls into Datanet storage for retrieval later.

Alice lowered her book a fraction and studied Marty quizzically over the top of it for the umpteenth time that evening. Marty pretended not to be conscious of her and kept his eyes riveted on the movie that he had called up onto the large wallscreen in the living room. The movie was about a political family and their intrigues back in the 1980's, or something like that. Marty wasn't all that interested. He had put it on to give himself something to look at while he tormented himself with fantasies of the person who had been in his home forty-eight hours previously. Somehow Alice was managing to act calmly and with composure, as if everything were normal. It was inhuman.

"Marty, are you sure you're feeling all right?" she asked again. He grunted. Alice waited for a moment, then shook her head despairingly. "But you've hardly said a word since you came home. You haven't told me how the show went in Toronto or anything. Something's the matter. Didn't it go too well?"

Marty forced himself to look at her. She looked fresh and pretty in a loose orange blouse and white slacks, her long waves of blond hair tumbling in a soft cascade around her shoulders. The slacks were thin and tight, emphasizing the curves of her hips and thighs as she lounged back along the couch. Her pose made her look sexy and him feel worse. Act natural, Abe had advised. Right at that moment Abe was probably out somewhere, sitting down to a T-bone steak. Marty felt he could cheerfully have beaten Abe's brains to pulp. He tried to smile, but the effort fizzled out somewhere on its way to his face. Instead he tossed up a hand wearily and shifted his weight uncomfortably in his chair. "Aw . . . things went okay. It was a rough week. Maybe I've just had it. I'll get over it."

Alice waited for him to say more, but he lapsed into silence again and looked back at the screen. "Why don't you take a nice hot shower and get to bed early and rest?" she suggested. "I'll be fine for the evening reading this. It's quite good." An impish smile came onto her face. "I could wake you up later."

Marty swallowed hard. What new adventures did she want to relive? His imagination went into overdrive, and he had to squeeze the arms of his chair hard to keep control of himself. Act natural, he told himself. It's important. "I dunno . . ." he mumbled. "I don't feel all that good. Maybe I picked up a bug somewhere. I'll be okay."

"Then you really should get yourself to bed," Alice urged. "It's probably just nervous tension. How about it? A good night's sleep and you'll be as good as new in the morning."

"Just leave me alone!" Despite himself, Marty was unable to keep the harsh edge out of his voice. "I said I'll be okay." Hurt and indignation flashed in Alice's eyes. Marty slumped back and forced an apologetic tone. "I, er . . . I didn't mean it like that. It's okay . . . I'll be all right here."

Alice set her book down and looked at him for a few seconds. At last she gave an exasperated sigh. "I don't know what's got into you, Marty, but there doesn't seem to be much that I can do about it." She paused as if wondering whether or not to pursue the matter. Then she said, "I was going to wait until you got into a better mood, but you don't look as if you're going to. There's something I have to tell you." She swung her feet off the couch and sat up to look directly at him.

Marty went numb, unable to believe his ears. So calmly and dispassionately, she could bring it up like this? What kind of a woman was she? Had he been as completely blind as that? He lifted his chin an inch by way of reply and at the same time felt a gnawing, sinking feeling of dread taking hold deep inside. His mind was racing ahead and trying to decide how he would react, but nothing coherent would form in the confusion boiling in his head.

"I don't know if you knew, but the American Bioengineering Society is having its annual conference here next week," Alice said. "Margaret at the office wants me to cover it for a special-feature issue next month."

Marty blinked and shook his head uncomprehendingly. "So . . . what's the problem? Why ask me?"

"Because a lot of the functions and lectures will run late into the evening, and there will be social events even later after that," she replied. "To cover that kind of thing, you really have to be there all the time. So the office wants me to check in there for the duration." She smiled. "In other words, just when you get back, I have to take off, that's all. It's a shame, but I'll make it up. You don't mind, do you?"

Marty exhaled a long, quiet breath of relief. Things would probably be a lot better with her out of the way, he thought to himself. He nodded and did his best to look enthusiastic. "Sure, that's no problem at all. You go ahead. When does the meeting start?"

Alice bit her lip. "Well, actually . . . tomorrow. It runs through until next Saturday—the twenty-fourth. I'll be back that night. You can always call if you need me for anything. It's being held at the Sheraton Glendale."

It took a moment for what she had said to register. "Where?" Marty asked hoarsely.

"Glendale, the Sheraton. You know . . . the big place up behind the Rainbow Tower."

"You want to stay at the Sheraton Glendale next week?"

"Yes. That's where the conference is. What's wrong with that?"

"And you want to stay through to the twenty-fourth?"

Alice smiled sheepishly. "Well, actually the office has already made the reservation. You don't mind, do you, Marty? Marty, you've turned as white as a ghost! I didn't think you'd feel that way about it, honestly. But I can't go and let them down now that it's this late, can I?"

Marty stared back at her with glazed eyes and shook his head woodenly. "No, I guess not," he heard himself say. There wasn't a lot else he could do.

That night he slept in the guest-room. He told Alice it was because he had a temperature and a headache. His fans would have applauded.

"Coincidence, hell!" Marty retorted derisively over lunch at the Mardis Gras restaurant the next day. "It was the same hotel and the same dates. What do you take me for, Abe? Do you think I dreamed the rest or something?"

Abe looked up from a plate of spaghetti and meatballs. "Of course not. But the reason I said you had to play it cool was to get facts, not to start inventing fiction."

"Like hell it's fiction."

"You don't know that, Marty. You gotta admit that the gene-freaks are having a conference there next week. And it is the kind of assignment you'd expect Alice to get. And it's not unusual for people assigned to that kind of thing to be around for the duration. So what she said all adds up."

"It all adds up too much," Marty agreed scathingly. He stared at the shrubs growing in pots to one side of the table. "And to think I just stood there this morning like some kind of ass and watched her fly off in the cab. I even told her to have a good time! Can you beat that? What kind of guy stands there watching his wife walk out to go swinging for a week and tells her to have a good time? So help me, Abe, you'd better be right about this being for the best, or else I'm going to be looking around for a new manager."

Abe considered the statement stoically while he munched on a piece of garlic bread. "Did you call the Sheraton to see if she's booked in under her own name?" he asked.

Marty pulled a face. "What's the point?" he demanded. "I'm not going to get mixed up with playing games like that. Anyhow that wouldn't tell us a thing. Alice isn't stupid. She could have taken a room, sure, but never be there and just collect messages from the desk instead . . .

something like that." He fiddled over his coffee with a packet of sugar. It burst and showered sugar everywhere but in the cup. "They've got it all set up. She's there with a legitimate cover, and Vicenzo breezes in, rents a room, and makes it a nice, cozy togetherness week for two. And you say act natural. Jesus, Abe, I swear that if you'd been there last night I would have strangled you."

"The evidence is all circumstantial," Abe said, ignoring the remark. "She's there because the conference is there and she's got a job to do. Like you say, she's probably got a reservation to keep things straight. So this Vicenzo jerk happens to be there too. So what? What have we got that would mean anything in court? Nothing. We still need facts."

"Christ, Abe, what more facts do you want? He was at the house, and they're staying at the same hotel together. Do you expect them to mail me a blue movie or something?"

"We don't *know* they're there *together*," Abe pointed out. "Okay, he was at the house, but we still don't know who he is or anything about him. If you started turning on the heat now he'd simply go to ground, and then you wouldn't have a goddamn thing you could prove. All you could do would be to file for a regular split, the settlement would be fifty-fifty, and she'd walk away clean with armfuls of your money. Do like I say and sit tight for now. Sooner or later they'll blow it, and then you'll have facts. That's when you move."

Marty fumed and pummeled his napkin into a ball. "Dammit, Abe, what facts are we going to get sitting here talking like this? The facts aren't here, they're there. Do you expect me to sit on my ass for a whole week while this is going on? You're out of your mind. Can't you get it into your head that I need to *do* something?"

Abe shrugged, his fork poised halfway to his mouth. "What can you do?"

Marty heaved a deep breath and glowered down at the table. Abe watched in silence while he finished the last of his meal. At last Marty looked up. "I'll go there," he declared. "That's the place to be to find out whether she's in with him or not, not here or anywhere else. And if he's there and not anywhere else, then that's the place to find out who the hell he is." He nodded decisively. "That's what

I'm going to do. *I'll* check into the Sheraton too. Why don't we make it a real party?"

"Now, you're outa your mind," Abe said, looking alarmed. "I know it's a strain, but you don't have to flip all the way. Hasn't it occurred to you that your own wife just might recognize you? And with all the people that are gonna be at the Sheraton next week, she might see you before you see her. Then Vicenzo would be out of town inside an hour, and you'd never track him down. You don't even know what he looks like."

A strange light was creeping into Marty's eyes. "I didn't say I'd go as me," he replied. "Who says I can't go Arabee?"

Abe blinked at him. "What?"

"Arabee. I'll rent an Arabee and use that." Marty shrugged. "It's simple."

Abe frowned, started to say something, then changed his mind and thought about it. He fished a handkerchief from his pocket and dabbed perspiration off his head. "It might work," he conceded grudgingly. He returned the handkerchief to his pocket, picked up a toothpick, thought about it some more, and nodded. "Who knows? You might dig up something. What's to lose?"

"In fact I might just make it an outsize model and beat the hell out of the bum," Marty said, licking his lips and showing his teeth as he savored the thought.

"You get any damfool thought like that outa your head straight away," Abe told him in an alarmed voice. "This thing's complicated enough already as it is. You keep to one that's your own size, and that way you won't be likely to do anything stupid. If . . ." His voice trailed away as a new thought struck him. He sat back, cocked his head to one side, and looked at Marty thoughtfully.

"I wasn't really serious about that," Marty said, raising a hand. "But wouldn't . . . Why are you looking at me like that, Abe?"

"There's a problem with it," Abe said.

"What kind of problem?"

"You." Abe sat forward, spreading his hands palms-upward on the table, and explained. "You're unique. Your gestures, mannerisms, actions . . . they're like a signature. You've been perfecting them for twenty years. They're a part of you now. You use them unconsciously even when you're not on-stage. Alice would know you a mile off no matter what kind of Arabee you used."

"You're exaggerating," Marty said. "Not in the middle of all those people. And it's not as if she'd be looking for me, is it?"

"Maybe, but can we risk it?"

Marty threw out his hands helplessly. His voice rose. "I don't know, Abe. What other way is there? What I do know is that there's no way I'm going to sit on my ass in that house for a week and do nothing. Okay, so maybe she recognizes me. That's too bad." He thrust out his chin defiantly. "Yeah, I say we risk it. I say we have to risk it."

"Maybe we don't . . . at least not to that degree," Abe answered. There was a curious note in his voice. He looked at Marty thoughtfully again. "Maybe there is another way."

Marty eyed him suspiciously. "What other way?" he asked.

"Don't make it a 'he' Arabee at all," Abe said. "Make it a 'she.'"

Marty gaped across the table. "And you told me *I* was crazy?"

"No, I'm serious. Look, when you—"

"No way, Abe." Marty held up his hands protectively. "There's no way in this world that I'm—"

"Hear me out, willya?" Abe interrupted in an earnest voice. "Think about it. It makes a lotta sense. One, it would guarantee you stay outa trouble. Two, Alice would never make the connection in a million years. The idea was good, but it had risks. This way we get rid of the risks. It has to be a better deal."

Marty shook his head vigorously. "Abe, forget it."

"It's nothing to worry about," Abe insisted. "Freaks do it all the time for kicks. The Arabee people are used to it. They don't care. And you could be saving yourself thousands . . . hundreds of thousands. It has to be worth it."

"The answer is no," Marty told him firmly. "Definitely, finally, absolutely, no way, never. I won't do it. For the last time, forget it."

Unperturbed, Abe finished using the toothpick and tossed it into an ashtray. He brought his hands together on the table and interlaced his fingers in front of him. "Now let's go through this again and talk about it rationally," he suggested.

Late that afternoon Marty was standing in a corner of the reception foyer, as far from the desk as possible, of the Los Angeles area branch office of Remote Activated Biovehicles, Inc., or R.A.B., popularly known as "Arabee." He felt ridiculous in the false mustache, hat, and dark glasses that Abe had insisted on, and wanted to get the whole thing over with, but the customer talking in lowered tones to the clerk at the desk seemed to have sprouted roots there. The other clerk, who seemed unoccupied and was reading a paper a short distance back behind the counter, had mercifully refrained from pestering Marty with offers to be of assistance, but this didn't make Marty feel any less conspicuous and uncomfortable. He kept his back turned toward the desk and pretended to read the posters on the wall for what must have been the fifth time.

Technical matters had never been one of Marty's strengths, and he had never understood fully how the Arabees worked. To use a "Rentabody," you presented yourself at the nearest R.A.B. office, where you lay down on a couch with some kind of neural coupling device around your head. The next thing you knew, you were in another cubicle in New York, Tokyo, or wherever you wanted to be, "inside" another body that was yours for the duration of the trip. An Arabee was not regarded by law as a person, since it was cloned from synthetically produced DNA and did not contain a cerebral cortex or any of the higher mental faculties held to be essential ingredients of personality. It was, in effect, a remote-controlled biological robot, human in physical form and appearance only. All the information collected through its senses was relayed via an electronics package contained in the skull back to where your real body was, and somehow injected directly into your brain; at the same time the signals from your own voluntary nervous system, for example to control movement and speech, were relayed in the opposite direction to complete the loop. Thus you could move around, see, hear, feel, and talk through a body that was thousands of miles away in a way that was indistinguishable from actually being there, and be home in an instant. The method was not suitable for all purposes, of course, but many members of the business community and other classes of habitual globetrotters had found that the majority of their journeys were made simply to put bodies in places where they could assimilate or convey information, and it was much cheaper and faster to bring the information to the bodies instead. And as often happens, once money was involved, hearts and minds hadn't needed a lot of convincing.

At last the customer at the desk concluded his reading aloud of the Los Angeles area phone directory, or whatever he had been doing, and disappeared through one of the doors at the back of the foyer. Marty glanced around furtively to make sure that nobody else had come in, then braced himself and walked stiffly up to the desk. "May I help you, sir?" the clerk inquired.

Marty spread his elbows along the counter and leaned forward to speak without raising his voice. "Yes, er . . . my name is Green. I called earlier this afternoon about a reservation . . . You said it would be ready."

"One moment, Mr. Green." The clerk activated a terminal beside him and turned his head to inspect the information that appeared on the screen. "Ah, yes. Female, white, mid-thirties, class three-B figure and stature, red hair, green eyes. For collection right here and return next Saturday. Is that correct?" Marty winced inwardly and wished the clerk would keep his voice down. The other clerk, however, continued reading his newspaper in the background with no show of interest.

"That's correct," Marty replied. Somehow he was unable to raise more than a whisper. It made him feel like a spy in a bad movie divulging "ze plans." "Er . . . it should be for cash in advance. Nothing to sign. That right?" People didn't cheat with Arabees. True, you had one of their bodies, but then again they had yours.

The clerk checked the screen again. "That's fine, Mr. Green. It comes to five hundred fifty dollars."

"Okay. I've got it right . . . here." Marty reached into his coat and fumbled with the wad of twenties in his inside pocket. The wad caught on a pen, breaking the rubber band around it, and exploded into a cloud of fluttering bills when he wrenched it free. The clerk collected together the ones that had fallen on the counter and watched impassively while Marty scrambled around scooping the rest up off the floor. Marty straightened up hastily and thrust a fistful of notes across, at the same time feeling his mustache working loose. Unruffled, the clerk accepted them and returned a plastic document wallet.

"If you'll go on through to cubicle nine, Mr. Green, everything should be ready," he said. Marty snatched the wallet with one hand, clapped the other to his face, and fled through the door at the rear of the foyer.

"That was Marty Hayes," the clerk at the back murmured without looking up from his paper. "Why didn't you get his autograph?"

"I know." The other shrugged. "What can you do? There must be a weird party on somewhere tonight. The guy who came in just ahead of him was into the same thing."

Marty walked along a corridor flanked by doors on either side and entered the one marked number nine. The cubicle was small, containing just a padded couch on one side and the usual bank of floor-to-ceiling electronics and equipment panels on the other. He ignored the sign inviting him to press the button indicated if he needed instructions and sat down on the edge of the couch. He took a deep breath, composed a silent prayer for Abe to be smitten by indescribable torments and biologically impossible tribulations, then swung his feet up, lay back, and allowed his head to sink into the support provided.

"Everything is ready," a pleasant voice informed him from a speaker somewhere in the room. "Are you set for departure?"

"Go ahead," Marty replied. A few seconds later the biolink helmet swung away from its stowage position above his head and slid smoothly into place.

He was lounging back in an upholstered recliner in a small, cheerfully decorated cubicle with soothing music playing in the background. His hair felt too long, and his legs felt too bare. He looked down. He couldn't see his waist. His chest was sticking out too far behind the thin shirt of silky lilac material that he was wearing, and the legs protruding from the short pink skirt below that seemed . . . obscene somehow. He looked up again hastily and swallowed hard. He raised a hand in front of his face and stared disbelievingly at his slender fingers and tapering red nails.

And then he panicked.

He looked around frantically for some way of communicating to call the whole stupid thing off. There had to be a microphone somewhere, a screen . . . something. He stood up, tried to move, and catapulted himself across the cubicle when his heels wouldn't go down to the floor. To hell with this, to hell with Abe, to hell with . . . He clung to the wall and shook his head to clear it. No, there was no way out. He had to see this through. He straightened up cautiously and tottered back to put on the summer top-coat and pick up the pocketbook that were lying on a side-table by the recliner. Abe would pay for this, he told himself grimly. How, he didn't know, but Abe would pay for every minute of this.

He took a moment to compose himself, then opened the door a fraction and stuck his head out. He was in a corridor similar to the one by which he had entered, but not the same one. A second later one of the doors opposite opened, and a tall blond woman looked out. They gaped at each other, horrified, and slammed the doors shut at the same instant.

Marty's breathing was coming erratically, and his blood was pounding. Pull yourself together, you turkey, he told himself. Nobody cares out there. They've all got their own problems. Get it into your head that nobody's interested. He calmed down, gritted his teeth, and turned again toward the door. The blonde was just disappearing through the swinging-door at the end of the corridor when he stepped out. He waited for a few seconds, then followed to find himself back in the reception foyer. Looking straight ahead and keeping his eyes averted from the desk, he minced across the foyer and walked out onto the plaza, where Abe was supposed to be waiting. Abe wasn't there.

He stopped, puzzled, and looked first one way, then the other. Abe was about ten yards away accosting the blonde. The blonde seemed to recoil in terror, and Marty caught snatches of a stream of obscenities that were most unbecoming for a lady. He closed his eyes and groaned to himself, then cupped a hand to his mouth. "Abe, you asshole," he yelled. "That's not me. I'm here!"

Abe looked around, startled, glanced back at the blonde, and came scampering back along the side of the plaza. He grabbed Marty's arm and hustled him quickly away around a corner and out of sight of the astonished passers-by who had stopped to watch. A short distance farther on they slowed to a more normal pace.

"Get some style into the act," Abe hissed from the corner of his mouth. "You're walking like a gorilla."

"What do you expect, for chrissake? I haven't exactly had a lot of time to practice. Honest to God, I'm gonna make you try this yourself sometime."

"Stop yelling and waving that pocketbook around like that. People will think we're married or something."

"Lay off, willya, Abe. I told you, I'll get the hang of it. Just gimme some time."

They walked on in silence for a short distance. "Did you get your reservation fixed at the Sheraton?" Abe asked.

"Yeah . . . all set. The hotel was all booked up for the conference, but they had a cancellation. I'm booked in as Phyllis Kronberg, Room Seven-three-six."

"Phyllis!" Abe sniggered uncontrollably.

Marty came to a halt and glared at him malevolently. "What's funny?" There was an icy menace in the tone, of the kind that only a female larynx can produce.

Abe moved back a step warily. "Nothing . . . nothing at all." He glanced at his watch and looked around. "We have to get you some more clothes and whatever other junk you'll need for a week. Let's look around in there." He gestured toward a door of Jordan Marsh that opened onto the concourse. Marty marched up to the door and stopped. Abe lurched ahead and held it open dutifully.

An hour later Abe was standing outside the door of the fitting rooms in the Ladies' Dresswear department, clutching an armful of packages and stamping around impatiently. Marty emerged with a pile of dresses and other garments over his arm and dumped them on the wrapping table by the cashier's terminal. The assistant glanced back over her shoulder from where she was just finishing attending to another customer. "I'll be with you in one moment, madam," she called.

Abe put the packages down next to the clothes. "Did you figure out how it all goes together?" he asked in a low voice.

"I'll worry about the finer details later," Marty whispered. "Those look like they fit, which is the main thing." Abe was giving him a funny look. "What's wrong now?"

Abe looked over his shoulder self-consciously, and then

waved a hand vaguely in the direction of Marty's chest. "You're all wrong there. They're not at the same level. You look like a Picasso with drapes."

"There's nothing you can do," Marty hissed back. "I tried. It's those straps and things. There's no way you can make 'em point the same way."

"There's gotta be. How do all the rest manage?"

"How the hell do I know? Maybe their mothers show 'em how." Marty looked around with a start and tried to smile when he realized that the assistant had come over to them and was waiting politely but not without a hint of curiosity.

"And how will madam be paying?" the assistant inquired as she began tallying the purchases.

Marty shot a venomous look at Abe. "Put them on my husband's account."

Abe grabbed his arm and drew him back a pace to whisper imploringly in his ear. "Be sensible about this, you jerk. How can I walk in here with you looking like that and charge a whole wardrobe to my account? I've got a reputation to think about. And suppose it got back to Joanne? How in hell would you expect me to explain that?"

"Don't give me that, Abe. Put it on the firm's tab."

"Why me?" Abe protested. "What about all the bread this is gonna save you?"

The assistant looked tactfully away and busied herself with wrapping the items.

"That's maybe, and only if this works," Marty retorted. "I'm doing all the work, aren't I? Don't tell me you're complaining about having to put a few lousy bucks into it. Are you telling me I'm not worth that much? To listen to you, anybody would think it was gonna hurt or something."

"Okay, okay." Abe motioned to Marty to shut up then felt inside his jacket for his billfold. "You should do just great," he murmured testily. "You're starting to think like a broad already."

The main lobby of the Sheraton Glendale was crowded with regular hotel guests going about their business and groups of conference delegates talking and mingling between sessions. Marty was sitting at a table on a shallow terrace that formed an extension of one of the bars out into the lobby, sipping a martini while he thought about what he was going to do next.

After checking in, he had posed as an old school-friend of Alice's to inquire at the desk where he might find her. He was given room number 1248, which was not Vicenzo's. Since then Marty had called the room several times, intending to dismiss it as a wrong connection if anybody answered, but nobody had. Just what he had been expecting. He had toured the hotel and mixed with the attendees of the various conference functions, but he hadn't seen her anywhere, which seemed to indicate that she had to be in Vicenzo's room, 494. It would have been a simple matter to call there—neither Alice nor Vicenzo would have recognized his face—but for some reason he hadn't been able to do so. Perhaps subconsciously he was trying to put off the moment of truth.

"Do you think you'll enjoy the conference?"

Marty looked up in surprise when he heard the voice. A large, florid-faced man was sitting down in an empty chair on the other side of the table. He was wearing a lapel badge that said he was Dick Williams, and a thinly disguised leer that said Dick Williams was scouting the territory. "Oh, you don't appear to have a name tag," Williams went on, as if he had just noticed. "I thought I saw you at one of the sessions earlier. I must have been mistaken." He looked at Marty expectantly. Presumably Marty was supposed to be curious and ask about the sessions.

"I guess you were," Marty said, and looked away.

"It's the American Bioengineering Society," Williams explained anyway. "It goes on all week. I'm here with an outfit called Calom-Freyn Biodynamics. You may have heard of us . . . we're the second largest in biotronics in the country. Over two billion a year turnover. I run the marketing side of it . . . international." He flipped a peanut into his mouth with his thumb in a way that was presumably meant to look cavalier and roguish. It didn't. He waited a second or two for a response, then took a more direct tack. "What brings you here . . . business, vacation, or what?"

"Oh, er . . . business," Marty said before he had really thought about it.

"Well, it's not all that bad a place. You here for the week?"

"Yes," Marty replied automatically. He began rummaging through the mess in the pocketbook on the chair next to him to find where he had put his cash so he could settle the tab and get out.

Williams was looking more interested. He slipped his left hand casually off the table and onto his lap. "Say, what do you know . . . we're both here for the week. You're very attractive, if you don't mind my saying so, and it is so refreshing to meet a girl who talks sense." Marty wondered what that was supposed to mean, since he hadn't said a damn thing. Williams hesitated for a moment, then added, "I, ah . . . I don't get to meet a lot of company since I got divorced. Er, maybe we could kinda . . . get to know one another just a little while we're here, know what I mean?" He winked meaningfully. Marty glared. Williams held up a hand and looked horrified. "Oh, don't get me wrong. I meant maybe we could get together for dinner or something . . . sometime in the week maybe."

"Maybe," Marty said, trying to squeeze all the interest out of his voice. Even as he spoke he knew he had said the wrong thing.

Williams smiled. "Say, you like the idea. Okay, we'll have to fix something up. I'm in Room Eight-eight-six, just so that you know. What about you?"

Marty swore under his breath. His predicament resolved itself when another man, lean and swarthy, and with a crown of curly locks of oily-looking hair, swayed over to the table and sat down heavily in the chair next to Williams, at the same time clapping Williams heartily across the back. Williams didn't look too pleased about it. "Dick, you old son-of-a-bitch!" the newcomer roared. "So this is where you're hiding, huh? So what's new?" He turned his head toward Marty as if noticing him for the first time. "So aren't you gonna introduce me to your friend?" He shrugged a mock apology across the table and grinned. "I guess he's not. Hi. I'm Larry. Dick'll tell you lots of bad things about me if you let him, but they're not true." He nudged Williams in the ribs and laughed. "That right, Dick? They're not true, are they? You make 'em all up because I always make out and you never do, and you get jealous." He winked across at Marty. "It's okay. He knows I don't mean it. We're great buddies really. That right, Dick?"

Marty looked around frantically for an escape. Out in the lobby a tall, ruggedly handsome man with shoulders like those of a football player still wearing his pads under his suit was striding slowly and purposefully toward the main desk. With the loose throng of people around him, he stood out like a battleship plowing its course majestically through a gaggle of coal barges. "My husband just arrived," Marty said on impulse. "I have to go. It was nice talking to you." He stood up, slammed a five-dollar bill down on the table next to his tab, and hurried from the terrace. Halfway across the lobby he slowed down and glanced back. Williams and Larry were watching him curiously. He looked around again. The dark-haired man was at the main desk, signaling for the attention of one of the clerks. Doing his best to look as if he belonged there, Marty sidled up and stood next to him. From close up the man was even more striking, with a face formed from lean, solid planes, well-formed lips that settled easily and naturally into a flicker of a smile, and dark brown eyes that twinkled and danced elusively. Everything about him said that he should have been in movies, but Marty couldn't place him.

And then he spoke to the clerk in a firm, resonant voice. "My name is Frank Vicenzo, Room Four-nine-four. You have an authorization for me to collect messages for Mrs. A. Hayes. Is there anything?"

"Just a second, Mr. Vicenzo." The clerk checked the pigeonholes behind the desk, took out some message slips, and passed them across.

"Thank you." Vicenzo inspected the messages briefly, then folded them and tucked them into an inside pocket of his suit, and walked away.

Marty almost died. Vicenzo was heading in the direction of the elevators, which meant he had to be going up to his room. And he had taken Alice's messages. That meant Alice had to be there too. Without really knowing what he was trying to accomplish or why, Marty tightened his grip on his pocketbook and hurried across the lobby after Vicenzo. Williams and Larry were still watching him with puzzled looks, but he didn't care about them any longer

He emerged on the fourth floor in a bay that opened out to corridors leading to guest-rooms on both sides. The wall of the corridor to the right carried a sign indicating Rooms

452 to 498, and Marty went that way. As he turned the corner into the corridor his heart skipped a beat. Vicenzo was a short distance in front of him, striding toward the far end, where the higher room numbers were located. Marty followed him breathlessly, finding that he almost had to run to keep up. Vicenzo stopped outside 494 and rapped twice on the door. He paused, evidently listening to something from inside which Marty couldn't hear, and then said in a loud voice, "It's me—Frank." He stepped back a pace to wait and looked casually back along the corridor. Marty turned toward the nearest door and started searching through his pocketbook as if he were looking for his key.

"It's never where you were sure you put it, is it?" Vicenzo called along the corridor. Marty looked up, startled. Vicenzo was smiling good-humoredly. Marty was too flustered to do anything but shake his head mutely and force the corners of his mouth to twitch upward. He was trying to smile. This wasn't real.

The door in front of Vicenzo opened. Vicenzo grinned at somebody inside and stepped through. The door closed. Instinctively Marty rushed up to it but came to his senses just in time to stop himself from pounding on it with his fists. With an effort he pulled himself together sufficiently to go back to his own room and down three straight Scotches one after the other. Then he called Abe.

Abe told Marty he was doing a good job and to keep working on it. Marty told Abe he was going to get drunk. He couldn't, Abe said. It didn't work with Arabees. Marty said that Abe didn't know what he was talking about; in fact Marty was beginning to feel drunk already. The power of suggestion, Abe said. Alcohol depressed the higher brain functions, and it couldn't work if the bloodstream with the alcohol was in one place, and the brain whose higher functions needed to be depressed was someplace else. Marty told Abe he was talking through his ass.

"You have to keep working at it," Abe insisted. "I just talked to Sam, and he says you gotta have witnesses. He's gonna show up there later on in the week and bring a photographer, but not until you've established the setup. I mean, for a start, have you actually seen her there yet."

"No," Marty told him. "But she's checked in here, she hasn't been in her room, and that Adonis creep's collecting her messages. What else do you want?"

"You need to see her there, with him, and you need witnesses who'll say you saw them," Abe replied. "Keep at it, Marty. You're doing great. The sooner you can give us the setup, the sooner we can get Sam in and you out."

Marty thought it over after Abe had hung up. Alice was definitely there in the hotel now, it seemed, whether she had been earlier in the evening or not. Possibly she and Vicenzo had been out for the afternoon, which meant there was a good chance that they would be around from now on, maybe to have a drink or to get something to eat. One thing was certain—Marty wouldn't find them together if he stayed in his room. He showered, unpacked the undies that he had bought earlier, and after spending some time figuring out what went on top of what, finally fought his way into a new outfit. Then he went downstairs again to have a drink at one of the other bars.

The only vacant barstool was next to a thin man with a neatly trimmed ginger beard who soon started trying to make conversation. Marty told him in no uncertain terms to get lost, and for the next fifteen minutes they ignored each other. Then the man asked the bartender for his check and showed his room key as he signed it. The room number was 494. He signed his name, B. L. Tyson, and then left.

Marty sat there nonplused. What in hell was going on? If Tyson was booked into 494, then maybe he had opened the door for Vicenzo. But if Tyson and Vicenzo were sharing 494, where was Alice? Perhaps she was staying in her own room, 1248, after all. Marty decided he had to know the answer to that. He finished his drink, paid the check, and went to a house phone to call 1248. There was no reply.

He paced around for a while wondering what to do. When he came into the main lobby, he noticed that a night clerk had taken over at the desk from the one who had been on duty earlier. This gave Marty an idea. He walked up to the desk, inflated his chest, and smiled across sweetly. "I have a small problem," he crooned at the clerk. "Do you think you could help me?"

The clerk's eyes widened with approval. "If I can, ma'am. What's the problem?"

"I've been silly and locked my key up in my room. Do you have a duplicate that I could borrow, by any chance . . . just for a minute?"

"Which room is it?"

"Twelve-forty-eight. The name is Hayes—Mrs. A. Hayes."

"Sure," the clerk replied. "I just need to see some ID."

Marty pouted. "I thought you might say that. That's the problem. All my papers and everything are in there too. I really don't want to have to start calling people and bothering them this late at night." He fluttered his eyelashes and lowered his voice to a husky, seductive whisper. "Come on, you look like a nice guy. You can trust me."

"Well . . . I don't know . . ." The clerk looked worried. "It's against the rules. You could get me into a lot of trouble."

"Who's going to tell anyone?" Marty said, winking. "You don't even have to give it to me. You could leave it lying on the desk there accidentally and be looking the other way. If anyone asks, I'll just say I took it."

The clerk slipped the key quickly across the counter. "Not more than five minutes," he murmured.

"You're really a sweetie," Marty whispered. "I knew it."

He went up to the twelfth floor, found Room 1248, and waited after tapping loudly several times. There was no answer, and no sound of any kind from within. Marty took a long breath, pushed the key into the lock, let himself in, and switched on the light. The room had not been touched. There were no bags, clothes, or any signs of occupation. A sick, sinking feeling slowly took hold of him as the final glimmer of hope that he had been nursing without realizing it at last faded away. He turned out the light, closed the door, and went down to the lobby to return the key.

So what did it all mean? The only other place that Alice could be was in 494. But two men were also booked into that room. He stopped dead in his tracks halfway across the lobby and went cold as a new thought struck him. Two men and . . . ? Surely not. Not *that*. He found himself shaking. Anything could happen in California. He had said that to enough people himself. For the next few minutes he seemed to be in a haze, not knowing where he was going or what he was doing until he found himself coming out of an elevator on the fourth floor once again. He turned to the right and moved mechanically into the corridor to stand staring along toward where Room 494 was situated. He wasn't really sure why he had come back here or what he was going to do next, but somehow he had to know what was going on in that room.

A small group of men was standing around outside the door of one of the rooms near him, drinking beer from cans and talking loudly. The door was open, and the sound of lots of raised voices punctuated by shouts and laughs was coming from inside. It sounded like a party—probably being thrown by a bunch of the conference attendees. A couple of the men turned their heads to study him with interest as he moved closer to them to get a better view along the corridor.

"Hey, baby," one of them called. "Wanna come to a party? Plenty of booze, lots of nice people. We're all pretty harmless." Somebody else guffawed.

"She ain't interested in ya, Benny," another man said. Then, louder, "Hey, I got class. How about just one drink?"

"Aw, she's too stuck-up."

"Just one drink. Don't take any notice of them. They've had too much already."

"Go crawl back under," Marty told them as he squeezed past to get farther along the corridor. At that moment the door of 494 opened ahead of him, and a man came out. Marty stopped and stared. It wasn't Vicenzo or Tyson but someone else, this time slim and distinguished-looking with graying hair and a three-piece suit. He stopped to fasten a button of his vest and straighten his necktie. Marty swallowed disbelievingly. And then Tyson came out. He said something to gray-hair, they laughed, and then began walking toward where Marty was standing rooted to the spot.

"She's some woman, all right," Tyson said to gray-hair as they passed him. "I don't know where she gets all the energy from."

"She often goes all night without a break," gray-hair replied.

"I can believe it."

They walked on by and stopped in front of the elevators. It was all Marty could do to stop himself from gibbering incoherently out loud. And then Vicenzo came out of 494, waving something over his head. "Tony," he called. "You forgot this . . . your watch." Gray-hair looked instinctively at his wrist. "Stay there or you'll miss the elevator," Vicenzo told him. "I'll bring it." He was walking briskly toward them as he spoke. As Vicenzo passed Marty, his eyes brightened with recognition. "Hi there, find your key?" he said, and walked on to where Tyson was holding open one of the elevator doors.

Marty turned around again and looked along toward Room 494. Vicenzo had left the door half open. This was his chance. Then somebody goosed him from behind—hard. He whirled around to find one of the party drunks grinning at him lewdly. Without stopping to think about it, he compressed his fist into a tight ball and delivered a straight, solid right to the jaw. Every ounce of the anger and frustration that had been building up for the past two days went into the punch. A sharp crack of teeth being snapped together sounded above the background murmur of voices.

"Holy Christ, a chick just slugged Benny!" a voice yelled behind him as he turned and rushed along the corridor.

"She's floored him!"

"Jesus, I felt it from here!"

He flung the door open wide and hurled himself through. There were men's clothes and papers everywhere, but no Alice. He rushed into the bathroom, tore aside the shower curtain, then came out again and began throwing open the doors of the closets.

"What's going on?" a powerful voice shouted from the door. Marty spun around. It was Vicenzo, looking mad. "Who are you? What in hell do you think you're doing in here?"

"Where is she?" Marty shrieked.

"Who, for God's sake?"

"You know who! Don't give me that garbage. I know what's going on." Marty snatched up the leather traveling case that he had found in the bedroom of his house and emptied the contents on the floor. Vicenzo stepped forward and tore it from his hands. Marty started opening the drawers of the vanity and hurling them onto one of the room's three beds.

"Stop that!" Vicenzo bellowed at him. "Are you crazy? There isn't anyone else here, I'm telling you." Marty pulled the covers off one of the beds, then wheeled around and started stripping another one. Vicenzo grabbed him and shook him roughly. "Goddamn it, will you listen to me, you stupid woman! *There isn't anyone here!* What kind of nut are you?"

"She's here somewhere!" Marty screamed. "You know where she is!"

"Who, for Christ's sake?" Vicenzo bawled.

"My wife, that's who! I know all about you!"

Vicenzo released his grip and stared at Marty in total bewilderment. "Wife? *Your* wife?" He looked Marty up and down, blinked, and shook his head. "Oh, God! You . . . you really are nuts." He tried to smile reassuringly. "I'm sure we'll find her. Now why don't you just take it easy, sit down, and maybe—"

"Don't try any of that on me." Marty stormed across to an open closet and dragged out a dark brown blazer with distinctive brass buttons. He threw it in a heap on the floor. "See that? Do you think I haven't seen that before? And this!" A necktie with yellow and brown diagonal stripes followed the blazer. "Don't tell me they're not yours!"

"Of course they're mine!" Vicenzo yelled, losing his patience. "So they're mine, and they're in my room. What the hell's supposed to be wrong with that?"

"I found them in my house, that's what!" Marty shouted, pushing his face close to Vicenzo's and contorting it in fury. "You want to know what I'm doing in your room? I wanna know what *you* were doing in my house, with my wife!"

Vicenzo backed away and looked wary. "You're insane. I don't know who you are. I've never been near your house. I don't even know where your house is."

"You know where it is, all right. Or maybe too much sex affects your memory. Newport Beach, Twenty-seven Maple Drive, that's where. Now tell me you've never heard of it."

Vicenzo's eyes widened. "You're crazy," he gasped.

"Well?" Marty challenged. "Are you still telling me you don't know it?"

Vicenzo raised his hands helplessly. "Sure I do, but—"

"Aha! Now we're getting to the truth. So what were you doing there?"

"I . . . I . . ." Vicenzo shook his head. "I live there. That's *my* house!"

Marty gaped at him. "Now *you're* being crazy. D'you think I don't know where I live?"

"I don't know where *you* live, but I know where *I* live," Vicenzo said. "And that's where I live, with my husband."

"But . . . but . . ."

The charge from the atmosphere in the room evaporated suddenly, and they stood for a moment staring speechlessly at each other. Then Marty said in a small voice, "Alice?"

Vicenzo stared in astonishment. "Marty?"

He looked at her. She looked at him.

"What the hell are you doing in that?" they both asked together.

Marty sat down weakly on the edge of one of the beds and spread his hands wide. "I got home a day early . . . on Friday." He waved toward the clothes on the floor and the traveling bag lying to one side. "Those things were there—some guy's things . . . and there was a hotel registration that said he was staying here." He gestured down at himself. "So I . . . It was Abe's idea. We thought . . ."

Alice looked at him in amazement for a few seconds while the meaning of what he had said slowly sank in. Then she threw her head back and laughed. "Oh, Marty, you . . . *idiot!* You thought . . ." She shook her head. "Really, it's too funny for . . ." She began laughing again.

Marty looked at her sourly. "Well, I don't think it's so goddamn funny. Would you mind telling me what the hell's going on here?"

Alice took a moment to calm herself. "It's very simple," she said. "You see, Margaret Sullivan, our editor-in-chief, had this idea about doing a story for women about what it's really like to be a man. She came up with this angle of having a couple of the girls renting male Arabees for a week and then writing up all the things that happened to them. I didn't tell you about it because . . . well, it's a bit strange, and, to be honest, you can be funny about things sometimes . . . and I did want to do it because it sounded like a lot of fun. We picked this week to do it so that we could use the conference as an excuse for being away from home. That's really all there is to tell."

"So who were those two other guys who were in here?" Marty asked.

"Nancy and Dianne from the office," Alice told him. "There are three of us doing it . . . sort of for moral support. We're all sharing this room. I did book another one in my own name, mainly in case you wanted to get in touch, but I'm not using it. It didn't seem a very good idea to have a man's body going in and out of my room all week. It's surprising how things like that can get around."

Marty was beginning to smile as he saw the funny side of it. "One more thing," he said. "What were you three talking about in here just before the others left?"

Alice thought for a moment. "Margaret Sullivan, I think," she replied. "We were saying what a human dynamo she is at the office. Sometimes she works right through until morning when she's got a tough deadline. Why? What made you ask that?"

Marty started to laugh. "It's doesn't matter. I'll tell you some other time." He stood up and studied Alice with renewed curiosity. "It's amazing," he murmured.

Alice tilted her head thoughtfully to one side and ran a finger along his arm. "You know, you're quite cute," she remarked. They looked at each other, wondering who would dare to voice the thought first.

Marty looked around. "It, ah . . . it's a pity you're all sharing," he said at last.

Alice's eyes twinkled wickedly. "Well, I still have the other room up on the twelfth floor," she reminded him in an off-handed voice.

"True," Marty agreed, keeping his tone neutral.

"It would be deliciously . . . different," Alice said after a pause.

Marty thought about it. "And Margaret would want you to cover the subject thoroughly, wouldn't she?" he suggested.

"Oh, definitely. She's very thorough." Alice's six-foot-plus body started to giggle. She slipped her arm through his, and they moved toward the door. At the last second they remembered and switched their arms around the other way.

"Who knows?" Marty said as they stood waiting for an elevator. "We might want to try this again sometime."

"Who knows?" Alice agreed.

The elevator arrived, and the doors opened. Alice and Marty stepped in, clung tightly to each other, and began laughing again as the doors closed. ✫

About the Authors

Terry Carr was born in the mountains of Oregon, grew up in San Francisco, spent ten years in New York City (working as a writer, an agent and an editor for Ace Books) and now lives with his wife Carol in Oakland, California. He has edited more than 50 anthologies and is best known for his *Best Science Fiction of the Year* series, now in its tenth year.

Paul A. Carter has been writing and selling sf stories since John Campbell published his first one, "The Last Objective," in *Astounding* in 1946. He has a Ph.D. in American History from Columbia University. He and his wife have four children and live in Tucson, where he teaches at the University of Arizona.

Leanne Frahm lives in Queensland, Australia. In 1979, Terry Carr was conducting a science-fiction workshop in Sydney, and she decided to give it a try. According to Mrs. Frahm, "I had reached that stage in married life when if I didn't do something other than help my husband's building business and feed the chickens, I'd go crazy." Since taking up this new career, she has sold several stories.

Ira Herman is managing editor of Mountain State Press, a book publisher specializing in Appalachian literature. His hobby is research and design of terrestrial solar power systems. He lives in Huntington, West Virginia, and is working on a novel about a genetically engineered crop of humans.

James P. Hogan, one of *Stellar*'s regular contributors, has provided this edition with not one, but two entertaining stories. A British-born engineer and former computer consultant, Hogan is one of the new breed of writers who understands science, who likes science, and who can put the excitement of science into his novels. He writes the kind of novel that was popular in science fiction's Golden Age.

Larry Niven, who has created a world unto himself . . . a Ringworld, to be exact, had his first story published in 1964 in *IF* magazine. Since then he has written some of the best-loved and bestselling science fiction ever and has been picking up Hugo and Nebula awards on a regular basis. Beyond the category, Niven and his frequent collaborator Jerry Pournelle produced a massive, genuine national bestseller, *Lucifer's Hammer*, in 1977.

Rick Raphael began writing sf in the late 50's and sold some 25 stories to *Analog*. In the 60's, Simon & Schuster published his novel *Code Three*, and short story sales continued to the various sf magazines. In 1963, Raphael, who as a journalist had worked for papers in New York, Denver, and Boise, took a job as Senator Frank Church's press secretary and eventually became his executive assistant, which put an end to his writing. Since retiring from government and corporate service two years ago, Raphael has written several novel-length thrillers and assorted short stories for the magazines.

L. Neil Smith is a self-defense consultant, a former police reservist, and has served on the Libertarian Party's national platform committee. He has published two novels—*The Probability Broach* and *The Venus Belt*—and is working on the next in his long and complicated future-history series set in a Libertarian alternate universe.

James Tiptree, Jr., long science-fiction's mystery man, much to everyone's amazement turned out to be Alice Sheldon, a delightful woman who existed for years behind the male pseudonym. His/her reasons were many, not all of them understood; but they—together and separately—write wonderful stories. Who gets the byline nowadays depends on the "voice" that comes through. In "Excursion Fare" it is definitely Tiptree's.

About the Editor

Judy-Lynn del Rey, editor of the *Stellar* series, was the managing editor of *Galaxy* and *IF* science-fiction magazines for eight and a half years. She has been a contributor to the *World Book Encyclopedia* on science fiction. In addition she is currently a Vice-President at Ballantine Books and the Editor-in-Chief of Del Rey Books, Ballantine's enormously successful SF/Fantasy imprint. Mrs. del Rey lives in New York City with her husband Lester, who has been writing science fiction and fantasy for more than forty years and who is now Fantasy Editor for the Del Rey line.

The Saga of the Well World

Jack L. Chalker's series is a futuristic phenomenon!

Awarded the Edmond Hamilton-Leigh Brackett Memorial Award.